PENGUIN BOOKS

A Tiny Bit Marvellous

'Engaging from the first page' *Heat*

'A wonderful writer – witty, wise, poignant' *Daily Mail*

'A delight' *Woman's Own*

'An engaging study of a British family close to meltdown' *Best*

'Dawn French has taken her gift for comedy and translated
it to the page to bring us a family teetering on the edge'
Sunday Express

'Funny, enriching . . . page after page I laughed out
loud' *Mail on Sunday*

'One to make you laugh out loud' *She*

'Brilliant. Beautifully real, utterly believable, engaging and
involving. Clever, unputdownable, heartwarming. The book's
title is an understatement' *Greenwich Time*

'You'll laugh, smile and maybe shed a tear' *Essentials*

'A heartwarming and humourous exploration of family,
the people we love to hate' Booksploring blog

'A hilarious, sharp and utterly compelling novel about the ups and downs of family, sibling rivalry and growing up. French's witty and engaging novel offers us an honest and insightful account into the relationships between children and parents' kalahari.net

'Hilarious. Typical French, laugh-out-loud funny in places, achingly poignant in others. She is particularly good on the disintegration, both emotional and physical, experienced by some women as they go into their fifties' *Irish Times*

'Written in a comic tone, it explores everything from teenage self-esteem issues to extra-marital affairs and a gay son who fancies men twice his age' *Edinburgh News*

'I laughed – a lot. The Battles are the classic messed up, normal family. There is a brilliant warmth to this book. French is quite obviously an astute observer of teenage behaviour. I do recommend it to anyone with teenagers – it will make you smile and feel relatively normal – for a bit' Sophia Whitfield blog

'French had me laughing from the first few pages. She has captured the voices of these characters perfectly. Lots of laughter and real life. It's much more than a tiny bit marvellous!' A Bookworm's World blog

'I went out this morning and ended up purchasing a copy of Dawn French's *A Tiny Bit Marvellous*. I hadn't planned to do this, but whilst killing time in WHSmith I decided to have a peek. I spent the next fifteen minutes laughing out loud and being stared at by the other shoppers. Soon I was actually handing people copies from the shelf. In the end six people bought Ms French's book between the hours of ten and eleven at WHSmith in St Anne's. To sum up, this book is hilarious' Alexandra O'Toole blog

A Tiny Bit Marvellous

DAWN FRENCH

PENGUIN BOOKS

PENGUIN BOOKS

UK | USA | Canada | Ireland | Australia
India | New Zealand | South Africa

Penguin Books is part of the Penguin Random House group of companies
whose addresses can be found at global.penguinrandomhouse.com

First published by Michael Joseph 2010
Published in Penguin Books 2011
003

Copyright © Dawn French, 2010

All rights reserved

The moral right of the author has been asserted

This is a work of fiction. All characters and events are the
product of the author's imagination. Any resemblance to real places
or persons, living or dead, is entirely coincidental

Pages 403–404 constitute an extension of this copyright page

Typeset by Jouve (UK), Milton Keynes
Printed in England by Clays Ltd, Elcograf S.p.A.

B format ISBN: 978–0–141–04634–1
A format ISBN: 978–1–405–93836–5

www.greenpenguin.co.uk

MIX
Paper from
responsible sources
FSC® C018179

Penguin Random House is committed to a
sustainable future for our business, our readers
and our planet. This book is made from Forest
Stewardship Council® certified paper.

For the best mum. My mum. Roma.

Between yesterday and tomorrow
There is more, there is more than a day.
Between day and night, between black and white
There is more, there is more than grey.

Alan Bergman, Marilyn Bergman
and Michael Legrand

Contra omnia discrimina

ONE

Dora (17 YRS)

My mother is, like, a totally confirmed A-list bloody cocking minging arsehole cretin cockhead of the highest order. Fact. In fact, I, of this moment, officially declare my entire doubt of the fact that she is in fact my actual real mother. She can't be. I can't have come from that wonk. Nothing in any tiny atom of my entire body bears any likeness to an iota of any bit of her. It's so, like, entirely unfair when people say we look alike because like, excuse me, but we properly <u>DON'T</u> thank you. And I should know. Because I look at her disgusting face 20/7 <u>and</u> excuse me, I do actually have a mirror thank you. Which I've looked in and so <u>NOT</u> seen her face, younger or otherwise, staring back at me. If I do ever see that hideousness, please drown me immediately in the nearest large collection of deep water. I would honestly be grateful for that act of random mercy.

At 5.45pm today she had the actual nerve to inform me that I will *not* apparently be having my belly button pierced after all, until my eighteenth birthday. She knows I booked it for this Saturday. She knows Lottie is having hers done. It was going to be our like together forever thing. Fuck my mother and all who sail in her. I hate her. She's fired.

TWO

Mo (49 YRS)

All things considered, that went rather well. Big pat on own back, Mo. I am definitely getting better at not letting her appalling language upset me. No one likes to be referred to as an 'evil slag', or 'hell whore', let's be honest, but I've suffered worse at the sharp end of her tongue, so ironically I'm grateful for these comparatively lesser lashings.

I am reminded of the trusty old David Walsh mantra I often recommend to my clients, 'When, in argument, you feel like taking the wind out of her sails, it is a better idea to take your sails out of her wind.' It certainly was no breezy zephyr I felt battering my aft as I purposely walked away, it was a Force 10 brute, but I am broad in the beam and made of suitably stern-ish stuff. As yet, unscuppered. If lilting a tad.

Yet again, no sign of Husband at the eye of the storm. He scuttled off to a safe port in the study to spend time with his ever-ready, ever-understanding lover, MAC. His endless muttered bleatings about female politics being a mystery are weak and wobbly to the point of jelly. Why does he constantly refuse to back me up at these critical moments? I have repeatedly explained the importance of consistency and continuity as far as the kids are concerned. We must present a united front. We should share my opinion at all times. I am, after all, the qualified child psychologist in this family. Other than fathering two children (total of six minutes' commitment to the project), I'm not aware of his training. However, have to give it to him, he is certainly a supremely skilled slinker-off-er when voices are raised, no one can better his retreating technique. He certainly gets the gold in *that* backwards race. Oh yes.

Then, he had the audacity to sit in Dora's bedroom with her for an hour whilst she apparently 'emptied out' and explained to him that she feels she and I are enemies and have been for years. I am not her enemy, I am her mother. Sometimes it's probably the same thing. It needs to be. I am <u>not</u> here to be her friend.

What *am* I here for actually? To be a guide, a judge, an inquisitor maybe? At the moment I am purely transport, bank and occasional punch bag.

Everso recently, it would have been me sitting next to her on that bed getting a wet shoulder complete with smeared mascara splats.

What a huge difference between fifteen and seventeen years of age. An entire personality flip has happened. Where has my sweet little goth gone? She of the smudgy eyes and red nylon dreadlocks and Tank Girl industrial boots and clamp-on nose-rings? It was so easy to love that one. That one was endearingly injured and tragic. Why have I been sent this Tango-skinned bleached-hair designer slave? I own a human Cindy. Her insufferable rudeness grows with every waking moment. And quite a few sleeping moments I suspect. I'm sure she doesn't waste any dream time <u>NOT</u> hating me. Does hate have a cumulative effect? If so, Dora will be earning buckets of interest on her massive deposits of mum-hate. I just have to accept it, she loathes me.

Today's particular loathing is about refusing to let her have her belly button pierced. In this particular respect, I feel entirely vindicated. Was there ever an uglier mutilation? The very thought of it makes my unpierced and considerably larger stomach turn. Her choice of 'parlour' is that nasty dirty little dungeon opposite the carpet shop in the high street, 'Pangbourne Ink'. Obviously I've never ventured in, but I know the sister of the troll who owns it and she had chronic impetigo last year, so if Dora thinks I am sanctioning such a dreadful thing and in such a dirty place, she can think again.

Of course, soon she will be eighteen and if she chooses to maim herself *then*, she can pay for the privilege. I am not a medical doctor, but if something terrible were to happen to her belly button, an infection of some sort, wouldn't that seal her umbilical tubes? How would any potential grandchild of mine get its nourishment? She is risking any future child-bearing possibilities. Is there no end to her selfishness?

THREE

Oscar (16 YRS)

The suffering of the last hour has been unutterably awful. Both of the Battle harridans, the monstrous mater <u>and</u> the dreadful daughter, have been shrieking sufficiently enough to wake as yet undiscovered molluscs at the pit-bottom of the ocean's silty depths. I have mastered the art of ear-fugging – the application of twisted curls of wet kitchen paper administered to the inner ears. One would imagine this would provide a merciful relief. Yet still, their damnable harpy squawking prevails.

What unlovely wretches they prove themselves to be, abandoning all vestiges of class and style, allowing the vulgarity of their lower-middle-class shackles to triumph. How very very very disappointed I am in both of them. It is so extremely tiresome. I am exhausted from the disappointment. I must needs take to my bed. The confines of my room offer the succour and solitude I sorely need. Increasingly, I discover that the delights of the Nintendo III Dance Mat Challenge are my only worthy companion. There, at least, the red fires of my passion are sated. Farewell, dear diary, 'til anon.

7

FOUR

Mo

New Year's Day. I vow it every year, but this year I mean it, everything is going to change. Radically. Last night was ample evidence that all sentient and valuable life in my home world has evaporated. Who have I become? Who is this? Who is Mo Battle?

I am, apparently, a person who goes to a scruffy pub like the Miller's Arms on New Year's Eve, to meet up with neighbours my community-minded husband has fostered. I have nothing in common with them, and hardly even like them. We meet in order to kill what seems like aeons of dull time until the final countdown of doom, heralding the flip into another potentially stagnant year. For God's sake, I spent two whole hours in that pub separated from the husbands, being forced to listen to the merits of turkey-turning with the wives. Yes, for easily the first three minutes, I was genuinely engaged in the science of it all – of course the juices of the bird would move about during the cooking, into the fattier parts of the corpse, especially the breast, and yes I acknowledge that rotating the beast might be advantageous and possibly tastier. Frankly that was the extent of my interest. But no, there were another 117 minutes of fowl-cooking minutiae to endure. As Karen blathered on incessantly about basters and thermometers and convection cookers and marinating and stuffing and blah and blah, my mind wandered, but for the sake of neighbourly relations I skilfully fixed my gaze on her yappy, overactive mouth and kept a convincing stream of responsive listening noises coming.

Whilst I was trapped in turkey hell with the heifers of our local, Husband was, of course, at the bar with the bullocks, lowing and chewing on their smutty Christmas anecdotes. As if there is anything remotely saucy about Christmas. There isn't, but they managed to make disgusting grunting noises all evening as if they were at Spearmint Rhino where discussing women in salacious terms is expected. Husband isn't ordinarily as blokeish as this, but when the herd convenes, the rules and codes are strictly adhered to. He assures me that their conversations are nothing of the sort and that they never refer detrimentally to the various wives.

Could this be an abandonment issue for me? For some reason his desire to be in their male gang, separate and away from me, always feels like a betrayal of some sort. I don't really want to be there at all, never mind being left with 'the girls'. I don't have anything against the other wives per se. It's just that they wouldn't be my choice of friends; they have been thrust upon me because Husband regularly drinks with 'the G-team' as he calls them. He doesn't worry whether or not they are suitable as his friends. They are *there*, so they will do. How curious. The idea that people you chance upon in a pub become a cohesive, supportive group of compadres, united in the pursuit of a nightly pint of Guinness (hence the G-team). The king of all tipples according to him, complete with its frothy crown.

As we sang 'Auld Lang Syne' and saluted the midnight moment with loud cheers and I was forced to clamp hands with a particularly limp, waxen chap with unfeasibly long fingers, who had just emerged from the Gents and who I knew perfectly well hadn't washed his hands, it dawned on me that I will not allow this to happen again next year. No. Next year will somehow, please God <u>somehow</u>, be different. I am determined to make it so.

There are important issues I must address this year.

I <u>must</u> be thinner.

I <u>must</u> be in a better relationship with Dora and she <u>must</u> respect me more.

I <u>must</u> tackle Peter's constant insistence that he is in some way channelling Oscar Wilde. It was an amusing family joke two years ago, but now I am finding it worrisome.

I <u>must</u> be further along with my book, and I <u>must</u> have a title for it. What would be a good title for a self-help book for parents of teenagers? Two possible ideas at the moment under consideration: 1. *Whatever!* and 2. *Teenagers: The Manual.* Hmm. Think the exclamation mark on the first suggestion might preclude it from being a serious contender.

Finally, I <u>must</u> give some serious thought to my fiftieth birthday in October. Can't decide whether to celebrate or hide in a deep cave. Not denial exactly, but maybe I *could* just ignore it . . . ?

My resolution is: by this time next year I want to know what the hell I'm doing and how I feel . . . about . . . everything . . .

I honestly have no sense of anchorage at the moment. I feel frumpy and unbeautiful, and cross, <u>all</u> the time. Could be the menopause. Mind you, I think there is still a bit of Southern Comfort coursing through my veins from last night. And from the large glass of it

I just drank ten mins ago. Hair of the dog. Shame that there was actually some hair of our actual dog in the disgustingly dirty glass which Dora hadn't even bothered to wash out before she put it back on the shelf. Oh, and that reminds me, the other member of the family I <u>must</u> pay attention to this year is ... Poo. Absolutely <u>must</u> get her spayed. This is the eighth year I've forgotten. Wonder if the vet would agree to do Dora at the same time ... ?

Happy New Year.

NB: <u>Must</u> arrest gradual sclerosis of hope for future.

FIVE

Dora

Fact. Sam Tyler is a cockheaded gitshit, a twatwanker, a coward and a gay. I can't believe I actually went actually out with him, how embarrassing. On top of it all, he is so rank, like, a total minger. Lottie always said he's like well below me and she's like <u>so</u> right. Why didn't I listen to her? I thought she was jealous! Of what? Of me going out with the biggest mong in Berkshire? – doubt it.

What I really can't believe is that I was thinking of finishing with him anyway and he just like beat me to it. At one minute to midnight. On New Year's Eve. In front of everyone – for max humiliation no doubt. And he had his next girlfriend all lined up and ready, so he'd obviously been like planning it or something? And she's like the second biggest mong in Berkshire after him. Good – well I hope they are happy together in mongtown where they can like live with all their mong friends and family and have mong babies who will grow up to be like more mongish than them.

Now at least I can admit how much his little twig legs always freaked me out and how disgusting his

13

teeth are because he hasn't properly brushed them since he was two or something and how his stubbly little moustache which he <u>so</u> believes makes him look like Zac Efron, <u>so</u> doesn't. It looks like a girl's moustache, like his next girlfriend's moustache. Which she got from her mother. And how useless he is at kissing. Like someone should tell him, 'Hello! You <u>can</u> move your mouth around you know and not keep like completely still like a dead corpse or something?'

Anyway it doesn't matter except all his friends were laughing at me and calling me BB New Year. I didn't know what that was until Lottie told me it means 'best before New Year' like I am past my sell by date like a packet of ham or something. Thanks Sam, you scrote. Can't believe I ever let him touch me. Thank God it didn't go too far, although I bet he's like told his mates it did. Liar. It didn't. He doesn't even know how many holes a girl has got – he said eight!! Good luck new girlfriend, you lie back while he stupidly humps away at every hole but the right one and all the holes of every other girl he like sets his eyes on. Hole-shagging freak.

I wish I hadn't cried though. I wanted to not show any reaction, like 'yeah, OK. Whatever', but I think the Tequila Punch was like *so* strong, that I went all like wobbly and before I knew it I was blubbing like a proper twat. Oh God!! Everyone saw. I hate him. I <u>so</u> hate him.

But, like today, I've woken up and like really miss him and his cute little face and now I'm thinking like maybe I really loved him or something? Like maybe he was like my soulmate or something and now I've lost him. I like, <u>so</u> loved him, and I still do. I still really love him. To the earth and beyond. Like we said. OH SAM —

SIX

Oscar

Families are a frightful inconvenience, true, but nowadays we are too hasty to dismiss them.

The Battle family. My family. Hmmm.

I am utterly convinced that if only a little glitter could be sprinkled on their blandness, they might yet spring up, and dance the dance of life. This, at least, is my theory where my ancient (sixty-nine whole years for goodness' sake) grandmama is concerned. Nothing ages a woman so rapidly as a diet of relentless *Jeremy Kyle* and *Emmerdale*. Evidenced by Grandmama, who carries the horrific strains and scars of years of loyal service to both of these demanding mistresses.

I offered her the benefit of my company this New Year's Eve, but informed her that as of midnight I should much like to insist that she refer to me as Master Oscar at <u>all</u> times. For that is whom I am, and I can't stress enough the importance of being Oscar.

Thankfully Grandmama acquiesced to this simple request. She is dreadfully dowdy but a perfect saint. Her name is Pamela. I ask you, how was she ever supposed to make anything of herself with that ghastly moniker as her albatross? As a rule, I would *never* trust a woman who sports anything nylon but, in Grandmama's case, all is forgiven due to the incontrovertible fact that she is gleefully ignorant of the joys of fashion and utterly unencumbered by a shred of style. I therefore choose not to taunt or goad her, it would only be cruelty, and poor wretch, she has no idea of the magnitude of her folly.

Bless her, she is famed in those parts of Pangbourne which are her closest environs, to be something of an expert when it comes to the preparation and serving of the finest of banoffee pies, and truly, in this respect, I am extremely fortunate, for banoffee pie in all its creamy bananaish toffeeish glory is quite easily one of my primary passions in life. To taste, to savour and to have culinary congress with it, is my pure rapturous delight and gives me, frankly, a reason to live. What else is there?

So, in pursuit of this pleasure, and at the set hour, I wended my way by means of two entirely separate and equitedious omnibus experiences to Grandmama's. I wore a high collar and one of Mater's faux fur hats against the biting wind. I fancy the ensemble was a mite enchanting, and suited me more than a little, and I detected not a few admiring comments en route.

Once at Grandmama's domicile I was horrified to realize that she had not reserved the evening exclusively for me, but had invited in, albeit briefly, her imbecile neighbour, the appalling Janice. A woman with the kind of face that once seen, is rarely remembered. Never was there a creature more appropriately placed to be the poster girl for euthanasia.

Why was Pamela born with such hideous contemporaries? I have no doubt that Janice was once the prettiest fool in England but now she is nothing more than a dull, agèd (sixty-two years) and ugly slattern, whose foremost crime is to assume she is always worthy of the post of centre of attention. She is blissfully unaware that this position requires the skill of being even the slightest bit amusing or interesting, if that's not requesting too much? I am accustomed to dullards, Lord knows I am surrounded by them daily in my family, but the awful Janice takes the biscuit. And the cheese and, by Jove, the crackers.

It was the hour to suffer and suffer we did. News of her wearisome family in Wales, her bargains at the sales and her monstrous bunions were among the ripest of the topics. I wished I were rather ravaged by wild dogs and torn apart and greedily gulped down than have to sit in her atrocious company, but mercifully, she was soon bumbling off muttering something about her neglected dog.

This left Grandmama and I to our familiar New Year's traditional schedule of a hand of cribbage, followed by the notorious banoffee pie in front of Jools Holland's *Hootenanny* where we both agreed that Dizzee Rascal was, frankly, dazzling. A satisfying evening with much to recommend it. I look forward to a decade of scandalous delights and I promise earnestly to remain forever Oscar.

SEVEN

Dora

Oh my complete and utter God. Mum is like a constant noise. She says the same things over and over again so much, that in the end, I can't even like hear her. She sounds like that noise you get when you're trying to tune the radio and you haven't got to a channel yet. The noise inbetween, that's her. Interference. I can usually pick up on a vague theme of whatever she's stressing about. Today it's something about revision and my UCAS personal statement. Duh. I know it's got to be done don't I? That's why I already finished like half of it already at school you dunce Mother. But if I let her see it, she'll just pick all holes in it and make me do it again, so why would I bother showing her?

Wish she could see what she looks like when she's in a major strop, she's hilarious. Her eyes bulge and her neck goes all red and she keeps slapping her head and the language is massive. She looks like an angry baboon. She's so over dramatic, she works herself into a psycho screaming fit. When she is swearing she doesn't even swear properly, and she always thinks of the worst possible thing that could ever happen. Today she banged on my door and said:

'Dora! Open this door immediately! I have been talking through it now for forty-five minutes! If you don't shitting wake up and realize that your cacking future is slipping away with every cocking second that you don't get that personal statement finished, you should expect to spend your fecking useless life walking around in Oxford Street, with those massive boards on you telling everyone where the endless arseing golf sale is. Yes, that is your future!'

This apparently is my only option!

And she doesn't even know how to write the bloody statement anyway. The last time she had to write something like this was when <u>SHE</u> went to uni, which was in the last bloody century for God's sake, over seventy years ago or something. She probably just wrote 'I, Maureen' ... something ... Don't know what her name was before she married Dad ... 'I Maureen Boring-Hair, do intend to attend this university of great learning so that I may learn all I need to know about being a crap shrink so I can tell everyone how to live, and boss them all about and convince them I'm cleverer than them, and charge them a bloody fortune and they can never tell me I'm wrong because it's not even a scientifically proven method, and there's no way of checking up on me whether I know how to like, even do this job properly atall. My hobbies are: talking, shouting, screaming, bossing, knowing best and getting really fat. I do hope this application finds a positive response because I really do want to boss people about for my job, and if I don't get in, I'll like, stomp about and shitting shout at everyone so please take me. I promise to be as fake as possible whenever I can, so my patients will always think I am a like calm and clever person who knows more about everything than they do.'

Yeah Mum, you're a *lot* of help, I really want your advice – not.

And she cracked off on a big one all about my Facebook site for bloody ages. She's got no idea what it is, or how it works, but she says I have put porno pictures of myself on there and apparently I send and receive messages with 'inappropriate language'. What would she know? She hasn't read them. And, actually those are the pictures me and Lottie took of each other and that is, like, a proper expensive bra thank you. Like, from Juicy Miss or something? So we're not sluts like she's making out.

She says any old perv could start talking to me on it but duh, hello old woman, you have to like <u>invite</u> people on to your page and like, why would I invite a perv? You div Mother, you honestly bloody embarrass me with your IT ignorance. Even her secretary at work has to type up her bloody patient notes stuff because she is so old and broken that she is too scared or something to learn how to like use a computer. Wake up you bloody dormouse! Everybody in the entire world has got a computer – except you. Even people in like mountain caves in Borneo or something? I learned how to use one when I was like, a baby for chrissakes!! If a baby can do it, can't a trained child psychologist use one?!

Dad says he is going to get her some stone and a chisel for her to write her next book on. I mean, who uses a pencil and paper to write a book? Even bloody Shakespeare must have had a better method than <u>that</u>. If the woman who writes *Twilight* had to do it with like a bloody pencil, it would take her like six years or something to write the first chapter, and I would like die of waiting. Get a life Mother, please! Wake up and smell the tea.

Anyway, I did do a bit more work on my personal statement, just to keep Mum quiet. I think it's really good now. After I finished it, I read it again as if I was like not me, but like I was one of the examiner people type of thing, and I think I sound like a truthful, honest person who is interesting and like, full of charm or something. I have lied a <u>bit</u> about some stuff, like saying I am Head Girl and that I am an accomplished public speaker and that I have ten A stars at GCSE when I only have one and that's for Art. Like they're going to check!! Actually, I'm really pleased with it and if I was like choosing who to take at Manchester Metropolitan uni to study Food Technology I would def choose me. Def.

Oh my actual God, I'm going to uni this year! I can't believe it, freedom at last! Go uni – go uni! I'm still deciding about a gap year or not but prob not because Mum has said that if I take one now, I have to like get a job and earn towards my travelling <u>before</u> I'm allowed to go off? What is she talking about? What does she think learning to be a snowboard instructor <u>is</u>? Just fun or something? No, the reason you learn that skill, cretin of all cretinous mothers, is so that you can teach kids and like <u>earn</u> <u>money</u> for it you damn fool, that's the whole point!! And in the evenings I would be like cooking dinners for skiers and their families in the chalets. That's what Lottie's sister did, so I know how it works.

Oh my days, it's going to be so great because there are like so many fit guys out there? Yea, though I walk into the valley of hot guys, let me always carry my camera with me so I can like upload tons of pics of me getting lashed on to Facebook so Lottie will die of jealousy. YAY! And maybe Sam Tyler might even visit my page and take a look at what he's missing, the idiot. Yeh Sam, here's me with loads of fit ski instructors, really like missing you – not!

Mum says that for def uni selection people are going on to Facebook sites to see what people are really like. Oh God Mum – you are one delusional mama, like I would invite <u>them</u> on as friends!

EIGHT

Mo

Dora is hell-bent on destroying her life. Her university application form is beyond awful. I tried, gently, to offer my help but of course she is rejecting all aid and encouragement presently. She has started the statement with a misguided attempt at a lonely hearts classified section-type joke which goes something like 'Pretty blonde girl, 17, with GSOH and own scooter seeks buzzin' uni with top class food tech department and fit boys for learning, fun and maybe more . . .' Dear Lord.

She then follows this with the old chestnut, the dreaded definition, so it goes:

'I ask What is a university? My trusty dictionary tells me it is a "high level educational institution in which students study for degrees and academic research is done". Well, that's handy then, because that's exactly what I'm looking for – except for the research bit – I won't be doing any of that atall. So hi Manchester Metropolitan University! I'm Dora and it looks like we're a match! . . .' Oh God.

She then goes on to actively lie about <u>many</u> things

including the bogus tally of her GCSEs and when I suggested she might elaborate on the sentence 'I like badminton' (she doesn't) she begrudgingly wrote 'I like badminton a lot'. She has sent it off now, so there is nothing I can do except scream internally. And I am screaming.

There was further annoyance when I returned to work today after the holiday period to find that George has agreed to take on two junior psychs to shadow us as part of some buddy scheme instigated by the Royal College. He mentioned this possibility to me before Christmas but at that stage, it was only supposed to be one, who would work with both of us alternately. That in itself was enough of an inconvenience – I always feel strangely self-conscious when there is an auditor of any kind. I find it hard to be natural when scrutinized; I'm distracted by their continual questions and judgements.

Fascinating that George has suddenly decided to take on two. Double fascinating that the one he has ascribed to himself is called Veronica and has unfeasibly huge tits and a constant pout and has already learned that George is putty in the presence of giggling girly flattery. How irritating that both of them would be so stupendously predictable and inappropriate.

I do hope they both actually do some worthwhile work with the clients alongside their revolting public foreplay.

Oddly, it is Veronica that I find most disappointing. George is just behaving like the reactive Pavlov's dog with many cocks that he is. Has always been. It's a given with him, mandatory, if there's a pretty girl and she shows any interest at all in him, he is helpless. Ring the bell, the dog salivates. He's not even choosy, really <u>anyone</u> will do, and they <u>do</u> do. Often.

I will never forget his arse-wrenchingly awful opening gambit to our previous receptionist on her first day at work:

'What the hell is the point of a heavenly creature like you wasting your lovely bum sitting on an office chair behind reception, when you could be using it to sit on my lap being adored, eh? Eh?'

He thought it was ironic and flirty. It wasn't. He thought it was funny. It wasn't. What *was* funny though, were the rivulets of muddy-coloured Grecian 2000 hair dye running down the side of his overexcited sweaty face.

Veronica obviously believes she is the one who can finally fulfil George's aching chasm of emptiness left by his wife's neglect. His surprisingly saucy wife Jess, who he clearly adores and who he leans on and remains with. There's no neglect that I can see, quite the opposite it seems. Safe in the confines of her evident love, he has grown a kind of mighty hubris, a confidence which allows him to play-act his bachelor stallion fantasy. All acting and all harmless ultimately. Slightly pathetic yes, and nothing new, but he's only made of the same emotionally porous bricks and mortar as almost every other chap.

I'm not sure quite where this relationship leaves Veronica and George when it comes to the work? Perhaps engorged George enjoys feeling swollen with confidence and thus displays himself as an exemplary specimen of a clever psychiatrist in order to show off? He peacocks himself with both his stocky physicality and his muscular mind. He is clever *and* he's in charge. A winning combination. His power is the aphrodisiac for himself *and* the women, I suspect. Admittedly, he is never less than marvellous at work. Never. I have learned so much from him. Got to give him that.

But Veronica. Poor Veronica, who is just the next one in a never-ending, ever-willing queue. And what about her betrayal of another woman, Jess, who has done her no harm? Oh I don't know, am I just a judgemental, jealous fool? I grew up in a time when the fight to be recognized for one's intellect and personality ALONG-SIDE, not instead of, one's fabulous tits was being fought. And it's still not entirely won, so I feel horribly let down by women prepared to present themselves as purely vessels for men's lust. God knows, being on the receiving end of a bit of lust IS gorgeous and I've certainly craved and luckily received my share of that, but that alone is a pretty miserable prospect.

Who am I to judge? Well, I'll tell you who – it is my job to persistently question why people define themselves in the way they do and why they relate to others in the way they do. Consequently, I cannot help but observe the behaviour of George and Veronica as a slice of social anthropology. However it may depress me, I still find it fascinating. On top of which, both of these particular people are of course prescribing techniques and asking others to monitor their own behaviours daily. That is their job. Do they ever self-analyse? I doubt it. They are interested mainly in each other's pants. And on we go . . .

I have yet to meet my intern. I'm told his name is Noel. He has apparently been abroad for Christmas and returns next week. Well, he will have to hit the ground running because the appointment book is fit to burst, always the case after the enforced jollity of family Christmases.

Talking of appointments, I must speak to George about Lisa. She is a poppet and an excellent receptionist, but I sense by just how often she now quotes her survivalist training techniques to me that her mind is elsewhere, and I fear we may lose her soon to one of the jungles, deserts or islands she has been so studiously preparing herself for. This morning she furnished me, from behind her desk, in the presence of a full waiting room, with all I might need to know when Preparing the Kill in the Wild. I now know too many details about Bleeding, Skinning, Gutting and Jointing.

'What's vital, Mo, is <u>never</u> to waste blood – it is rich in vitamins and minerals including salt that could be missing otherwise from a survivor's diet. Fact: When cannibals drank their enemies' blood apparently their eyesight got much better. Deal with it.'

It follows, then, that I might be able to save on my next Specsavers bill by drinking copious amounts of Lisa's blood, maybe. Just a thought. Meantime we ought to be keeping our inferior pre-blood-drinking eyes open for a new receptionist, perhaps?

NINE

Oscar

I must find a suitable tailor. I <u>must</u>. I am not well pleased with the pathetically paltry style offerings of Pangbourne nor indeed of Wokingham and God forbid I should be forced to descend into the ultimate cultural abyss: Reading, a large town, the capital of Hell. If one should be searching for any vestige of dandy, these harbours of evil won't suffice. The purveyors of supposed fashion in these infernal places are so very colourless and lack any individuality. All is repetition, all is uniform, all is bland. I consider the ugliness they are willing to peddle a kind of malady. A sickness of utterly rotten bad taste. A malaise of pandemic proportions, which seems to be spreading like wildfire across our green and pleasant land.

Last week, I attempted to purchase a simple cravat. I might as well have attempted to procure the soul of the Dalai Lama, it was so impossible. The store is a well-known gentlemen's outfitters. One may have presumed my intended purchase wasn't so rare a request, but the imps of Satan employed therein displayed their intolerable bad manners with repeated giggling and whispered insults. Well, hardly whispered. They were too unclever to manage even that. Rarely have I encountered creatures with such a complete absence of intelligence and such monumental incompetence. Veritable scoundrels and bounders.

I refuse to behave as though my predilection for jaunty neckwear is some kind of shameful dark secret. I simply will not allow the intellectually lost to dictate my personal aesthetics. The value of dress in relation to good taste is obvious to me. Just as obvious as the notion that the widespread infection known as the 'hoodie' has undoubtedly destroyed acres of taste in our currently crippled culture of couture. I shan't tarry around that subject too long, for fear of drowning in gallons of my own bile. Suffice to say that I bade my adieus and departed Burton's without a backward glance. They will not <u>EVER</u> profit from my not inconsiderable pool of pocket money. Since Christmas I have in excess of forty honourable English pounds. My exodus signified the end of what might have been a rewarding relationship for both of us, but Je ne staunchly regrette rien.

My search for a prince among tailors and gentlemen's outfitters continues apace. I tentatively suggested to the Pater that he might accompany me presently, on an excursion to London in search of the very same. The thrust and parry of our repartee was certainly invigorating. The Pater insists that he would clearly be travelling not as my companion, merely as my chauffeur. Of course, he is right. Although a thoroughly decent chap, he and I are hardly kindred spirits. Truth be told; I often ponder whether I can possibly be blood-related to him, since we have so little in common.

Admittedly, there are some irrefutable genetic similarities. I have his nose, his eyes, his jaw and his stature. I also have his flaxen hair colour, his eye colour and his exact same hands. My gait, however, is my own entirely. Papa is a gross lolloper. I prefer to propel myself with a tad more grace.

I'm reliably informed that my physical presence is variously 'interesting', 'imposing' and 'big'. Initially I took offence at the latter, but I was so very young at the time it was uttered, I was a mere fourteen years then, whereas I am much more resilient now that I am sixteen years and a full two months. A lifetime of fortitude has befallen me since then. I now accept 'big' as an undeniable compliment. I am, indeed, big. I fancy I carry off my bigness with a certain élan, with the aplomb of someone easily twenty years my elder. Someone like Stephen Fry or Dale Winton, perhaps?

Both of which fine chaps obviously benefit from the skills of some master of great style, and that, dear diary, is who I must find. A tailor of repute, a cloth-meister of renown. To London, Pater, and don't spare the horses!

TEN

Dora

I am thinking that going to Manchester Metropolitan to do Food Tech might be a like, giant mistake? I know all the uni experience stuff would be like really great and everything but would I just be wasting my time completely if it's not what I *really* want to do? It would take me <u>away</u> from what I *really* want to do for three years for God's sake, and I might never get the chance again, and after all, if you are going to really make it as a singer you've <u>got</u> to start really young.

I'm already wasting time. By my age Adele had been singing in public for like three years or something, really building up her profile. My profile is like, minus a thousand or something? Ask anyone, they've *never* heard of me. Which is totally like Mum's fault because I clearly asked her to book me a session in a recording studio or something as my birthday present last year. All the bloody usual excuses came out – 'You need to have a song ready' 'What musicians are you going to use?' 'Are you aware it costs two thousand pounds young lady' – all that sort of prime crap, the usual stuff she says to stop me having a singing career.

I mean, like excuse me, but who was the one who won the house singing competition in Year 9? Who got accepted for choir? Who was asked to be one of the backing singers behind Judith Taylor in the school band, Girls For Hire? Was it *you*, fatso Mother? Or was it *me*, the one with the really 'distinctive' and 'unusual' voice as Mr Solomons said, and he's only the Head of Music actually, so he should know.

It's not like this is some kind of pie dream I'm having – I've like really seriously thought about it, and I know with all my heart that I am destined one day to live my dream, and be as famous as like Cheryl Cole or something? Oh my actual God, I'm not thirteen or something, I will be eighteen in August so I know myself. Who I am, what I am and what I can possibly be. If only my cocking parents weren't bloody stopping me by like, ruining all my dreams by pissing all over them every time I suggest it.

Lottie says I can, really, sing, better than anyone on *American Idol* and like loads better than bloody Susan Boyle. Who <u>is</u> she?! I know it sounds like totally random but I've had an idea and I really really think I'm going to do it and that is, to go up for *X Factor*. They have auditions in London, I could easily catch the train. Hope they're on a Saturday because they're being like so strict at school now about absence and stuff. Just because of exams or something.

I will have to choose a song but I think I already know it will be 'Beautiful' by Christina Aguilera because I know the words and because I can like so relate to it. They always say you should really <u>feel</u> a song and with that one, I <u>so</u> like, do. Because in that song it says, 'Now and then I get insecure from all the pain, so ashamed,' and that's exactly how I've felt since Sam dumped me.

Lottie's the only one who knows how bad I really feel. All the others think I don't really care because that's what I say but ... <u>why</u> did he dump me? Am I ugly? Well, I know I <u>am</u>, but not as bad as some people. Have I got like zero personality or something? I know plenty of other girls are like way more interesting than me, and funnier and prettier and everything. Is it because I wear glasses? I'm going to get the laser thing done but not yet because my eyeballs have to fully grow first or something, Mum says.

The awful thing is I think he was right to dump me because to be honest, he can do better than me. Still, least I had him for six weeks. That's my longest boy-friend yet. Maybe I'll find someone more my level next.

Maybe I shouldn't aim so high then the boy will stay with me a bit longer in future because he will be grateful too. I need someone who likes someone like me. Someone who is, like Christina says, 'Full of beautiful mistakes'.

ELEVEN

Oscar

Well, the fact is, my life would be vastly improved if only we could move lock stock and both barrels to London. For that is where I truly belong, my dears, it's so frighteningly obvious. The thought of remaining in boring Berkshire is perfectly monstrous, unthinkable in fact. No, I refuse.

Every visit I pay to London reminds me that I am alive. One can live for years sometimes, as indeed I have, without truly living at all. To live is the rarest thing in the world. Most people exist and that is all. Like my own dear papa who is apparently a living human being to all intents and purposes, all outward signs and definitions, but who, frankly, seems to barely eke out an existence as a person.

He very sweetly agreed to drive me into our fair capital in search of the suitable tailor, but he virtually destroyed the joie of the outing with his relentless babbling. I know he means well but we have very little in common and I find it unutterably tedious to keep answering relentless questions about my schooling, my friends, my life, my future. Might we ever, I wonder, have engaging discourse on the merits of a good cigar or when might be the appropriate occasion to sport a cummerbund? I doubt it.

He is a good enough fellow though, and awfully kind. I am prone to carsickness and I am not well pleased with the M4 at the best of times. This outing was particularly unpleasant including several bouts of violent vomiting with which to contend. The Pater was especially attentive and each incident was accompanied by his patting of my back and a regular supply of baby-wipes stored in the Volvo for that very purpose. We took refreshment at every opportunity, including Heston Services, my least favourite of the stopping-places. Here also, Papa swung into action with a bravura display of fatherly protection as I was exiting the lavatories and, as so often happens, some vulgar young men began to mock me. Mainly, it seems, with reference to my yellow checked trousers, which had somehow mortally offended them. The Pater was quick to reprimand them with a gentle 'move along you rascals and leave him alone' initially but when that didn't suffice, he employed the curter and more effective 'FUCK OFF! NOW!' which did the trick. Sometimes, actually, he *is* useful to have around.

Not so successful was our foray into Savile Row and

Jermyn Street. I have long dreamed of the moment I would enter one of those hallowed halls of bespoke delights. A proper gentlemen's outfitter. I was swollen with anticipation and breathless with excitement. A bell rang above the door of the first establishment we entered and the smell of the place was oh, was divine. The smell of tweed and citrus shaving lotion and new leather shoes. The smell of style. I explained that I was looking for a good day suit and possibly a frock coat? Papa took a seat and read the *Independent* all the while, looking not a little embarrassed.

The delightful assistant, Mr Berry, took great pains to show me bolt after bolt of splendid cloth from which my garments might be hewn. Pinstripes and herringbones and Duke of Windsor checks, wools and silks and linens. Each more exquisitely beautiful than the last. We agreed that one should never wear brown in town, that it would be outré so to do. We also discussed the merits of the correct titfer for each season. When to choose a Panama, a Homburg or a simple Fez? Which is exactly le chapeau juste? Bliss. He measured me and, with my guidance, he drew a miraculous flash-sketch of exactly the attire I required. At last, somebody finally understood my needs and could service them splendidly.

I was about to place my order when the thorny issue of payment raised its ugly head. Why does it always have to be so vulgar? In hushed and grave tones, Mr Berry explained that the suit would cost 'about £800' and the frock coat would be about '£1,200. Sir.' I found myself breathless with shock and, whilst the silence was quite unbearable, I had no option. I had no speech in me. All was only air, no sound. Followed by some severe gasping. Then I had to sit to regain my composure. At which point Papa stepped in and explained that my entire purse was £40.

Mr Berry very kindly showed us the choice of neckerchiefs in my price range and I chose a splendid red silk cravat. Papa added the necessary £12.50 to my £40 to purchase it and we left post haste. I managed to round the corner, out of sight of Mr Berry, before another episode of violent vomiting gripped hold of me. And I wasn't yet in the car!

I think I may remain in mufti for the foreseeable future. These London tailors, whilst undoubtedly maestros conducting their orchestras of style, are also, frankly, cads.

TWELVE

Mo

Damn it. Just as I was settling back into the flow of work after Christmas I've been struck down by a horrible case of the flu. The whole family taking great delight in treating me as if I am infected with a planet-destroying pandemic-sized uber virus. They are all wearing the facemasks Husband uses when painting, plus my Marigold gloves.

Peter, of course, personalized his, and has added a back-to-front dressing gown and an old flowery bathing cap. He thinks he looks dramatic and surgical. He actually looks sinister. Bit like the mother from *Psycho*. Not a comforting sight when you're feeling vulnerable. I really wouldn't have the strength to fight him off if he came jabbing at me with a Sweeney Todd knife right now. I don't think he will, because he simply wouldn't be able to bear the idea of splattered blood. Too messy. When I shake off this flu, I may ask George to see Peter for a couple of sessions and try to interpret exactly what's going on with this whole 'Oscar' business.

God, flu is awful. Is it my age or does it genuinely

gain strength as a virus? Flu used to mean aching, hot and snot for about two days then up and about. Spit spot. Now it means at least a week in bed rendered entirely useless and a bit weepy. I think the constant bouts of crying are mainly to do with an overwhelming sense of helplessness due to lack of actual physical strength. I feel feeble. Oh God I'm crying again now. For heaven's sake, Mo, get your act together.

During this wretched illness, the family really have had to help out. Headed by Husband, they have taken it in turns to bring various forms of sustenance or diversion. Oscar brings a well-laid tray with a paper doily and a flower in a vase to accompany a plate of garibaldis and some cold, ready-to-eat prawns from M&S, which he perceives to be the height of sophistication, 'the fruit of the sea'. He reliably informs me that the oil in fish is beneficial for my hair, nails and, most importantly, my IQ. The latter is apparently where I am most lacking. Are prawns fish? No idea. He also tells me that he has informed the doctors' surgery that he thinks I have chronic swine flu, citing all sorts of symptoms I simply don't have, like 'beady with perspiration', for instance. Consequently I now can't go there to get any antibiotics because I must remain in enforced isolation and monitored quarantine.

Oscar is loving this, the drama of it all. He wants to look after me, but only if it can be like Bette Davis looked after the crippled Joan Crawford in *Baby Jane*. Only if I am glamorously ill and wholly dependent. This morning he brought me a fan and a bed jacket from the Oxfam shop. The 'bed jacket' is an ancient crocheted lime green shrug, a stained monstrosity with ribbons to tie at the neck. It smells of camphor and caramel and cigarettes. It's disgusting and he refuses to wash it because, he tells me, 'it will diminish the history, and inherent faded beauty, of the thing'. So, I sit in bed, fanning myself and being grateful for biscuits. At least Husband rustles up a decent vegetable broth and although he enjoys referring to me as 'm'lady' a bit too often to be funny, he knows me well enough to bring the paper and a sharp pencil for the daily attempt at the crossword that regularly disintegrates into a similarly failed go at the elementary sudoku.

Dora came in last night with some prawn crisps (what is it with my kids and prawns?) and cheese string she had bought with her allowance. I was so touched. Remarkably, we very nearly had a conversation, for the first time in recent memory. She sat on the bed, and although she couldn't exactly look at me, she answered my questions about her day. Grumpy, evasive, monosyllabic answers, admittedly, but answers nevertheless:

Me: Good day?

Her: OK.

Me: What did you do?

Her: Learning.

Me: Learning what?

Her: Stuff.

Me: What stuff?

Her: Stuff stuff.

Me: How's Lottie?

Her: OK.

Me: How are you?

Her: Same.

Me: Worried about anything?

Her: Yeah.

Me: Want to tell me?

Her: No.

Me: Want me to shut up?

Her: Yeah.

This is a seismic step forward. We even managed to have a quite comfortable silence whilst I attempted the revolting prawn crisps. Out of that quiet, she walked to the big mirror on the wardrobe and I watched her inspect herself. She was strangely unself-conscious. She used to do exactly that when she was tiny – twist and turn in front of the mirror, closely scrutinizing her hair, her skin and the lines of her body. Of course <u>then</u>, she was on an adventure of discovery, exploring all the many shapes she could throw and checking out the mysteries of parts of her physical self she couldn't easily see, like her back or her ears or up her nose. Secret and new places. The revelations were ever more exciting and her curiosity knew no bounds.

Here though, and now, I witnessed an entirely different kind of study. Her face slowly crumpled as she vetted every inch of her evidently disappointing body. I could see that she thought absolutely <u>nothing</u> was right. Nothing. She pinched and slapped and jabbed at all the perceived imperfections, even her shoulders and her fingers are vile and offensive to her. It was shocking to witness her hate herself so much. She loathes her reflection.

The irony, of course, is that Dora is beautiful. I know she is mine and yes, perhaps I forgive imperfections too easily because – why? – because they are sometimes the exact physical imperfections I saw in myself years ago? The plumpness of her cheeks, the fleshiness of her knees, the roundness of her hips? All facets I now know to be <u>SO</u> attractive in the young but which the egocentric blindness of youth prevents us from seeing.

The fact is that Dora is a real beauty, a gorgeous, vital young woman with so little self-belief that she denies herself even the slightest bit of approval. It would only take that. A little bit. The tiniest fragment. She could build up from that foundation. I attempted a tentative launch of her self-esteem by telling her, utterly truthfully, what I see – a vibrant, healthy, shining girl with a lovely body and the skin of an angel.

I reiterated again, whilst I had this little window of opportunity, and whilst she was sort of listening, how much I dislike the constant bleaching of her hair. How it has sadly ruined it, how it looks like straw, how it looks cheap and how very much I prefer her natural hair – its curliness and brown-ness. On reflection, this latter approach might have been misguided and she flounced off in a major huff. Yes, I might have done better there – possibly quit whilst I was ahead and whilst she was listening?

Nevertheless we *did* manage to have a few moments of positive reinforcement and, with any luck, that's the part she will remember … hopefully …

THIRTEEN

Dora

Well thanks Mum, for ruining my life. I'm glad you've got flu, you utterly deserve it and I hope you die in a horrendous choking in your own snot incident. I bloody bought you crisps and stuff! You are so beyond selfish! How dare you give me this kind of stress? As if I'm not like stressed out enough at the moment for fuck's sake. I've got coursework stress, uni stress, *X Factor* audition stress, Sam stress, money stress, phone credit stress, Facebook picture stress and now she only goes and adds to it with bloody major hair stress!

I'm bloody fed up of explaining it over and over again. Listen up, sucker – I <u>HAVE</u> TO HAVE THIS HAIR!! If you have brown curly hair at my bloody motherarseing school, <u>NOBODY</u> like bloody talks to you. End of. You are a leper. You are a mong. You are a brown curly-haired leper mong. And you might as well die of loneliness and pain right now, coz that's what's going to happen in the end anyway. Make the choice Mum – blonde hair or death?!

Maybe you would prefer death for me? – then you

wouldn't have to like keep looking at my so-called 'straw head' all the time? Yea, that would like so make your bloody life so much better. Admit it, then you'd be able to like get on with your work and writing without the annoying distraction of what's it called again? – oh yeah – A DAUGHTER!!!

Sorry for existing, sorry for breathing – sorry for offending you with my hair, and my face and every-thing else about me and my body that you loathe on sight. Is it too late for you to look in the offspring cata-logue and choose a like more perfect one? Then you could return me and order a flawless daughter with ideal brown curly hair who looks like a bog brush on legs and fits exactly with you in your pretend immacu-late family with no faults or defects. God forbid the child shrink should have a kid with such a hideous flaw. Blonde hair – how disgusting!

And stop calling me a 'wannabe plastic'. I'M NOT a plastic. I might look plastic on the outside yes, but that's nothing. A real plastic is plastic on the inside and that's exactly where I am not plastic if you just bothered to stop and notice. On the inside Mother, I am fully natural. I am 143% real. Are you?!

FOURTEEN

Oscar

Who would have thought that a simple mistake could prove to be the portal to my personal nirvana? Who could have predicted that anything so very wondrous could possibly occur on a Thursday? In Pangbourne? But tarry a while, haste is the arch-enemy of delight, and I need to fully explain today's miracle from the beginning.

Mama is so very quaint. I can't help but admire her resistance to all of this 'new-fangled' technology. I have done a good deal of resisting it myself, but I am accustomed to the very inevitability of it all, so I have availed myself of the knowledge and advantages a computer can bring. We are all of us, more or less, barbarians in these befuddling times we rashly refer to as 'modern', but needs must, and, frankly, I can do without the wrath of Mr Gilicone, my irascible IT teacher. It's as well to keep him equable. Perturbed, he is a danger, and can render my life intolerable should he choose to impose yet another strict regime of detentions and break-time restrictions. Break time is, after all, my only chance to convene with The Enchantings.

What's that, I hear you cry, dear darling diary? 'Who are The Enchantings?' Well now, since The Enchantings are an exclusive, secret and elite band of brothers, I shouldn't rightly inform you. However, in the sure knowledge that one day, when I am notoriously well known, these meagre scribblings will no doubt be published as a tome of some note, I ought to edify you. But pray, keep it to yourselves do, for the very motto of The Enchantings is 'semper arcanus' which denotes that we should never speak of it or otherwise perish for ever. I cannot perish. No, no. I have too much to offer, I am whole volumes in folio. I must not deprive the world of me, that would be nothing short of selfish.

So, The Enchantings. I founded this institution as a conclave of excellence. It wasn't hard to identify potential members since my school maintains a steady paucity of anything remotely excellent, especially human beings. In the end it came down to three. Including myself. I am the chairman. Roddy Hargreaves in my year is the vice chairman and Wilson from Year 9 is also a member. Roddy brings to our merry table his extraordinary knowledge of musical theatre and his affable wit along with his ability to play the pianoforte.

Wilson gains admittance by dint of only one qualification – his ravishing good looks. He appears to have been plopped into Year 9 directly from heaven. Surely one so beautiful can't possibly have been created from mere mortal homo sapiens? Angels must have been involved in the manufacture of him somewhere along the line.

I, of course, bring me. We all agree, that alone is more than sufficient.

We meet each Wednesday in a clearing in the dingle by the old tennis courts if fine. If wet, we repair to the cupboard at the rear of Big Hall where the large vaulting equipment is stored. This is capacious enough for our purposes. Our typical rendezvous consists of a password (usually the name of the most enchanting person in the news that week) followed by a fifteen-minute discussion concerning all that enchants us. At the end, we swear allegiance to Aphrodite, the most enchanting of all the ancient goddesses, give each other a little kiss, and hasten off to class. I have no doubt of it that this charming ritual makes my entire experience at that dreadful vulgar place nominally called school, even slightly bearable. It is one of my greatest pleasures, and entirely necessary if I am to survive there.

So, to reiterate, I do not at any cost need Mr Gilicone to have reason to cause me to miss The Enchantings and Wednesday break is when detentions occur. Thus I endeavour to meet the strenuous demands of 'Glans' Gilicone's IT homework schedule. This, and only this, is the reason I know how to use the computer. I remain suspicious of it at all times. However, I regularly log on to question Google about who might be deemed Enchanting – on more than one occasion, its most popular suggestion has been someone named Paris Hilton. I think <u>not</u>.

Even with my rudimentary knowledge of technology though, I surpass Mama's ability a hundredfold. I suppose this will never change now since Mama is so hopelessly, irreversibly ancient. Unbelievably, she will see her fiftieth birthday in October should she last that long. Fifty?! My Lord. Is it possible that she can survive much after this age without becoming a public nuisance?

Should she become infirm, I would, of course, offer to assist, but only on the strict understanding that it would be in my capacity as a companion and entertainer. I would, for instance, happily read the classics aloud to her, or regale her with stories of contemporary scandals and malicious gossip. I would, under no circumstances whatsoever, touch her or tend to any base physical needs. That is the work of women, husbands and paid help. No Enchanting should be required to perform such menial and degrading duties. Mama wouldn't wish it anyway. She adores it when I amuse her and that is what I would do. Let us hope decrepitude befalls her later rather than sooner, for both our sakes.

So, to the fortuitous 'simple mistake'. Owing to Mother's ill health this week, and her lack of technological expertise, Ditzy Dora and I have agreed to alternately collect various work folders to bring home to her during her confinement. Today was my turn. It was clearly specified to me at breakfast by the Pater who requested that I drop by her office after school for just such a purpose, which I dutifully did, only to find Dozy Dora already ensconced in the reception area and mistakenly receiving the aforementioned files. Is it possible that a mortal can live, breathe, walk and talk without the benefit of a brain? If so, Dumpy Dora really is a staggering example.

In the meantime, I had the more pressing matter to attend to, of persuading her that she had come on the wrong day, and that her turn was tomorrow. She remained impervious to any reasonable argument however, and insisted that she was in the right. I may be taller, bigger and undoubtedly brighter than Dodo Dora, but sadly, she is the more violent and less controlled. A lifetime of painful and sometimes eventually septic pinches and punches have taught me to keep my distance and to always allow her the victory. This way, I'm permitted to keep my skin, eyes, hair and all extremities intact. That is my preference, it is the civilized route. Since the Pater was coming to pick up the assigned courier – me – I decided to bide my time, wait with Dim Dora and enjoy a lift home.

This is when I first laid eyes on Noel.

What a thing temptation is. Just at the moment I believed that Wilson personifies all that is necessary to be beautiful, there is Noel, and I'm compelled to posit the question 'Is beauty enough?' Till today, Wilson was, indeed, enough. To look upon him was all the lusty sustenance I needed. But Noel . . .

Oh Noel. How did you come here? Did Father Christmas accurately name you, and let you ride on his sleigh all the way from New Zealand with him on Christmas Eve so that you could be the best, brightest present of all? Ordinarily, I don't care for the bitter twang and ting of a Kiwi accent to be frank, but emanating from you, Noel, it somehow becomes an aria of syrup. Honey. Elixir. What were our first words? Ah yes:

'I haven't met your mum yet but I'm looking forward to it. Here are the files she wanted. Send Mrs Battle my regards.' Yes. Yes, Noel, I will. I will do your bidding.

Let me tell you all about him, diary: Noel is tall, solid and blond. Not Dishonest Dora blonde. Genuine blond. Like Marilyn Monroe. Or the Archangel Gabriel. Or Adonis. He is about thirty years of age, I think, with a good jaw and a full mouth. His eyes are green, the green of a kiwi fruit's fleshy inner. He sports linen slacks. Linen! In Pangbourne! Hallelujah! How divine. The answer to my prayers at last. He seems utterly unruffled by anything, even the prospect of working with Mama, which might put the willies up the boldest of fellows. He shook my hand, and I don't exaggerate when I say that there was unquestionably a shudder of frisson that passed stealthily between us. Something mysterious and important. Something that spoke of wonders yet to come . . . 'how do you do, sir? May I acquaint you with all things Enchanting here-abouts . . . ?'

FIFTEEN

Dora

Oh my actual God. My brother is a mega moron. Mum says he's eccentric or something and it's like just a phase, but how embarrassing is he? I can't believe we are related. Especially today. He went off on a big one about who had to collect Mum's files from work, whose turn it is. Idiot. Then, when the new guy was giving them to us, he just stood there like a silent mong and didn't say a bloody like word! Thanks, Pete, like leave me to do all the talking, and the guy was just trying to be nice.

He's Australian or something – looks and sounds like that old Crocodile Dundee bloke.

He said, 'Wow, you're so tall! I didn't expect that in England, don't know why.'

What *did* he expect? Midgets? Like from Victorian times or something?

'Is your mum tall too?'

Peter didn't answer, didn't speak atall, just stared at him like a bloody goldfish, so I had to say,

'Yes, she's very tall. As tall as a block of flats.'

Luckily he laughed, coz Mum said to be friendly

coz she has to work with him for the next year or something.

There was a new girl there called Veronica who is working with George. She's really pretty and everything. Mum should of got her – why don't they put the girls with the girls and the boys with the boys?

You can so see George loves showing off to Veronica – he is doing that thing to her, where he looks over the top of his glasses at you really close up to make you feel like you're the only important one. It's a bit creepy. He did it to me once, and it made me feel nervous. It's scary. I think he just likes acting the big one. Like, 'I'm the boss, OK? And I can make you do what I say.' Yeah, well he's not the boss of me, and anyway, hello George, I know your like, *wife*, Jess remember? – because she was the one who like helped me with that project on Shakespeare I had to do in Year 10. She's lovely, so what do you think you're doing looking over your glasses at Veronica's mega jubblies? You twathead! My sixteen yr old weirdo brother is like, more mature than you! Be a bloody adult. Like Dad. He wouldn't dream of behaving like that. Maybe coz he doesn't need to keep making people notice him all the time. He doesn't mind if no one notices him. That's how he likes it. Mr See-Through.

Dad made fajitas this evening. Oh my actual like utter God or something, I just like bloody <u>LOVE</u> them. I would so marry a fajita if I could. Yum Yum. Coz a fajita is delicious and would like, never disappoint you or like dump you or anything.

Saw Sam today. He was in the baker's at lunch break getting a sausage roll. God, yeah, we used to do that together and like, he would like always choose the most burnt one or something? Those are his favourites. He said they were like the rejects of the sausage roll world, the unloved ones no one else wants, like as if they've committed a crime or something, against pastry.

Sam always stood up for injustice, and that's one of the reasons I like totally fell for him, even though Kitty Cook, the head plastic in my year, said he was a troll-boy. She doesn't know him like me though because all she cares about right, is what somebody like looks like. How shallow is that? Mind you, she *is* a plastic and that is the first rule of a plastic – you must be shallow. No depth required. You have to be able to like, see the bottom? I may be blonde, but you can't see my bottom . . .

Anyway, it was weird seeing Sam. Dunno. As if he knew I was there but couldn't look at me kind of thing. He got his phone out and started talking on it so he didn't have to speak to me. He pretended it had just rung, but it hadn't otherwise I would of heard his ring-tone coz he's got the *Mission Impossible* tune on there and it's really loud and he never has it on vibrate. He just suddenly started talking to obviously no one …

'Yeah? OK. Yeah. I will. Yeah. Really? OK. Yeah. Yeah. Yeah. Me too. Yeah. OK. Yeah . . . . Yeah.'

Honestly, it was so bloody embarrassing. I get the picture Sam. You don't want to talk to me. Fine. Think he is like ashamed or something that he went out with me? I might be shit, yes, but you don't have to be such a tosser about it Sam. I'm not ashamed I went out with <u>you</u>, and like <u>you're</u> the one with dwarfish legs! I would never ever make him feel bad so why is he doing that to me? It would almost be better if he like spoke to me and said something really nasty instead of ignoring me like this. What am I supposed to feel? Proper crap. That's what I feel.

Actually I really do feel crap. Like, in my gut. I added some of Peter's prawns to the fajita and I think they're out of date or something? Thought you could always eat prawns if they're in the fridge? Dad says they put the sell by date on to scare you. Well, yes thanks for that comfort Dad, but I can feel bad stuff going on inside. Going to bed.

SIXTEEN

Mo

Am exhausted. What a night. Was already feeling pretty rubbish on the tail end of this flu. Kids brought my pending files back, and I was able to work on those in bed for most of the evening although my head is still pounding. Husband made a spectacular hot toddy incorporating cloves and malt whisky, which did the trick and I was just nodding off . . . when Dora came in to start what has now become a regular occurrence, the nightly battle.

I <u>think</u> she is still feeling raw about what happened with the boyfriend at New Year, but that isn't what she discusses. She opened this particular night's hostilities with a rant about the need for even more highlights in her already utterly ruined hair and then she accused me of patronizing her by telling her the other day how beautiful I think she is.

'You are *such* a wonk, Mum! I absolutely need those bloody highlights. They're the only thing that take people's eyes away from all the other stuff that's so disgusting. Look at my legs, they're gross! I'm just, like so revolting. I'm *so* fat. Look at my bloody hips.

It's like I'm wearing someone else's hips on top of my own hips. And my arms! Oh my God they are so rank, they look like meat or something. And my feet. Just look. They're not feet, they are like two slabs of trifle. Not trifle ... I mean bloody cow's guts ... what's it called? Offal! Two slabs of slimy offal. With nails. Urgh! If you can't see how disgusting I am, you must be like, blind, deaf and dumb or something? And if you're not any of those, you must have noticed what a deformed bloody wretch I am, so you are actually just a big fat liar to be telling me the opposite aren't you?!'

Either way it was clearly my fault. I have made her feel worthless and ugly apparently. She flounced out when Husband shouted up that her fajitas were ready, and as she left the room, she threw one last mumbled insult over her shoulder – 'You sicken me, you lying bitch.' Nice.

Well, after taking a few moments to remind and reassure myself that these irrational verbal missiles are projections of her own insecurities and that she lightens herself by hurling them at me, and also that she <u>cannot</u> diminish me unless I allow her to, I took some deep breaths and managed to get off to sleep. I have no idea what time Husband crept into the bed, I just know he was there when I awoke suddenly at about 4am to hear Dora by the side of my bed sobbing, 'Mummy, Mummy.'

I put the light on to discover her standing there, shaking and covered in prawn-inspired vomit. 'I've been sick, Mummy!' She was suddenly two years old and in a flash we were both back then, fifteen-odd years ago. Husband jumped out of bed and automatically went to clean up her room. I ran a bath with Matey bubbles in, undressed her, and put her in. I stroked her hair and sponged her back whilst her sobbing changed slowly to wailing then weeping then snivelling then occasional whimpering and eventually to quiet calm. I rinsed out the nightie, and marvelled at the phenomenal amount of small whole prawns that were amongst the carnage. Fucking prawns.

I dried her and we even managed to giggle when I covered her in talc with my fabulous big pink powder puff I had for Christmas from Husband. We giggled more when I put her in one of my old nighties. She looked so tiny in it. Husband brought sweet tea, and I tucked her back into her newly made bed and kissed her goodnight. So <u>that</u> relationship – the mother and toddler one – is still intact then … How interesting. And how lovely. Am now knackered.

SEVENTEEN

Dora

Was like, spewing up like a blue whale's blow hole last night. Am staying in bed today. Dad called school and they said so long as I did some of my work at home, it would be all right and I won't get too far behind. The only really big thing I have to do is compose a song for Music. Should be easy coz I like sing songs all the time. And, if The Saturdays can write a bloody song, I def can! It was supposed to have been done in stages last term, but I didn't have time then. Now I've only got 'til next Friday to hand it in.

Think I'm going to write it about love or something and like about having a broken heart from being chucked or something. I would like really be able to connect with that. Maybe it would start like:

> *Oh baby I feel so sad*
> *Oh baby you got me so mad*
> *You gonna be sorry you let*
>   *me go*
> *No one else gonna love you*
>   *so . . . good.*

Then the chorus would be like

> *Love you so good, so good.*
> *Love you so good . . . yeah.*
> *Love you so very very good*
> *Love you sooo good.*

I could even put a little rap bit in, like Alesha Dixon does, like:

'Tell me baby, tell me true – who de lickle gal wot did love you? She be me 'n' I be gone. So you have to cry all night long. Come find me baby, in my lickle house. Come find me honey – cryin' like a mouse. Mash it up!'

Yeah, think that would work. Might need more lyrics for a second and third verse maybe. Right good, I've done that so now I can read the new *Heat* Magazine and maybe watch *Cash in the Attic*. Dad is coming back from work at lunchtime to make me something and check on me coz Mum's still ill in bed. Dad asked what I'd like for lunch. I said Pop Tarts. He said OK, but don't tell Mum. He's got to go and get some coz Mum won't have them in the house coz they apparently immediately poison you on contact, with like their evil sugar substitutes or something. Dad will have to go to Tesco and smuggle them in. Is his work near a Tesco? Don't know – no idea where he works. Think it's somewhere on the other side of Reading or something? He does something with computers or something? Anyway, he will def find the Pop Tarts. No doubt about that. If Dad makes a promise, he keeps it. Lunchtime is 3 hrs and 55 mins away from now. Countdown to Pop Tart lift-off.

Actually, I might have some Jaffa Cakes to keep me going . . .

EIGHTEEN

Mo

Still bedridden. Too much thinking time. I am convinced I am now in the foothills of the menopause. The perimenopause. It's a bit like being under starter's orders – you know it's all going to kick off any second now, but presently you are in limbo with just a few warning signs for company.

It's not at all what I imagined. It's mainly to do with my brain, my mind. I seem to be employing entirely different methods of processing information. Methods which allow for a small but perceptible amount of memory loss or a deal of confusion I've not experienced before. It's like I'm making allowances for being a tiny bit slower. I know for instance that it's slightly more difficult now to keep ten concurrent thought balls in the air. I can manage eight, but not ten any more.

Part of the problem, of course, is not wanting to admit it, especially at work. What would I say?

'George, can I have a tiny word? Just to give you a quick heads-up that I'm simply not as clever or quick as I used to be, and I'm certain it's going to get incrementally and significantly worse. OK?! Thanks.'

I am operating inside a kind of pink fog, which has blurred the edges of me. Ironically, it's only now of course that I realize the edges are the bits of me I most like. That's where the brittle and more dangerous verges of my mind-reef are, where I am most inexperienced and unbalanced. That's where I experiment and where I am a teeny bit deranged, and a lot scared. I feel like the fog is urging me to go back on to the safer, sturdier centre of the reef where I am well supported by habit and familiarity.

The most alarming part is the dawning realization that perhaps I have reached my limits. Up 'til now I have never once questioned that I can push my own limitations, intellectually and even sometimes physically. Now, slowly, I think perhaps I have unknowingly reached and touched that perimeter and am never going to journey beyond it. Like those huge sharks in massive aquariums, constantly swimming about at the edge of the glass, seeing beyond, but not being able to go there. It's a cruel trick of nature really. I've got the muscle, I am fortified by years of experience, I even have a chassis of sagacity, but the glass is too thick. That's the head part. The body part is another whole story. Whereas the brain treacle has been a slow, gentle, even barely perceptible pouring in, the body change has happened with alarming speed. All on one day, in fact. Two Tuesdays ago.

I went to the mirror to put on my face. When I started to dab on my tinted moisturizer I realized that I didn't entirely recognize the face staring back at me. There were enough vestiges of my familiar face to assure me it <u>was</u> actually me. But ... what were these folds and crevasses and blotchy red veins and big open pores? Who did <u>they</u> belong to? I knew immediately who they belonged to – to Pamela. To my bloody mother. I had seen this Ordnance Survey map of a face before, many times, but never in the mirror. It's not that I don't <u>like</u> my mum's face; it's just that it belongs on her, not on me.

I turned the mirror round to the magnified side and experienced what can only be described as genuine horror. The kind of fright that makes you eat a tiny bit of your pants with your bum hole. What fresh hell was this?! So <u>much</u> has changed. All of it not at all as I imagined it would. I expected sag and wrinkles yes, but not in this formation. My features look as if they've been in a vice, clamped hard on to either cheek and squeezed tight then left overnight to set. So, most of the lines are deep rivulets going from the top to the bottom of my face. Eh?! Gulleys down the side of my nose and mouth and chin, crevasses on my forehead and, the strangest of all, huge vertical wrinkles on my eyelids from the brow to the lash. What?! I have never seen this before, on <u>anyone's</u> face. It gives me the appearance of a corrugated roof. I am well designed to repel driving rain. No rain is ever going to enter my face, no sir. My facial downpipes and guttering will see to that.

I also seem to have grown extra eyelids. On top of my eyelids. Like molten lava skin has spilled down from my eyebrows and is now spreading out over my eyelashes, which can barely support the weight. Where has all this skin come from? Has it been hiding behind my hairline and ears waiting for my fifties to pounce? Well, hardly pounce, more like dribble. My face has surrendered. Two weeks ago it still had some fight in it, but now it wants a permanent rest. I can't say I blame it. It really has had to work hard in the past, what with all the reactions and expressions and everything. Never mind the weather erosion.

So, my face is my mother's.

Has my mother lain within me all the time? Has she nestled just under my skin, so close to the surface, that, as time has peeled off the layers she is more and more revealed, like a sphinx rising out of the sand? I don't know how to feel about that. My life has been an exercise in exorcizing her from me. I have made every effort not to become her. She is a good person in so many ways, but I didn't want to inherit her faults. I wanted to acknowledge and identify them, and then change. I wanted to move on and past her, to create my own person and my own place to be.

Some of the elements I wanted to alter aren't even faults, they are facets of her nature that just irritate me; her endless tolerance, her passive acceptance, her attraction to tragedy and trauma and her seemingly endless ability to cope. It's irrational and unpleasant of me to find all this annoying. But I *do*, and now I discover that she has been lurking, all these years, just inside me. She is physically arriving more and more every day, so is she eventually going to entirely body-snatch me? Character, personality, soul and spirit all consumed into one massive mother monster? A parasite of giant proportions who will eat me up, who <u>has</u> been eating me up all these years slowly and steadily without me knowing?

Oh God help me – I know what this bloody means! It means I am connected to her. Attached to her. Still. Whether I like it or not. I am tethered. But am I trapped? No, because that's where my free will comes into play. Having her face growing on mine steadily as a mum-mask is one thing (and not such a terrible thing – her

73

face is actually quite nice, very appealing, if ankle-deep vertical furrows are your thing) but I do not <u>have</u> to <u>become</u> her. I am an adult. Apparently. I can be whom-soever I wish, and I wish to be entirely *me*. So move over, Pamela, I'm coming through!

In the meantime I'm going to spend an exorbitant £80 on a miracle cream which I'm perfectly aware won't work, to try and grout some of the deeper trenches in my poor cracking face. It will make me feel better to spend the money. At least that way I have actively taken a stand. After all, I'm worth it . . .

Oh Christ. Am I?!

NINETEEN

Oscar

I do not eat. I rarely sleep. I merely breathe. I do not live a life worth living. I am a husk of my former self. I must certainly fade to nothing within the month. All is storm and calamity within. I have yielded my heart. It is entirely yielded. Peek inside me and you will discover only a heart-shaped chasm, a place where a heart used to be. Mine is no longer at home. It abides within another. Another who has little or no idea that he has stolen it. A thief, an innocent thief. The thief of my affections. That wonder of wonders. That clever, darling, dazzling dear gentleman. Dare I name him? Dare I let my lips dance around his moniker? Oh I am a silly silly boy. Yes. I will. Dance, lips, dance.

Noel

There . . . there . . . and there. Noel, Noel, Noel. Oh, the giddy whirl of it. Noel. One has to form a kiss to say it. Noel. Oh, I detest every pointless waking moment where I am not saying it. Noel. There's something of the rascal about it . . . Noel. And the angel, might I suggest? Noel. Let me die with his name on my lips and I will die happy. Noel. Perfect in every way. Noel, my dear Noel. It's absurd to imagine a life without you, Noel. Oh, when one is so very in love, the rapture of it is unbearable. I am dying of you, Noel, I am in bliss with you. I love you, damn it. I love you!

TWENTY

Mo

Not feeling quite right yet, not 100% chipper, but cannot possibly remain one more day at home. By yesterday I had begun to loathe the fuggy ill smell of my sickly self and my bed. I'm convinced that after a week or so of bedridden festering, the bed itself catches the disease and ingests it into its very structure and fabric. If you don't recover quickly and get up, the bed will take direct action and reinfect you back but ten times more virulently, as a punishment for being a pathetic wuss.

Anyway, I was up and out today. My legs were slightly surprised by the sudden and swift action required of them, bit creaky, but once in the car to work, all seemed usual. The same old journey, past the same old shops and school and cricket pitch and war memorial. I sometimes wonder if my eyes get bored flicking over exactly the same landmarks on this journey every samey day? I think I could do this journey with my eyes closed. I bet I could, I would <u>feel</u> the road, wouldn't I? I would instinctively know when and how much to turn the wheel, to put my foot on the accelerator, to stop, to start again.

Obviously the unpredictability of other cars might present a problem, or a rogue pedestrian maybe, but otherwise I'm pretty sure I could do it. Maybe early on a Sunday morning when no one else much was around? Would I have the courage to do it? Would I test myself like that? Would I behave so irresponsibly? It would be totally out of character. Would I just be too afraid – want to be safe? What would I choose to do if I wasn't afraid? If I didn't want to be safe or sensible? Yes, I would definitely do it then. Definitely . . .

But for now, here I was, driving to work like any other day. I was looking forward to catching up with my clients. Most of them cancelled last week when they discovered I was off. I know they need their therapy but I can't help feeling a little bit pleased that they prefer to wait 'til I'm back. George has covered for me where necessary apparently and the intern has sat in. My intern, not his. Am glad about that. Really not sure what some of my teen boys would make of the extremely well-blessed and underdressed Veronica. How would they concentrate with those in the room? Awful thing is, I suspect she would relish the attention. I wish I could defend her right to present herself any way she chooses at work. I certainly would feel strongly about that in relation to myself, but how do you legislate for the irresponsible?

Oh, shut up, Mo, and listen to your bitter self. What about if she just _is_ sexy, full stop? Does that mean she should be banned from this profession, then? No. Of course not, but I can't help feeling she is inappropriate, however clever she might be, because she makes a conscious choice to use her potent female sexual power in all interaction she has with men or boys. She has obviously never learned to do otherwise.

We used to call it 'DWB' at uni. 'Different With Boys'. We applied it to women who betray their entire gender by constantly operating in a submissive, teasing, coquettish manner, setting us all back by decades. Those signals which are all wrong for this particular workplace. For any workplace actually – unless it's a lap-dancing club. Please, Veronica, do me a favour, and don't teach these young men to only interact with you on such a frivolous level. Please display your cleverness, cover your baps up and save the faux milkmaid act for the bedroom where you can fake it as much as you need. (Personally, I think that's the prime place you shouldn't fake it, but . . . each to their own.) At least don't play those tricks at work with chaps that you are well aware can't resist it. Be classier than that. Don't give sceptical professionals like me, and especially the men, reason to dismiss you as lightweight. As a fluttering, flittery thing. As a kitten. As weak. As insignificant. Instead, use your considerable invaluable intellect and leave us in no doubt you are formidable, that you are of consequence. Oh – why does it bother me so much?! Maybe instead of ranting about her, I need to just get on with my job and leave Veronica to her methods. Just not with my patients, thanks.

I was greeted by Lisa who unless I am much mistaken (inconceivable), is gruffer than ever. 'Mornin'.' Gruffier than a Gruffalo who's been on a gruff-refreshment course. It's not the ideal first impression of a child welfare clinic, to be frank. It is the ideal demeanour for a fearless survivalist explorer. She is looking more and more like the unfortunate love child of Bear Grylls and Ray Mears. A union that doesn't bear imagining . . . the sheer khaki overload! Bit by bit, she is adopting her eco gear as normal workaday wear, and because I have been off for a week, it's crept up to quite a commitment at a staggering rate. Today, she was wearing combat trousers, hiking boots and a short-sleeved beige shirt. She looked like a keen junior staff member at a safari park. Nothing about her says 'I'm the receptionist – welcome – how can I help you?'

Everything about her says 'If you provoke me in any way, I will attack you with my alarming teeth and I will eat you.' So, we have a killer on the front desk and a strumpet in the therapy suite. Here come the girls . . .

My office was much as I had left it, save some extra folders on the desk and 126 emails awaiting my attention. George popped in and hugged me to welcome me back.

'Ah, the divine Mrs Battle returns to order our chaos and shine her light in all our dark and naughty places! Welcome back, Mo, you old slapper. Missed you big-time.'

He was sporting a floral Paul Smith shirt that I've seen him wear before, but only when he needs to impress. Veronica is obviously receiving some quality impressing.

She swanned by and gave me a little wave. 'Hi, Maureen, gorgeous to see you!' She was wearing a turquoise low-cut Indian smock-top with sequins sewn into the cleavage, and white trousers. Perhaps she believes we are about to launch our practice as a Mediterranean cruise? Enough. Shush. Back in the knife drawer, Mrs Sharp.

George invited me into his office for a catch-up meeting with the interns in attendance, before the first appointment. I took my pad and walked down the hall. I love my pad. Well, I love the leather holder – it's so battered now, it's seen nearly thirty years of frontline use. Husband gave it to me as a passing-my-degree present. It sits perfectly on my lap, holds the pad in place and has a holder for my pen. It shields the paper from the patient's gaze but isn't unfriendly. It's worn and weathered, like a trusted friend – to me and to the patients.

George was sat at his desk and we sat in the armchairs – me, the turquoise tartlet and Noel, my new shadow. He seems perfectly pleasant, not too cocky but nicely confident. I like New Zealanders; they have a freshness about them. Dora told me he looked like Crocodile Dundee. Not at all. He looks more like a serious cricketer. He is tall and lean like they are, with an easy manner. He seems respectful. Yes, I think we'll get on fine, and after all, it's only for a year. He will only annoy me if he is too needy or intrusive or arrogant. I have my Maginot line of mental fortifications at the ready, should I need to raise them. Thus far, no need. Mercifully.

TWENTY-ONE

Dora

Things I hate about me:

1. Am fat.

FAT face, fat nose, fat neck, fat ears, fat eyes, fat belly, fat arms, fat hips, fat thighs, the fattest knees in the whole sixth form, fat calves, fat feet, fat toes. Only thing not fat is hair, and that's like the only thing I actually want, is fat hair.

2. Am ugly.

Eyes not level and far too small. Scar above eyebrow from falling off scooter. Disgusting spots. Dandruff. Teeth uneven and yellow however much I brush them. Eight chins. Neck looks like a foreskin. I think. Haven't actually ever seen a real one. Arms look like an old fat retired wrestler's arms. With cellulite all over. Tits too small and face outwards. Nipples not even and look like dried apricots. Could never EVER show them. Torso too long for leg length. Really disgusting middle bit looks like three ugly people's middles sellotaped together. Could never show.

Fanny – like, <u>so</u> revolting. Looks like I bought it off the deli counter. Can't believe that's normal. Too many flaps. Could <u>NEVER</u> show anyone. Tree trunk legs with no shape. Shins are weird colour, spotty red and white. Feet are huge and more like flippers than feet. Small toe curls under, hardly there. Hands, fingers, nails – deformed.

3. Have hair everywhere.

Am like Mexican werewolf-boys. Eyebrows too thick and each hair too long. Hair on sides of face like Mr Darcy. Hair on top lip. Small thin hair under chin. Hair in nostrils. Hair under-arms in repulsive clumps. Small hair on arms. Hair on fanny – grows sideways and made of iron. Hair in bum crack! Not much, but there. Oh God I am vile. Not human. Hair on legs, full length. Hair on toes. Like hobbits. All above hair shaved on daily basis with Dad's sharp razor. Mum says to wax but like can't wait that long for it to grow. Hair all over me. Made of hair.

4. Skin.

Dry skin on knees, elbows, scalp, feet.
Oily skin on whole face.
Eczema elbows, knees, back of knees.

Spots – whole face, back.

Scabs – scalp, one on arm, two on legs.

Porridge-cellulite – belly, legs, tops of arms.

Colour – mostly pale grey-ish or bright red.

Except fanny – weirdly brown and purple.

5. Hair on head – normally disgusting brown and curly.

Has blonde highlights but they look shit and can't afford to get them done as often as I need so roots grow through and look sooooo like chavvy. Have clip-in extensions but they are different colour and get matted and look wrong. Blonde dye has made it go all dry so won't go right in the straighteners or in the giant rollers. Just sits on head and looks like a long dry disgusting hair hat or something. Can't even put it up coz then you see brown bits underneath. So completely disgusting that I have to hide it all under a woolly cap. Conclusion – I am a vile disgusting Gollum girl. No wonder I haven't got a boyfriend. Even I wouldn't go out with me.

I am hateful.

Hideous.

Ugly.

TWENTY-TWO

Oscar

Though Mother is a thoroughly good woman, it has lately come to my attention that she may not be best acquainted with a little friend I like to call 'taste'. She has entirely failed to note the dazzling beauty of the brightest star in all God's firmament, who just happens to be working in her office. My mother can now be officially registered as aesthetically blind deaf and dumb.

Poor dear wretch. She will miss so much. I fear she will simply be looking the other way whilst life displays its glories to her in all its splendid magnificence. She will die having lived the most tawdry of lives. It is naught but tragedy, especially since her advancing years indicate that she doesn't have much time left to arrest this lamentable spiral. Her life will have been a series of dull and colourless episodes. One following another, like the chimes of doom. Ding. Ding. Dong.

No matter. I have come up with the most inventive of plans, and poor dear dull Mama has no inkling of my cunning devices. I have offered my services to George, to voluntarily do some 'filing'. I'm not really sure what this task involves, but I have heard Mama mention the practice. I fancy I've heard her refer to various gap-year students in the past being employed thus to do. George was his usual affable self and said I could come in next week after school on Tuesday. Tuesday! Oh, Tuesday. Please be my 'good news day'. Please bring me into the orbit of my beloved, so that we might circle each other in the same constellation. Let Mother's office be the galaxy wherein I am the earth and he is the sun.

What to wear? I need to appear casually dashing. Elegant, without the slightest apparent effort. I can't believe that at our first encounter he witnessed me in school uniform. It is so dreadfully unflattering and appallingly dull. The school rules prevent me from personalizing it too much, although I occasionally slip a jaunty pochette in my blazer top pocket and if I spy a fresh bloom that matches en route to school (I carry miniature shears for that very purpose), all the better. Thus far I haven't been reprimanded for my attempt at élan but I was thrust into 'uniform detention' for the seemingly heinous crime of wearing a mauve shirt and a braided waistcoat on speech day. I was helpless to resist it. The thought of going up on the stage to collect my 'best reader' certificate and book voucher attired in nothing but the mandatory, dreary grey slacks, white shirt and green blazer of the indescribably unimaginative uniform, filled me with dread. What would people think? That I am some kind of automaton, a drone who falls in line? On such an auspicious occasion? An occasion that begs to be honoured with colour and flair. Those are my two mistresses, along, of course, with the great master – style. There isn't a single authority at school who would deter me from these, my true teachers, my gurus.

I think I will choose my white linen shirt with the ruffles on the front, and my yellow check slacks. The ensemble will appear casual but, at the same time, mischievous. He will be compelled to notice me but he won't quite know why. All kick pleats, French cuffs, bustles, trains and tiaras can bide a while in my box of tricks. For use later, when the fly is on the web. For now, subtlety must be my keyword, as I journey ever on, ever closer to my North Star. My Noel.

Speaking of dressing, and how to do it appropriately, today heralded a new low in Dirty Dora's panoply of distasteful attire. The floozy cretin came into the drawing room sporting a clinging pink T-shirt, intended by all accounts for a four-year-old child. The shape of it was entirely artless, grabbing viciously at her bosoms, and displaying her mass of wobbling stomach flesh. Across her chest was emblazoned the startling fluorescent logo, announcing her to be a 'Porn Star'. Charming. Not only is it sordid, it's supremely inaccurate. Dippy Dora could out-virgin Mary.

TWENTY-THREE

Mo

Parents' Evening at Dora's school was on Monday. Same at Oscar's (still finding it hard to call him that) school on Wednesday. The two experiences were polar opposites as always.

It becomes increasingly apparent to me that the education we offer our kids is a game with unfair rules. If you play by the unfair rules, you are a success like Oscar, but if you are a person for whom the rules are not only unfair but impenetrable, like Dora, you are a failure. There doesn't seem to be a system which measures personal growth or personal achievement. Uniform, standard measurements are all. You pass or you fail each exam. If you were previously 'failing' spectacularly but now you are 'failing' by only a little bit, it doesn't matter. You are failing. That's all. The exam system doesn't commend you for improving. I have been apoplectic with rage after every one of Dora's Parents' Evenings for seven years now. I can identify and attribute individual indelible furrows on my brow to each year. I'm waiting to watch the seventh rut appear ... like a branding, which is code for 'frustrated parent'.

Dora's school, Brook's Meadow, is a supposedly friendly, arty, sporty school. The reason we chose to move her there for the sixth form at ENORMOUS bloody expense, was because Dora was in hell at her previous school. We know Dora isn't an academic kid, but actually I believe she is more intellectually gifted than she or the school gives her credit for. She learned very early on that if you plod through the school process a little slower than your peers, if you are a tub gurnard, a bottom feeder, eventually teachers tire and you are left behind. This system can provide a haven for the idle as well as the unclever.

I think Dora is more of the former than the latter because on occasion, when truly motivated and interested, she has made the elementary blunder of opening the curtain around her brain treasure, allowing us to peek inside momentarily, and see just how much shiny stuff she's got stored there. It's quite a stash, actually. If you are ignorant, you don't ever have the ability to let your treasure glitter, but if you are hidden, like her, it's there all along. It is the duty, and should surely be the pleasure, of her teachers to locate it and help her display it.

Occasionally, very rarely, I have been able to creep in, and she has allowed me to momentarily witness her collection. It's at these times I am overwhelmed with pride. Not so much at what she has there, but at her courage to show it, even to me. Because she knows through experience that what she's got probably won't be enough. That's what has happened again and again, so she chooses the route of light-hiding and bushel. It is comfortable and familiar there, and strangely offers her, as a bonus, a place of higher social status. The position of outsider, the supposedly dangerous and fearless rebel. It is cool to be in either the anorexics' tribe or the couldn't care lesses'.

How she accomplished ANY GCSEs at all at her old school I don't know, and actually that is testament to how fundamentally clever she _is_. I don't think anyone at that school appreciated what strength it took for her to even turn up on the exam days. She was entering the firing range as far as she saw it, as the target, confronting exams which had a steady aim. But she went, and each morning when I dropped her at the school on exam days, her inner conflict was evident: attend and fail? Or abscond and fail? Absconding carried more credibility and came with the added bonuses of assumed control and power. Attending meant losing face by admitting that you do, after all, care about the outcome.

And look at the outcome! She passed four of them. Yes, C grades, but passes – and she goes and manages an A star for her art! Utterly incredible. Thank goodness in that particular instance, for her observant and sympathetic art teacher, Ray, who noticed that she was attempting to sabotage her grade by refusing to hand in her coursework, a project about fathers containing a beautiful pop art portrait of Husband. She had worked so hard on it, yet she felt it had little or no merit. She <u>predicted</u> failure. Even of something so obviously good.

So, this was the Dora we took along to Brook's Meadow. We told them she was seriously melting down to the point of vanishing, and they convinced us that this was 'exactly the kind of kid they welcomed'. The Head assured her that this was her opportunity to reinvent herself, to show herself and to participate fully, should she choose. I know she was excited at the prospect of becoming this whole new, motivated 'achiever', and we had to get behind her positivity, but I also knew in my heart it would be difficult to pull it off overnight. She would have to shake off the habits of a lifetime. A short lifetime, but an entire lifetime nevertheless.

We stood helplessly by as she fought them all for

her first year, retreating into the same old patterns of behaviour, hell bent on self-destruction. She was endlessly in detention. Detentions she refused to turn up for, eliciting further detentions. Which she didn't turn up for ... and on ... and on. The teachers were pulling their hair out and called us to various excruciating meetings to discuss it. Husband was my saviour at these. He steered me through, nice and steady, whenever I was prepared to rant, defend, overexplain, or just cry at the sadness and the hopelessness of it all. At one point, I felt his calming hand on my arm when Mr King asked if we thought Dora could 'even achieve the lowest levels we accept at our school?' There was the rub, right there – '<u>our</u> school'. Not Dora's school, <u>their</u> school. Where Dora wasn't that welcome, perhaps? Didn't really belong? Didn't fit?

Husband would constantly remind me that this was just school, that Dora didn't legally even have to be there any more, that in the end what mattered was her happiness. He kept repeating 'she is fit and healthy. She is not a drug addict. She is not an alcoholic. She is not pregnant. She is beautiful. You are beautiful. Everything's beautiful. Shut up.' He was, unusually, right.

And in any case, these past few months I've been heartened to spot real changes in Dora. She goes to school *willingly* every day. Unheard of. How can I explain to them that in Dora world, a Herculean attempt is in progress, that she is really trying, in her own reluctant, grumpy way, to take part in life. To invite herself in from the cold. To include herself. From our point of view, this is a seismic shift and we are hanging out the bunting to celebrate. In fact, I decided to make some bunting myself and send it to the rather sardonic Mr King, her Head of Year, to encourage him to also celebrate her astonishingly few attendances rather than admonish her for her failure-fuelled withdrawals.

So finally here we are, in her last year, and Dora has given up the fighting and is much more engaged. Better late than never. I sort of wish she could start again at Year 7 and this time believe that school isn't a hell where demons perpetually prod you with hot irons called SATs. Or exams. Or coursework. Coursework has replaced leggings at number two in my list entitled 'Things that are unnecessary, evil and plain wrong'.

Anyway, enough bile. Dora's Parents' Evening was the usual joyless standing about, waiting your turn to be slightly patronized by a series of various Gorgons and dragons. Of course, for me in particular, there is always an added pressure. I am a kid-shrink. They teach kids. It goes one of two ways:

1. Their utter delight and schadenfreude about the fact that I have an imperfect kid. A kid I can't 'save' or 'treat'. They savour that. That's a lovely chewy treat.
OR
2. They feel threatened by my analysis of the way they misunderstand my kid. In other words, they think I can psychobabble my way up my own arse. They believe I overthink my kid and her problems.

Probably a bit of both is quite accurate, but a lot is <u>NOT</u>. When it comes to Dora and Parents' Evenings, I am just her mum, and that's what renders me helpless with emotion. I can't bear for her to be attacked. I definitely take it too personally, because I see the effect their careless undermining has, and I feel it for her.

It wasn't as bad as it's been before. The usual lemon lips and rather pitying tone from most, but they had to acknowledge that she was putting in more effort than before to the A levels. The labyrinthine complicatedness of deciding which subject to do only 'til AS level, and which to continue on with totally baffles me, as it does every other parent.

Eventually Husband and I were both repeating the simple phrase 'I see' just to make them stop explaining. We don't 'see' at all. Dora and the teachers will have to make those decisions. As long as she keeps up her art and gets the grades she needs to get into the uni she fancies, I don't mind. Currently she is thinking of going to Manchester Metropolitan to do Food Tech. That's fine by me. Cooking. Yes please. At home, she has only ever made one omelette – with an unfortunate anchovy filling – but if she thinks this is her destiny, so be it.

The five-minute window we had with her music teacher was revealing.

'Hi there, Mr and Mrs . . .'

He looked down at his list, scanning furiously:

'Battle. Ah yes, the lovely Dora. What a friendly, very musically talented girl.'

Husband chipped in with, 'Yes. We think so.'

I shot him a do-shut-up glance, which worked.

'This term, Dora's set have been asked to compose an original song. Dora *was* slightly late with hers but she did do it. So let's not forget a big hurray for that. Hurray!'

We were transfixed by the sheer optimism of the chap.

'Admittedly the song is a tiny bit ... how should I put it folks? ... erm ... bland. Yes, a bit, generic, with lots of "ooo baby's" in it, like they do, ha ha, erm, but it certainly shows promise, so a big whoa for that. Whoa! Yes, bags of promise, that is, until verses two and three, which go as follows:

> Sweet dreams are made of this
> Who are we to disagree?
> Travel the world and the
> seven seas
> Everybody's looking for
> something.
>
> Some of them want to use you
> Some of them want to get used
> by you
> Some of them want to abuse you
> Some of them want to be abused.

He wondered whether we thought it sounded at all familiar? Just a bit, we agreed. He then pointed out that, even as an exercise in plagiarism it was pretty shabby. She had only bothered to change the words 'am I' to 'are we' in the second line. I'm guessing that she will have probably been distracted by *Cash in the Attic* on the telly and not really bothered.

Husband and I had a large drink in the pub afterwards and couldn't help laughing all the way home. Oh Dora. How we love you in all your splendid naivety.

Oscar's Parents' Evening at St Thomas's couldn't have been more different. He has had a few detentions, mainly for abusing the school uniform rules, or being a bit too precocious and cocky in his handling of some of the less-experienced teachers. His choices are spot-on though; he always successfully identifies the tossers as wankers. We had to agree on that. His judgement is sharp and accurate. He can sniff out anyone disingenuous or pretentious. He confounds them really. He is a true eccentric and as such he is unique, so the system doesn't have a comfortable place for him. They would love to be rid of him really, he is a bit of an eyesore, an embarrassment, but they can cope with that, because he's clever. He is on target for all A stars and he is their champion chess boy, public-speaking hero and quiz king. They can't afford to lose him. Their stats wouldn't look so good. So he is forgiven <u>everything</u>, whilst Dora is forgiven <u>nothing</u>. Repulsive.

TWENTY-FOUR

Dora

Oh my actual like holy God. What a totally amazing day. Just goes to show you shouldn't judge a book by its title, because I could never EVER of believed that Nana Pamela was <u>so</u> like, amazingly amazing. I was only supposed to be going over there to drop off Poo. She's being spayed tomorrow and Nana Pamela lives nearest the vet so she's taking her in. Mum wouldn't have been able to deal with it really, she gets so stressy about anything to do with the dog.

What <u>is</u> spaying anyway? I think it's taking out her eggs or something so she can't get pregnant. Hope she gets one of those huge cones they put on dogs' heads to stop them licking the stitches. She had one of those when her leg broke, it was mega hilarious. Kept banging into furniture and you could creep up on her from behind and scare her to death. Sooo funny.

I wish she wasn't getting it done though. It would be like sooo sweet if she had puppies, I would like sooo love it. With their tiny tiny teeth and tiny tiny hot tongues licking your face. I'm sure we could find homes for them. All of my friends would want one, especially if they could be, like really small, and fit in your handbag or something? Poo is <u>quite</u> small, border terriers are, but she would have to like mate with a boy chiwoowoo or something to make the puppies really tiny. Has a dog ever mated with a cat? That would be, like sooo sweet.

The dad dog would have to be white or something though because Poo is brown and if the dad was black or brown and small as well, the babies would be like really small and brown. So Poo would give birth to a lot of tiny poos. Be better if the dad was white or something, then the puppies would look more like dogs. I <u>love</u> it when the dog like <u>so</u> goes with the handbag? Like if the bag is pinky glittery and the dog coat and collar is too. It's sooo great. I know it's like totally plastic to want a mini-dog but that's the only plastics' thing I'm jealous of. Just that. The tiny dog thing.

Anyway, when I was at Nana Pamela's she made some hot chocolate and asked me all about Sam and stuff? It was good because although Mum and Dad know what happened, they haven't really talked to me much about it. Think Mum just reckons it was some kind of like teenage thing or something like it didn't really matter but it like so did because he was the longest boyfriend I've ever had and as well, he was the one I got closest to doing it with and that makes it like so special? We didn't actually do it, which I'm like so glad about now, but he really actually did want to, twice. So I could of.

Anyway, I was telling Nana Pamela all about him and she was like so listening. And it was so lovely and I was looking at her lovely face, which has looked at me like that all my whole life, always interested in what I'm saying and never talking about *her* all the time like Mum. And she hasn't got a phone that always goes off or writing to do or other teenagers at work to be more interested in than me, <u>her</u> <u>own</u> <u>bloody</u> <u>daughter</u> excuse me? So I just kept talking and talking, all about Sam, and school, and Lottie and stuff. Then she like totally gobsmacked me when she said, 'And tell me, sweetie pie, did you bonk each other?' Oh my actual God. Just like that. With that weird word old people say to make it sound like you're not actually doing it, you're just jumping about or something. Like Tigger.

Anyway, we just started laughing and it was really good. And I told her I've never actually done it and then we just kept talking about it and she said we should like play a sort of game where I ask like ANY questions I like about like sex stuff, and she has to answer really honestly. So it went like:

ME: OK. How long does sex actually take to do?
NANA PAMELA: Well, the cuddling and stuff can take ages but the in and out and done stuff is about five minutes usually. If you're lucky.
ME: Oh my God. I thought it took hours.
NANA PAMELA: No hon. Only if you are Sting and his lovely wife Judy and even then, most of that is just talk. And endless awful meaningful staring. I should imagine.
ME: How do you know if you're good at it?
NANA PAMELA: All girls are good at it. Being a girl automatically means you're good at it.
ME: Does cling film work as well as a condom?
NANA PAMELA: No, never do that. And conversely, don't ever keep your sandwiches in a condom either.
ME: What is a female condom?
NANA PAMELA: A bad idea.
ME: Should you ever let a boy put his you know in your bottom?

NANA PAMELA: Entirely up to you, but personally I think that's the exit not the entrance.

ME: Could it happen that he might wee in you instead of the other thing?

NANA PAMELA: No. Never. Men have plumbing that tells them exactly when to do which thing. The only time that goes wrong is when their brains mistake car parks and shop doorways for toilets.

ME: Should you believe him when he says his ball bags are filling up and it could back up into his body and poison him or even just burst if you don't help him out?

NANA PAMELA: No. But you could offer to puncture or lance them with a sharp implement in order to facilitate drainage. See what he says then.

ME: When should I say yes to going all the way?

NANA PAMELA: When that boy is a beautiful generous spirit who loves you and cares about how you feel and doesn't pester you to do it before you're ready. When you know he will understand how golden the moment is, for both of you. When you can honestly say he's a top-notch fella who thinks you are the cat's pyjamas, and wants to make this moment matter . . .

And then Nana P started to cry and I didn't know what was the matter. She told me it was all right, it just made her remember Granddad Ted and how lovely he was when they were young. I like, so couldn't believe it when she told me they did it when they were both sixteen! Oh my actual God. In a sand dune in Dorset! Apparently like, after it was over and they were lying there, he told her she was 'a gem of the first water', and Nana P says that's when a diamond or something is the best ever quality, when it's the clearest, like water, or something? She said she felt 'exalted' and that's what I deserve too because I'm splendid she said. Yeah. But, like how can you 'exalt' someone with fat knees? Then we had some delish pineapple upside-down cake she made, because she knows that's my favourite. She said 122% fact it wouldn't go to my knees.

TWENTY-FIVE

Oscar

So, Tuesday finally deigned to arrive. I was Tuesday's slave for a week, and he was my master. What a cruel master. How could he tease me thus, by purposefully putting the brakes on time? Each twenty-four hours has meandered past, a snail-like sluggard, mocking me with its retarded impertinence. All life has been in slow motion. Chug chug chug. I was on the verge of acute melancholia when, as if by magic, Monday was upon us heralding the glorious and imminent advent of Tuesday.

As if kick-started by the school klaxon at four-fifteen, my underarm sweat glands commenced their damp attack, firstly on my school shirt and thencely on my white linen shirt with frontal ruffles which I changed into in the toilets, along with my yellow check slacks, and the winkle pickers I purloined from the back of the Pater's wardrobe. On closer inspection of the said shirt I noticed that it was less than white, in fact it could more accurately be described as grey. Sadly, not a bold, purposeful, brave grey. More like a limp, 'I was thrown into the machine with a careless leaky young black sock' grey.

It has been said of Mama, and with much truth, she is no expert laundress. The whole family have, at one time or another, fallen victim to her ineptitude in this, the very epitome of womanly skills. Ah me. I had no option but to soldier on enrobed in dull grey. I had no doubt and took comfort from the fact, that my irrepressible wit and sparkling bons mots would be the focus for my dear Noel, not my disappointing shirt.

I shovelled my uniform into my school briefcase and took a few moments to attend to my toilette. It is the mark of a gentleman to arrive upon the scene well groomed and fragrant. I hoped that a liberal spraying of the Pater's sports deodorant would help to staunch the underarm flow, and if not, at least perfume the offending area. I splashed some of Pamela's lavender water about my neck and face and tugged some Brylcreem through my unruly shock. I let alone my chin where I am pleased to note a small but significant display of hirsute manliness has recently sprouted. I fancy I cut quite a dash on a final glance in the broken mirrors. Unfortunately I had to don the God-awful blazer to leave school (rule) but all in all, I knew the effect was pleasing.

The journey to Mama's office was a delight. It might have taken considerably longer had I been condemned to walk on the pavement but of course, I had a ticket to ride on a cloud. My step was light, my transport was air and my companion was joy. The quickening beat of my heart helped to hasten my passage, and the very essence of Noel called me on. The sky was bluer, the sun was brighter, the flowers were more colourier than ever. All was verdant and fresh. Although admittedly a 'big' fellow, I was but a wisp, being carried along by the sweetest of zephyrs. Tumbling, whooshing ever onwards towards my destiny. Towards my love. Towards Noel.

In less than a fairy's tinkle, I was at the door. Now, my heartbeat was calling strong and refusing to be quiet or still. My heart urgently wanted to physically connect with his, and was trying to escape from my chest to find him. Lisa greeted me with the fairly offensive 'Ha! Here he is, Giant Lord Fauntleroy, come to work amongst the mortals!' She directed me towards the back room behind her desk where the filing cabinets are.

Lisa has become increasingly strange. She is looking more and more like that mad Australian crocodile man who died in a stingray attack. Steve Irwin. Yes, Lisa is becoming him. The thought flashed across my mind that one inconceivably awful explanation for her odd metamorphosis could be that she was attempting to allure Noel by making herself familiarly Antipodean. I dismissed the thought pretty quickly – it was too horrible to countenance.

She gave me a cursory demonstration of the archaic filing system they have there. I can't quite believe they still use handwritten notes in this way, but I suspect much of it has to do with Mama's allergy to technology. It is positively Dickensian, but at least my task is pathetically easy. Put files in alphabetical order. Yes, I do believe I am capable of that. In fact, I quickly realized I was going to have to feign a deliberate slowness in order to stretch it out. All the while I had to come up with bogus excuses to emerge from the back room so as to catch sight of my paramour.

That's the damnable thing about these mind doctors – they work in sealed rooms with tightly closed doors. One is not permitted to enter during their 'sessions', even to offer refreshments. I learned that very early on from Mama, when, as a young boy of thirteen I barged in and sat down whilst she was mid shrinking. I thought it would be fine to join in as it were, and enquired whether their particular problem was anything I could contribute to? This was, apparently, an outrage, and I was quickly ejected with a lengthy lecture about propriety to follow over the kitchen table at home later. So tedious.

Thus, in order to catch sight of my beloved, and to allow him to feast his eyes upon me, I must appear as if out of the ether, utterly coincidentally, by his side. It must be supremely casual. Nothing deters a potential lover so much as the whiff of desperation. In order to know when he might be approaching, I needed to be positioned at the front desk, near Lisa. This meant concocting numerous reasons to come out and station myself by her. I dreamed up endless questions to preoccupy her, mostly practical requests and banal enquiries, like:

'Do you enjoy working here?'

Or:

'What time did you start this morning?'

Or:

'That's a lovely practical haircut you have there.'

But she was soon flagging and in need of a more fruitful line of enquiry so as to elicit lengthier stories, thereby allowing me to tarry awhile longer.

I hit a rich vein when I chanced upon her obsession with outdoor pursuits and her survivalist lifestyle. Her attire should surely have been the clue, but I was after all otherwise distracted. After nearly two hours of relentless information on the subjects of hammocks and their many uses, poisonous plant life and the merits of cooking a rabbit in an underground hangi, Maori-style, I was nearly beaten. As yet, there had been no sighting of Noel, so I raised my metaphorical white flag and retreated to the back room.

I had little to no interest in the filing but did find some solace in the contents of the files themselves, which were immensely enjoyable to read. Mama writes quite well. Obviously these documents are in note form and consequently severely précised, but still, a vibrant and engaging style shines through, mostly very pleasantly expressed. Judging by the multitude of supposed 'behaviours' brought to her, I can only conclude that she is the very saint of patience. People really are beyond the pale. What on earth do these young folk think they're doing when they speak aloud of 'feeling dead', 'hating Dad' and 'want to cut myself'? For heaven's sake, you silly nancys, just take a brisk stroll and cheer up! Stop depressing my mother and wasting her time with your pointless whingeing, you great babies. If I were your therapist I'd get up and stroll over to where you sit and give you a proper slap. With the full force of my hand. What a dreary shower of Olympic-level moaning minnies you are. The least you could do would be to invent a malady with the merest modicum of originality. What despicable bad manners – to bore your therapist into a torpid oblivion.

The reading occupied me for the best part of an hour until Lisa surprised me by calling out 'That's it, mates! Time to shut shop. Last orders, please. Could the deluded, misguided and lost make their way to the exits. Followed swiftly by their patients. Thank you and goodnight.'

Quelle horreur! The day was over and not a moment had been spent with my darling dreamboat. Terrible – all is terrible! Mama emerged from her drab room and offered me a lift home. I was initially reluctant, because perhaps now, at this last moment, I <u>might</u> catch a glimpse of him? Of his dear dear lovely visage? Perhaps now, as the workday ended, he too would reveal himself and appear alongside the other weary day-enders? Might he appreciate a reviving Dubonnet and lemonade in my company at some nearby hostelry? Might he be thankful for a quick neck rub perhaps? I enquired of Mama, as casually as I dared, 'Is Noel not finished too . . . ?'

Her answer was brief but devastating.

'He doesn't work on Tuesdays.'

Curses.

TWENTY-SIX

Mo

I have an angry rash on my face from my allergy to the expensive anti-ageing cream, AND ... The bloody dog is bloody pregnant. It's sod's law, isn't it? I finally get round to having her spayed and the vet tells me this. I did notice she was a bit fatter, but we're all a bit fatter. I'm fatter and I'm not pregnant. Dora's fatter and she's not pregnant ...

Oh God ... Please say she's not pregnant! Surely not? She'd tell me if she'd started having sex ... She couldn't possibly have had sex without telling me – could she? And surely not with that boy – can't remember his name – Ben? Tom? – not with him, please. He's only two inches tall. Please tell me she hasn't had sex with Tom Thumb, without telling me? No, I genuinely think she would. There is already precedent for open dialogue on that subject – we definitely sat down and had a proper eye to eye across the table frank conversation about sex and what it involved, when she was about thirteen. Definitely. The channels are open. Yes. Sure of that.

Anyway, the dog is the far more pressing thing at

the moment. The kids are delighted of course, even Husband thinks it is 'cute' for Poo to get the chance to be a mother. Yes, we all love puppies but what the hell are we going to do with them? Who's going to take them? How many will there be? The vet reckons they will be born in six weeks or so, which is just around Dora's birthday. Great. Two separate major stresses converging at once.

Dora is asking for a 'prom party'. What has happened to British teenagers? It's as if they've taken a communal drug that convinces them they're in a cheap American horror flick. I didn't know what a prom was at her age. I didn't know what a sleepover was. I didn't know what an actual nightmare Halloween could be. Why do they all want to dress up in tuxedos and cheap satin and have beauty pageant hairdos and tiaras and pretend they're from the Midwest? Whatever happened to warm cider and a few joints at a mate's house followed by a frantic fumble in a graveyard? That's a party. Oh, it doesn't matter. We <u>can</u> go down the route of the dread 'prom', I suppose. I tried to point out that she will have already just had the school 'prom' (the entire school have obviously taken the same delusional pill) weeks earlier but she assures me that 'duh, it will be sooo completely different'. How?!!

Why is it that I have a nagging feeling of failure when it comes to kids' parties? It began when mine were both small and the fierce competition started up between all the mothers as to who was giving the best parties. I freely admit I was drawn to it like a moth to a flame. The phases were clear. Early on, the aim was to have the best clown or puppet show or storyteller. Ruby Bond's mother easily won that when she had an 'in' at the BBC and secured an actual *Blue Peter* presenter. Then there were the eco-friendly and arty parties. Make your own piñata and paint a plate. Again, Ruby's mother was the champ, ensuring all ugly plates were glazed and delivered to the parents accompanied by a mug with an adorable picture of the birthday girl emblazoned on the side. Damn her to hell, I was still struggling to find the correct party-favour bags to impress.

It was Nell Barlow's mother who trumped us all in the end though, when she arranged an entire petting zoo to be present including hugging a koala, a boa constrictor experience, and a donkey ride to finish. *Plus* the kids were all given documents to prove they were now adoptive parents to individual, personally named, specific, orang-utan babies. One each. Bugger. I threw in the party towel there and then. You win, Nell's mum.

I must banish all these irritating distractions and crack on with my book. I have settled on *Teenagers: The Manual*, as the title. In order to write it well, I am having to remind myself constantly that I am good at my job. I know fundamentally I am. People recommend me. People return to me. I have, on occasions, worked with two different generations of the same family, so I must be doing something right. I am doing a <u>lot</u> right. You don't get to be forty-nine without discerning at some level whether or not you are successful. It's one of the facets of this job that, in time, one gets 'a nose' for it. I can often detect the root cause of the trouble within a few sentences.

Of course, I <u>may</u> be proven wrong, but honestly, not often. That may have something to do with my strongly held beliefs that pretty much <u>all</u> toddler and teenage malaise can be rooted in the parents. The parents, of course, don't want to hear this, so that is always my first hurdle, to reassure them that A. they've taken the brave step by coming and B. that it's not their fault. I am usually telling them by session ten that it <u>is</u>, in fact, their fault. Of course, I don't use that word. No blame is apportioned in my room. Ever.

Today, I am writing a chapter entitled 'Time and the Teenage Clock'. I'm hoping to try and explain some difficult neuroscience in layman's terms. I have been reading up on the teenage brain and finding it fascinating all over again because the adolescent brain differs from the adult in virtually every way. Not only is it not yet fully cooked in terms of development, but it actually seems to have functions that are present only in teen brains. Like the whole idea of 'teen-lag', where the night-time troughs and daytime peaks of melatonin secretions occur two hours later than in adults. This puts teens in their own time frame, two hours adrift from the rest of us, hence a possible explanation for the really tricky grumpy mornings, and the very late nights. Although, frankly, with my own teens, their idea of time is aeons out of synch, not just two hours.

Dora is still clattering away on Facebook at two in the morning quite regularly. I wake from sleep and instantly know she is still at it. Of course, I had no such possession as a kid her age. I'm sure I would have found it equally as mesmerizing. I'm grateful it wasn't an option. The more I think about the time she gives to machines, the more I realize, with horror, that at the root of my constant fury about them, is something like jealousy. It's as if I am locked out. Locked out of her life. It's preposterous. I don't want to be her friend. It's exactly the advice I most find myself giving to my clients. Parents who wish to be liked by their children are on a doomed route. And yet ... I do find myself longing for a closer relationship, where we properly speak and listen and, most importantly, HEAR.

If I'm totally honest I really mean that <u>she</u> properly hears *me*. After all, nothing Dora says is anything I haven't heard before, from countless other teens. I am already ten steps ahead of her, I can predict how it will pan out. So easily. The difference in *our* family is that both Dora and Oscar have access to a mother who is trained to *understand* teenagers and their problems, who knows that what really counts is to listen to them and give them healthy amounts of quality time, where only <u>THEY</u> matter.

Damn it! Husband is shouting up the stairs for me to come and join them all for lunch. I don't want lunch, for God's Sake, I don't want to talk, I want to press on with my book. When will I get <u>my</u> quality time? Bloody never.

TWENTY-SEVEN

Dora

Had such a weird conversation with Mum. Sometimes she is like so deranged. She shouldn't be allowed to do her job really, coz how would people feel if they knew how nuts *she* can be? She's supposed to be the calm clever one but I swear to God she gets it so wrong sometimes. Mostly it's coz she's such a drama queen. Everything is such a big deal. She just can't seem to chillax atall. She's gonna like die of a heart stroke or something if she doesn't chill.

It all started with her telling me that Poo is having puppies. Yay! Me and Dad and Peter have been longing for that for eight years. It's not fair for her to have the spaying done before she even gets the chance to have just even one little puppy of her own to love and cherish. She doesn't get a say in anything, stuff just gets done <u>to</u> her, she doesn't choose at all. We choose her name, her collar, her bed, her food, when she goes out or stays in, everything. Now she's really struck out for herself. She's gone and done it with some other dog. We don't know which one, it could be the manky poodle from the sweet shop, it could be the Labrador from the park – it could be like, _any_ dog.

Apparently they do it really quickly? Maybe that would be the better way for us as well. Meet a guy in a park, look each other up and down, make a quick decision yes or no, have a sniff of their toilet parts ... Actually, no not that bit. Then just mate. Over and done with, then walk on without even like looking back. Thank you. Trot on. Very nice. Goodbye. That way you wouldn't get your whole heart broken in two and made to feel like a big fat loser by Sam Tyler the world's smallest freakboy. And you could do it with the next one you meet in the park two minutes later, without having to like, get your highlights done and your bikini line waxed and have a bath and get new clothes and stuff. They wouldn't care. You wouldn't care. You'd just do it. It's more honest, to be honest.

Actually, I am like _so_ over being a virgin now. I really want to _not_ be a virgin soon? My eighteenth birthday is coming up and omigod I'm like, still a virgin? It's so like embarrassing. Omigod.

Anyway, Mum was yapping on about y'know, 'what's going to happen with the puppies? Where's she going to have them? We'll need to get the vet here so she doesn't die ...' Blah Blah. Panicking on and on. And me and Dad are like, 'It's going to be fine. She will know what to do instinctively. We'll make a little corner up for her. We can put an ad in the local paper to sell them.' Like that, but she's not listening, and suddenly, out of nowhere, she asks me to come and sit at the table. That always means it's going to be bad if it's not a meal time. We like <u>NEVER</u> sit down at the table like that. Looking at each other.

She started off pretending this was like some kind of normal girly chat thing like we always do or something? Not. Then, out of bloody nowhere, she suddenly says, 'You're not pregnant, are you Dora?' Like that. Like a bloody gunshot or something. The dog is pregnant, so I must be pregnant? Eh? What is she talking about? Like somehow you catch pregnancy off dogs? What is her bloody planet? And thanks for assuming I'm some kind of slut or something. Doing it all over the place with, like <u>ANYONE</u>. And thanks for like rubbing my nose in it just when I'm feeling so 188% virgin that no one wants to sleep with me anyway coz I'm so bloody fat or something. And thanks for pointing out how much fatter I've got that you even bloody think I'm bloody pregnant you bloody idiot Mother.

She makes my skin creep. Why is she my mother? Why couldn't I have one like Lottie's who just, like listens and doesn't say stupid untrue stuff all the time just to bloody hurt you? Why did I get the mad one? Dad just got up and walked out, he was just like, so grossed out.

'No Mother, you major douchelord, I am not pregnant. Shall we put that in the paper to let people know? Like, "Mr and Mrs Battle are delighted to announce that their daughter Dora is currently unpregnant." Would that do?'

She went on and on about how she is 'entitled to ask' and perhaps if I 'included her' more she would feel like she is a part of my life. I don't want her in my life full stop – never mind telling my private stuff to. I only live with her because I have to. I can't bloody wait to get away from her. I full on proper hate her. I do. I hate her.

Look what she's bloody made me do now. I have to eat like this whole packet of Jaffa Cakes to even feel a tiny bit better. So thanks Mum, for all your endless belief in me. Perhaps if you stopped thinking I'm a slag, I might actually <u>like</u> myself a bit more and then I might <u>NOT</u> eat so many Jaffa Cakes? Excuse me. Who is the shrink now?

TWENTY-EIGHT

Oscar

Well, really. Is it my lot to be so unutterably disappointed my whole lifelong? Today I was forced to come to terms with the undeniable notion that even The Enchantings might ultimately prove to be shallow. With the exception of myself, of course. One hopes against hope that one's choice of members is sound and well judged, and yet . . .

We convened at the usual hour, in the dingle. Today's password was 'Audrey Hepburn'. Hargreaves knew well enough who she was, but Wilson commenced a litany of atrocious transgressions by pronouncing her name to be 'Angela Hopburn'. What a beautiful fool he transpires to be. He claimed never to have heard of her. Thus followed a full fifteen-minute briefing on the many attributes of said Ms Hepburn. Hargreaves employed words such as: 'elegant', 'tiny' and 'posh'. I rather fancy that I was a jot more eloquent, parrying with the likes of 'gamine', 'flawless' and 'dainty'. I even dared to posit that very naughty word, 'pert'. Ultimately I reduced them to a respectful hush with 'paragon'. Yes, a fitting victory.

We endeavoured to move on to various other topics including the necessary withdrawal of Anton Du Beke from the top ten list of Enchantings' Icons, due to his recent ill-mannered trespasses, and of course the ever-thorny and controversial issue that is Peter Andre. Hargreaves was generally chatty and willing to contribute whereas Wilson was bafflingly inadequate, revealing himself to be pathetically wanting.

Have I massively overestimated him? Perhaps I have been blinded by his beauty. I suppose if I were charitable I would remind myself that he is, after all, only a Year 9er, rendering him a good couple of years junior to myself and Hargreaves. He simply hasn't lived as we have. The sheer paucity of his Enchantings-worthy knowledge ought to be excusable, yet I find him to be increasingly irksome.

It could well be that he simply pales in comparison to Noel. I am acutely afflicted with Noelitis, that's a cert. Even Hargreaves's hearty attempt to lift my spirits with a breathy rendition of Gershwin's 'Someone To Watch Over Me' didn't do the trick. My heart remains leaden. I took the opportunity of a willing and captive audience to recite some lines from an Ode to Noel, which I have been working on.

O my racy pulse stops, and a
  sleepy sorrow starts
My mind, as though of serpent's
  sap I had sipped
Or spilled full lull into the dear
  sweethearts
Of two star-crossed buds, hence
  been nipped.

Admittedly I owe a certain debt of gratitude to Keats but I feel sure he would commend my attempt. Wilson seemed somewhat saddened when I spoke the lines. Perhaps he guesses that he has been usurped in my heart by Noel. I admit it. I have Noel fever. Help me, doctor.

TWENTY-NINE

Dora

Got a letter this morning. Well not an actual letter, but a kind of appointment card thing to tell me the date – omigod – of the first round of *X Factor* auditions in London!! This is like, so boom! This is it, baby. Stage one. Passed it. I can continue on in my goal of my dreams towards becoming Britain's Next Top Singer.

I so cannot tell Mum and Dad about this. They just don't understand. They are both old and they've like totally given up on their dreams now. All they do is their jobs. Whatever *they* are. Well, Mum does therapy with teenagers and families and stuff and Dad . . . has a job too. On computers or something?

Not me, I'm not going to waste my life on a bloody job where you just go to the same place 24/11 and die of boringness. I just *can't* for God's sake. I've got a talent and it would be oh so wrong not to let it out, not to let other people hear me. How would I feel if I just go to uni, get a degree, get a job, get a family, get a dog, get a house? It would <u>kill</u> me. Proper dead. I want to <u>LIVE</u>. I want to sing, sing, SING! 'I believe I can fly. I believe I can touch the sky . . .'

THIRTY

Mo

Interesting day. Am feeling somewhat unsettled, but not unhappy. Little bit muddled. Nothing serious.

I agreed to give some time to Noel at the end of the day, so that he could fire any questions at me. Thus far he has been the perfect shadow – hardly ever in my line of vision and taking up very little of my time. Of course George's experience with Veronica seems to have been rather different – but then, George is only too keen, isn't he, to find time to answer the slightest query and to assuage any doubts his needy protégée might have. Ho hum.

Noel is practical and, frankly, more professional. He is fascinated by the fact that I am amongst the very few who still keep session notes in longhand. I have always taken minimal notes during the sessions, other-wise essential eye contact is lost, and frankly it's just a bit rude. But I don't think anyone is put off by my occasional scribbles in my lovely battered old pad holder. As long as I write up my notes after each session verbatim, I see no reason to log everything on the computer. I also feel that, ironically, the files are safer in this tangible form, where they are filed out of sight, securely. The computer seems so dangerously accessible somehow. George is constantly telling me that passwords and suchlike are fierce protectors but I prefer to stick with my old tried and tested system. Until someone can prove me wrong, I will continue to do that.

Noel seemed fascinated by all this when we sat down together. I thought for a moment he might be suppressing a scoff, saving up a snigger for later, but I realized I was wrong, he was genuinely interested in my methods, which for a young buck in his thirties is fairly impressive. He was attentive and curious and his subsequent questions proved that he was listening. I suspect he's a bit frightened of me. George is forever telling me that I am regarded as a Jekyll and Hyde figure – calm and patient with my clients, but rigorous and brusque with everyone else. Fine by me. Totally true. Ask my family – none of them are my clients and consequently I'm sure they'd agree that their mother is chiefly evil Mrs Hyde. A little bit of nominal fear from a trainee is no bad thing, it keeps them on their toes. In Noel's case, though, he seemed to be bravely battling his misgivings in order to find out more, and so I felt inclined to be helpful. Even though I have very little time.

Actually, I am completely snowed under, a fact I was describing to him when he tentatively asked if I would like to continue our talk in the pub since Lisa seemed to be actively kicking us out of our own offices. She has taken to violently jangling the keys as she stomps up and down loudly announcing the end of the workday. Lisa has assumed the role of warden. More baffling is that we have all willingly assumed the roles of inmates. Or rather, outmates, since we aren't permitted to be 'in' past Lisa's strict curfews. I'm pretty sure this is the wrong way round.

Anyhoo, I didn't see much amiss with the idea of a quick drink since George and Veronica are regularly to be found in The Keys after work. Not, it seems, on this occasion.

Noel bought the drinks, I had a half of cider, he had a pint, and we sat by the door on the only available and very draughty table. Initially, he continued his line of questioning about various aspects of work, and he was extremely engaged. There's no doubt that he is bright and he is definitely confident about his prospects for a career in psychology. He is less of a Jungian than me, more Kleinian, more interpretive, but nevertheless, he's clever, I think. Even a little argumentative when pushed, which I like. We had quite a rewarding wrangle over confidentiality, and he became quite heated:

'The fact is, Mo, that if I get a kid in front of me who finally opens up and admits he is feeling suicidal tendencies, what am I going to do? Not tell the parents? Or what about criminal activity? Not tell the parents then? Or the police? Or you? It's bloody difficult . . .'

It was really invigorating. Great. It was nearly time to leave when the conversation turned to our own families. He seemed amazed that I have been married for twenty-six years. No more amazed than me, I assured him. I genuinely <u>am</u> amazed. Twenty-six years with one man. Even at the altar, when I was happily pledging my <u>whole</u> <u>life</u>, I didn't really mean as much as twenty-six years. I suddenly realized that I have been married for more of my life than I haven't been married. I felt alarming, ferocious waves of degeneration. I have been closing down for more years than I was opening up.

Noel said that he 'admired' me for 'sticking with it through everything'. What 'everything' does he mean? He doesn't know me from Eve. He has had no part whatsoever in my 'everything' – yet oddly I was grateful for his appreciation. He can't possibly know any specifics, can't possibly. Surely he was being general, meaning my general 'everything'. That must be what he meant. Yet his comment has stayed with me, and I'm wearing his admiration like a favourite cardi.

I'm still enjoying it, now. Why? Maybe it's because I don't feel I've been admired for a long time. Not 'admired'. It's a professional word, I know it, but it's taken me a little bit by surprise how quickly I wrapped it round me, how pleased I was to hear it. He's a sweet chap, Noel. Easy to be around and easy to teach. The time whizzed by and before I could ask him anything about his family, I realized it was late and I'd missed picking Oscar up from chess club. I'll hear about that for weeks no doubt ... pretty sure there will be a monumental lack of 'admiration' coming at me from that department.

THIRTY-ONE

Dora

Lottie was sooo late coming over this evening, she was supposed to be here at like six or something but she didn't show up 'til after nine. I could tell Mum was stressing but she put on that fake thing for Lotts, sort of like pretending that our house is some kind of easy-come easy-go sort of place where you can drop in any time you like coz we're all so relaxed. 'Open-house' she called it. That is 108% <u>so</u> not true.

Mum hates people coming over, coz it means she's got to pretend all evening, and she gets tired from it. She even came up to my room with a tray of hot chocolate and like snacks and stuff . . . crisps and stuff. She <u>NEVER</u> does that but she was acting like this happens all the time. Yeah she just brings up trays of nice drinks and snacks all the time because, hey y'know, 'these kids are working sooo hard for their exams', and like, 'what is it with all this endless measuring and assessing of kids these days' – it's 'monstrous' and 'inhibiting', they should be allowed to just 'be kids' instead of 'exam robots' apparently. Then, when people have gone, she goes right back to like, 'Have you done your coursework?! It's due in by half-term. You've got to do it by yesterday! Switch the TV off immediately!' And she's back to being this like totally freaked out stress queen. Like, why don't you decide who you are and stick to it you psycho.

Lottie was well happy with the hot chocolate though and when I said it was all fake she said her mum does exactly the same and anyway, who cares because we've got hot chocolate so –YAY! That was a bit weird, because every time I've been round hers, I always think her mum is like, so cool. I never thought she was faking it atall. She's just like a normal natural lovely kind person who I wish my mum was more like.

Think Lotts is just saying that to make me feel better. She's sooo kind like that. Today I said she was my sister from another mother and she sooo like agreed. I really love her. We've got no secrets atall. We share everything. I so know that like, if someone was going to shoot her, like in a bank robbery or something – I would sooo say like shoot me instead, and I would jump on her so no one could hurt her. And she says she would do the same for me. She says that if one day I like, can't have a baby or something, she would have one for me? That is sooo precious. Like she would use her womb for me?

We tried to figure out how it would actually work and it seems like she would have to get my husband's sperm or something somehow. I said I'm not sure I would like that and she said it wouldn't actually <u>mean</u> anything, she would, like not even look at him or get drunk or something and they would like totally have to promise not to actually feel anything when they do it, and the thing to remember is that they would both be doing it <u>for</u> <u>me</u>. Like a sort of present kind of thing. It wouldn't mean *anything* for the two of them *atall* with each other, *not atall*, it would *only* be for me.

I feel a bit weird about it though, because like I would so love him and I would so think he would totally fall in love with *her* instead, especially if they're always doing it, even if it is just to give me a baby. And then, when the baby happens, and I took it home, I would have to keep looking at a baby with *her* face on it all the time? It kind of creeps me out, so I might say no to that. I didn't want to tell Lotts that though because she was just being kind.

She thinks I've lost weight, and she's right because I haven't been eating any main meals atall, just snacks, so I think it's gradually coming off now, especially around my hips. I noticed, because my jeans are sitting back down on my hips where they are supposed to because they're hipsters, but when my belly is bigger the waistband goes under the belly and the flab goes over the top and they hurt. I don't think jeans should hurt. And anyway, no one cares about hipsters any more, they are like <u>so</u> gone. Lindsay Lohan has got these really great high-waisted blue trousers that are like <u>so</u> cool so I want a pair of those now, so I'll have to look for that type. No hope in Pangbourne, I'll have to go into Reading. Maybe me 'n' Lotts can go at the weekend. Dad will give me the cash and drop us off. Mum will say we can only go if we do our work and 'earn' it.

Maybe I shouldn't get the trousers now coz I'm obviously going to lose loads more so maybe I should just wait, or at least wait 'til just before the *X Factor* auditions. That way the trousers will be new and I'll be thin so it'll be perfect? I'll wear them to the audition.

Omigod, me 'n' Lotts had to act like we were so doing our coursework but really I was practising my song and she was being Dannii Minogue and like telling me what to do. She loves the Christina song and she thinks I do it even better than Christina because like, Christina actually <u>is</u> beautiful but when I sing it, it's more true coz I say, 'I'm beautiful – no matter what they say,' and that's more like real life coz no one could say Christina Aguilera isn't beautiful. But they could say that about me.

Which reminds me, I'm not going to wear my glasses on the audition day. Lotts says my eyes are my best thing, so I'm going to show them. She's def going to come with me. I so can't wait but we're not telling the parents coz they'll just freak out. Anyway, we've got loads of time coz the exams and the prom and my party happen before that. I am now thinking that maybe two prom things in a row might be a bad thing, so I might change my party to a Bunnies party instead, where all the girls have to dress like cute bunnies type of thing? That would be, like so hot. After Lotts left, I Facebooked everyone and told them about the Bunnies thing. No replies yet but it's ages away.

Soooo tired. Going to sleep to dream about Simon Cowell doing that big-eyed surprised face when he hears me sing for the first time and saying, 'Omigod Dora. You are like, so the best singer we've ever heard. You are what this show's about. You are gonna be a star, little lady. And what's more, you've got gorgeous eyes and Dora, you are beautiful, no matter what they say.'

THIRTY-TWO

Mo

I'm so glad Dora has Lottie. For a while she didn't seem to have any real friends, then up popped Charlotte who broke ranks from the dreadful 'plastics' to support Dora when there was a massive fuss about which of the American TV vampire shows was the best. The entire lower sixth form came to a shuddering halt one lunchtime whilst the incendiary stand-off took place. Dora was in a group of one, until cheeky Charlotte took up her cause, and argued the case for *Moonlight* against the behemoth juggernaut of vampire triumph that is *True Blood*. Only when Lottie *also* pointed out that both factions were in total agreement about the unquestionable supremacy of *Twilight* the movie did the whole brouhaha dissipate, with relatively little collateral damage on either side.

No lives were lost on that occasion, although many confessed that death via Robert Pattinson's fangs would always be a welcome end. I sort of get it ... but then I don't. He's too girly for my liking, as if Jude Law, Orlando Bloom and Bela Lugosi had been melted down to create a wispy vampire offspring from their combined smoke.

Anyway, Lottie was, and still is, Dora's advocate and the only one that has hung in there. It's sweet when she comes round so that they can study together. Not that they study at all, but at least they are together, hatching plans and whispering and giggling, exactly as you're supposed to when you're seventeen. Lottie seems an unlikely amigo for Dora at first sight. She is petite and fragile-looking. The type of girl with indeterminate but interminable asthma. She is the physical opposite of Dora and they both, endlessly, pointlessly, wish they looked like the other. Lottie wishes she was tall and strong with Dora's blossomy skin and sheets of rain-straight hair. Damaged, but straight. Dora wishes she was smaller and more feminine with the mixed-race mocha beauty of the fabulously freckled Lottie. Lottie has the most audacious hair I've ever seen, an afro-tousle of tight curls that shoots out in all directions like a firework. She hates it, and complains about how uncontrollable it is, whilst Dora can't wait to get her hands in it and play – tying it up, plaiting it, slicking it down, putting thirty different-coloured shiny butterfly clasps in it. Anything Lottie will let her do, hairwise, Dora delights in. Dora wants more hair, Lottie wants less.

Lottie always wears funky hats or big fabric flowers in her hair, and Dora falls asleep every night dreaming of such opportunities to be so casually exotic.

If they were blooms, Dora would be a yellow sunflower and Lottie would be a fuchsia orchid. Of course, neither of these typically adolescent beauties can see the beauty in themselves, only in each other. For this, I am so grateful because Lottie's bountiful praise is the only type Dora allows to land on her, so it is such a nourishment when I hear Lottie piling it on. Long live Lottie and her generous wonder-working spirit.

I can't help it, and I know it winds Dora up, but when the two of them are together, I am overcome with the desire to nurture their friendship with plenty of motherly gestures. I like nothing more than to prepare a tray of treats for them and slide the goodies into Dora's bedroom. This is what Pamela used to do for me during the dreaded uni revision, and I've never forgotten the delicious comfort of it. I suppose I'm trying to pass on some of the care she showed me back then. It's not entirely altruistic of course. The sense of satisfaction I get from providing like this is enormous and I suppose really, at the heart of it, I'd love them to invite me in to share it all with them. I wouldn't go in of course, but it would be lovely to think Dora might want me to . . .

THIRTY-THREE

Oscar

The majority of today was supremely unlovely. Dippy Dora displayed the true dimensions of her monumental ignorance at breakfast when she announced with giant confidence that she was hitherto only eating white food. She claims that she has been reliably informed (*Heat* Magazine, I suspect) that should one limit oneself to only a singular colour of food, one will certainly lose weight. I suggested that blue might be a wiser choice since she would then be restricted to a diet of blueberries, blue Smarties and toxic Slush Puppies. On second thoughts, these are representative of Delusional Dora's favourite food-types and she would be sure to gorge 'til the statistics of the breadth, height and girth of the silly girl were shockingly identical.

I do wish she might demonstrate <u>some</u> restraint, if only because somewhere, under all the paunch and plastic, my sister is hosting the possibility of something akin to beauty. So, Dreary Dora <u>could</u> one day be Dreamy Dora, should she prevail.

I am well aware that I am no David myself, but I'm afraid the bald unjust truth is that it matters less for chaps. A solid bulky frame such as mine can be viewed as not unattractive. It carries the markings of stature and importance. I am a man of notable bearing. At the risk of pronouncing myself as vain or arrogant, I think I can safely claim that I am a significant person. Physically, at any rate. Dizzy Dora presently appears to be someone who couldn't care less. The irony is all too apparent because, of course, she cares very much, certainly about what others make of her. I know from some of the louder, more gauche fellows at school that she is thought to be very nearly pretty but far too apologetic.

If Dreadful Dora could only know her potential, I do believe she could thrive. However, this latest show of madness will not assist her in that respect. White food. What means she? Perhaps she will live on a diet of clouds.

After that inauspicious start, I had to face the fact that it was Tuesday again and I must inevitably fulfil my promise to George and finish the filing, despite knowing there was absolutely no prospect of viewing my darling. If I were to withdraw from this commitment, I would only alert them all to my passion, so I must needs do these last few pointless, fruitless Tuesdays.

I could hardly bring myself to connect with Lisa, who insists on yabbering incessantly, blissfully unaware of my failing interest. Today was a particularly grue-some diatribe:

'Right. Listen up. Amputation. Sounds unlikely but, supposing, Peter slash Oscar, that a person was trapped by a limb in a burning wreck, yea? Imagine that. Ter-rifying. Immediate action is required. One! Application of a makeshift tourniquet using garments as restric-tors. Two! The precision of the incisions, to exclude important arteries. Three! The correct severing of the muscles and retraction of the skin are crucial to suc-cessful recovery. And you are going to need your buddy to recover fast, mate, believe me, to help you ward off wild animals who will for sure be circling you for the kill once the fire is out and they've smelled the blood.'

All these details were apparently crucial, and had to be explained at length. At spleen-wrenching, vomit-inducing length. I was tempted to tie off Lisa's arteries and, using all the tricks she'd taught me, relieve her of her tongue. Instead I gradually shuffled my way to the door and finally withdrew to the back room.

I only had the last five letters of the alphabet's worth of files to sort, meaning mercifully, not many. I was interested to see two generations of a family of Vick-ers had been regular clients, with depression and low self-esteem at the centre of their various difficulties. The problems of the Walker family were mildly entertaining also, including one incident of self-harming with a Stanley knife. I had very nearly finished my task when I noticed a file under 'W' was out of place. On closer scrutiny I was curious to find the surname attached was 'Wilson'. Of course, I had to read on, despite the fact that Wilson is a very common name and it would be highly unlikely that these folk would be attached or related to my particular Wilson.

The case was beyond tragic. It seems that when the boy Luke was three, he and his father were fishing for dabs in the sea when they were cut off on a sandbank by the tide. The boy, at his father's behest, climbed on to his shoulders to remain above the rising tide. The mother and older brother on the shoreline had called for assistance, but the older brother who was twelve couldn't bear to wait and had frantically swum out to help. When he reached his father and brother, he discovered that his father's legs had sunk into the muddy sandbank and he couldn't get out. Meanwhile the tide was quickly rising and starting to lap over the father's head. The brother dived down repeatedly to try and extract his father's legs, to no avail, and gave his life in the attempt. When the rescue boat arrived to gather up

Luke, he was still perching precariously on his drowned father's shoulders.

I found myself in floods of tears reading this awful account, movingly told to my mother by Luke himself. How would one ever recover from such a disaster? I could see that Mama had been incredibly sage in her analysis of this woeful boy's long-held guilt. Much of his poor record at school and all-round underachievement, which his distressed mother was so worried about, could clearly be assigned to this tragedy. He was often predicting his own failure, and then living a self-fulfilling prophecy. He was having regular weekly sessions with Mama and was trying to work his way slowly out of the big wretched cement boots of guilt he was clonking about in. Poor Luke. My heart was bleeding for the sad little mite he must have been.

I then looked at the contact details on the top of the last page of the file. Luke's mother, who attends the sessions with him once a month, is called Karen, and she's a dinner lady. At my school. Wilson's mother is a dinner lady at my school. LUKE WILSON. I've never known his first name. Year 9s don't have Christian names. Luke is Wilson.

THIRTY-FOUR

Dora

Right, I've <u>GOT</u> to finish my art coursework by the end of this week so what I'm going to do is: I'm going to make a list of all the things I need to get and do for the school prom and for my bunnies party before I start that.

<u>School Prom:</u>

1. Purple Prom Dress (below knee, strapless with netting petticoats)
2. Bag to go with dress (small, but must fit phone in)
3. Shoes to go with dress (at least 3½ inch heel)
4. Strapless underwired bra. 36DD
5. Pants to match. Not underwired
6. Hairpiece. To match own hair but be able to curl and put up
7. Tiara or flower or blingy hair slide
8. Short jacket or, like fake fur wrap thing
9. Tights (won't need if legs are tanned)
10. False eyelashes with sparkle on
11. Jewellery – necklace, earrings, rings (expensive-looking or borrow Mum's)

12. Book a tan session, hairdressers, full manicure and full pedicure with tips
13. Book limousine or check if I can go in someone else's
14. Get a camera. Only got the one on my phone and it's crap
15. Charge up and borrow Dad's video recorder
16. Get boyfriend or date for the night

Own Party. 18th Bunny Bonanza:

1. Book a big room in hotel
2. Get Bunny outfit. (Ordinary, sexy outfit but with bunny ears and tail)
3. Fishnet tights
4. Shoes (at least 4 inch heel), black, shiny
5. Big earrings (hoops but not chavvy)
6. Tiara (with BIRTHDAY GIRL written on)
7. Huge cake (with funny but flattering statue of me on top) OR loads of different-coloured cupcakes with like glitter on
8. Book DJ (don't let Mum do this)
9. Get flashing disco lights
10. Rent karaoke machine
11. Book Hummer limo for me to arrive in
12. Loads of lager, vodka, coke etc.

13. Glasses (with umbrellas, cherries etc.)
14. Get badges with 'Dora is 18' printed on for everyone
15. Try to book a boy band or something. (Like maybe an old one like Blue or something to make it cheaper?)
16. Get someone to make a film (get loads of friends and family to wish me happy birthday and say nice stuff about me. I will look surprised and cry when it's shown on the night – should also film)
17. Organize food – (8 family buckets of KFC?)
18. Get boyfriend or date for the night

THIRTY-FIVE

Mo

Caught sight of myself today in the window of the bank at lunchtime. For a tiny millisecond, I genuinely did not recognize the reflection. Firstly it was moving very fast and so I only glimpsed it momentarily, the way you sometimes see a bird dart into a bush. Swift, sudden, hardly there. It was only after I had passed and was starting to process what I had just seen, that I realized I was moving fairly fast myself, in fact I was entirely in step with the blurry bundle of grey I had just spotted beside me in the window of the bank. In the window. In the reflection of the window. In the reflection.

So then, that must have been me.

The shock of this realization slowed me down 'til eventually I stopped. Right outside the estate agents. I turned to look again, this time in a different window, which was full of property details suspended in clear plastic, behind which was an office of eager, attractive young liars at desks. I wasn't looking at them, I was confirming my suspicion that the reflection I'd already seen was in fact me. The stack of haggard grey was indeed staring back at me with frightened eyes in a face that was similar to mine but much older, and more like Pamela. No doubt, though. It was definitely me, just not the me I imagine myself to be.

I suppose that if I think about it at all, I would imagine that if anyone met me, they'd meet an above-average-height woman with a good French-ish shortish darkish haircut, a long face with large very green eyes (often commented on), a fine nose, and a large mouth with lots of tidy teeth. A face that says I'm clever but not intimidating. I have never relished being tall, so I don't think I read as a tall-and-therefore-more-important-than-you sort of person, but I've somehow always imagined my physical persona permits people to know I'm in charge if needs be, that I'm not to be messed with.

I'm not super-fashionable and of course I have to wear the appropriate clothes for work, but even so, I'm pretty sure I've got a fairly good sense of style. I know how to wear tonally correct, simple classic clothes. I wear a lot of linens and layers, subtle blues and greens and browns. I like a pashmina and, unlike many tall women, I like a heel. I <u>love</u> jewellery that makes a strong statement. Big necklaces hewn from amber and tiger's-eye are among my favourites. I prefer stockings to tights (sole reason Husband proposed), and a fountain pen to a biro. I wear fresh sharp citrus scents, nothing sandalwood or musk. I always have one very good coat that I'm prepared to spend a month's wages on once every two years.

Today I was wearing that good expensive coat, which is one of the reasons I was so shocked to see a tired middle-aged woman in a cheap coat looking back at me. An ill-fitting dreary grey coat. How could I have misunderstood the grey so thoroughly? I thought it was an elegant, mysterious, timeless rich grey, for rich people with immense taste. It's not, it's ageing and wersh and weak. My coat is insufficient, and so am I. Everything I have always feared becoming was staring back at me. I seem to have already become it while I am pointlessly fearing it. I looked tired and desperate somehow. I look as if I have been savaged by life. This shouldn't be happening. Not ever, never mind *yet*. I look like some bad clothes wearing a woman. I am tall, yet I seem to be a woman of impoverished demeanour. How the hell have I ever assumed that I am even slightly powerful? Evidently . . . I am a wreck.

Why hasn't anyone told me about this? Why hasn't Husband shown signs of shock and dismay? Why hasn't Pamela given me a warning shot across the bows? Did it happen so gradually, imperceptibly, and that's why I haven't seen it? I've noticed the surrendering of my face, but when did the entire person give up? I am walking about in this body believing that I am underpinned rather well, but obviously I have subsided, and no one has got the inspectors round or informed me. Is it that I only ever really look in small mirrors, so I haven't seen the full-length effect?

I was so supremely shocked by the sight of myself that I attempted to walk off several times to escape the reflection, but I had to keep returning to that window, to confirm that what I'd seen was in fact true.

Eventually, one of the young pretty liars emerged from the gloom on the other side of the glass to flash a knowing smile at me. He was mouthing something . . . What? Smiling and beckoning. Oh Lord, he thought I was looking at one of the properties in the window, when I was actually looking at myself. He came to the door and invited me inside. I was so taken aback by what I'd seen and so embarrassed by what he'd thought I was looking at, that, for some inexplicable reason, I meekly followed him in. Forty minutes later, I emerged from there with a handful of particulars for gorgeous little country cottages that were, apparently, in my price range. My entire lunch break was misspent with a young man I didn't like, looking at houses I don't want, pretending to be a person I'm not. What the shitting cock is going on? That's forty minutes I won't get back in a life that's already six months in arrears.

I hurried back to work and spent the few precious remaining minutes of my lunch break in the toilets dabbing away furiously at my face with make-up, in a vain attempt to staunch the horror, applying my own Boots-sponsored mask.

I was amazed that none of my afternoon clients recoiled in shock, so I can only deduce that I am correct in thinking the decline has been gradual and no one wants to be the first to notice it. Or perhaps, worse, none of them ever actually take any note of me whatsoever. They listen to me and they hear me but they don't really look at me – is <u>that</u> it? Have I become invisible? Would I be more effective as simply audio? Have I become so unfortunate to view that it's simply easier for everyone to slightly look through me, just as you do when you are face to face with a person with a disfigurement of some sort? We sort of look beyond, we distract ourselves with the importance of what we are saying rather than dwell on the difficulty of the looking.

No one is looking at me, they're not seeing me. I'm a ghost.

THIRTY-SIX

Oscar

This week I have been on close terms with Master Regret and his mother, Lady Shame. How could I have treated Wilson so shabbily? I have cast unbecoming aspersions on him ceaselessly. I descended to depths of such despicable arrogance when I actively deplumed him in the presence of Hargreaves.

True, Wilson was revealing himself to be an unquestionably tiresome hobbledehoy, but I wasn't to know the seat of his grand sadness. A suffering that has undoubtedly eaten up his confidence and joie de vivre. How can he possibly learn anything when he is so very sunk in misery?

I am a clumsy bungling insensitive fool. It is usually beneath me to be so singularly odious, but on this occasion I have surely triumphed as the world's unkindest twot. I ought to be beaten by psychopathically violent nuns and have my eyes stabbed out by deranged woodpeckers. My heart should be wrenched from me by slavering wolves and I should be grateful to have my limbs removed by a drunk woodsman with a blunt axe. I am a treacherous hateful shitcock who should, at the very least, be murdered instantly.

Wilson is a prince, a ravishing masterpiece and an utter cutie. I should heap adorations upon him and drown him in valentines.

Yet. I cannot. For I am besotted with another. I am prepared to die at the mercy of this greedy infatuation. Noel. He is the flame. I am the moth.

THIRTY-SEVEN

Dora

Think only eating white food is going like really really well? It so 120% works, and I can't believe all the great stuff you can eat. In the last day, I've had bread, pasta, egg mayonnaise, bagels, white chocolate, vanilla milkshake, white candy floss, marshmallows, white cheese, milk and loads of other stuff. What's amazing is that when you've had a meal, you feel so like bloated that you don't want to eat anything else 'til the snack or the next meal. I can't feel that my clothes are any looser yet, but in the next few days I expect the pounds will just like, start to drop off. Can't wait.

This week has been one of the most boring of my whole life so far. Everyone is moaning on about exams all the time, school, home, everywhere. Do revision, do learning, do exams, do school, do prep. That's all I hear. Well, sometimes, I would like to take a break if that's OK? I heard on the radio that if you, like, stop for fifteen minutes every hour, it like really helps you to study better? So if you are going to study for like six hours that's

15

15

15

15

15

15

---

90 minutes

I just think it's best to take that time in one lump chunk, just after my lunch hour but NO, apparently that is a sin and an 'utter misuse of time' according to Mum. So, I sat down to make a study plan this morning. Got out the card, the felt-tips, glitter, etc. and by teatime I'd finished it and it is so like beautiful. It's one of the best things I've ever made. I've used neon felt-tips to make the grid, and different-coloured fabrics to indicate the different days and subjects and stuff? Then I got some of Mum's ribbon from her wrapping drawer to connect up all the subjects with the study sessions. I've made flaps to go over all the subjects so that it will be like a little surprise when I lift it up and see – oh, OK this morning I have to do Home Ec. theory, that's a surprise, wonder what it'll be this afternoon? It's like a giant advent calendar and at the end of each revision session I have stuck on a little matchbox with a suggested snack inside (white only, of course).

So, say you have studied art stuff for forty mins, you slide open the box and ta-da – 'Hi Dora! – you are allowed 8 white chocolate buttons' etc. etc. Y'know, for a treat for working so hard. Then, at the bottom of each day, is a sliding door-type bit of cardboard I made with sellotape and Post-its which you open when you've finished and it says stuff like – 'Hey well done Dora! You can watch an episode of *True Blood* coz u've earned it, lady!' then, all over it I've done like, little sayings and work mantras to cheer me up, like WE DON'T DO PERFECT HERE! OR EXAMS ARE FOR SCHOOL, NOT FOR LIFE! OR STUDY YOU HORNY BITCH! Stuff like that.

I went on Facebook to tell Lottie all about it and posted up pictures of it for everyone to see. It's sooooo cool. Everyone wants one now, so it looks like that's my weekend gone. I've got such a cool idea for Lottie's one – to put like all furry stuff everywhere coz she like so loves fur, that's SO her.

I bloody hate bloody exams. What is the bloody point of them? And the teachers are a load of bloody hypo-crites because they keep telling us how bloody important it is to get these subjects coz apparently they 'open your horizons' and stuff but look at *them*! What did *they* bloody do? They learned bloody Geography at school then went to uni to learn harder Geography and now they're teaching loads of kids who hate it – Geography. Yeah it really opened *your* horizons Mr Parker.

And I've got hormones at the moment as well, which makes revising bloody impossible even if you do get a treat every forty minutes. *And* my back aches, *and* I've got bad eyes, *and* I've got period pains, and anyway, my Psycho. Ed. Report said that I'm a kinaesthetic learner, so the bloody teachers aren't supposed to give me notes, I have to do mind maps, I've told them that, but no – just get on with it Dora and do the hard slog. I WOULD IF I COULD YOU BLOODY MORONS!

Anyway, the point is, there is no point me even tak-ing the bloody exams because nothing I've been taught, except in Music, is going to be any use to me. Ask Leona Lewis when she last used some English language? Never! That's the point! If I get through those *X Factor* auditions to the next round, then they'll see . . .

When I'm a huge mega world star, I'm going to go back to school and ask the Head if I can have a meeting with all the teachers in the staff room. When they're all sitting in there with their special mugs and Ryvitas, I'm going to say 'Yeah, thanks very much for teaching me Maths and English and Geography and History and Home Ec. and Art and everything, but guess what? – I haven't used a *single* word of *anything* you've *ever* said you losers and what's more – I'm a huge star, and every three minutes – yeah click your fingers – every three minutes – I earn more than all of you put together do in a whole year. Revise THAT, you mothersuckers, and spank you for coming. Goodbye!'

THIRTY-EIGHT

Mo

Today was full of surprises. I am allergic to surprises. Nothing makes me feel sick to my stomach more than a surprise. It's a good thing a surprise <u>is</u> a surprise because I would dread it long ahead if I knew about it.

Actually the start of the day was far from a surprise. Breakfast, kids, Husband, dog – same old same old. Sometimes I find a kind of comfort in the familiarity of it all. Knowing for sure that Husband will go to the cupboard, intent on wholesome muesli but will submit at the first sign of bread or croissant or the night before's left-overs. If he maintains his resolve and has the muesli, he looks terribly dejected as he sits with his *Independent* and his jacket on the back of the chair, as if he has been denied any last jot of joy in his life. If he gives in to temptation and has a plate of something he really wants, he is like a naughty school-child who's just been let off detention. He bounces about, cracking gags and kissing us all. Such simple, small, easily attained pleasures are the stuff of life to him. Personally I think he should abandon all attempts to eat healthily and just be happier instead, but every morning he puts himself to the test. Oscar asked him once why he bothers with the notion of the healthier option at all?

Husband replied,

'Well, thing is, as the dad of this family, I am the protector, the provider, the hunter-gatherer.'

I couldn't stifle my giggles at that.

'What am I? Chopped liver? Think you'll find I do a fair bit of providing, mate . . .'

'Shut up, cave-wife, or I will have to club some respect into you. I am the man here, I am head of the cave, and as such, it is my duty to stick around as long as possible.' He started lurching around the kitchen doing a silly caveman impression, looking more like a gorilla than a Neanderthal.

'I go out, kill sabretooth with ug bare hands and ug drag home to cave to eat. I haul massive boulders for many ug miles and heave into circle forming ug blockade around home enclosure to ward off all other cavemen and beast attacks. Ug. Ug. This is my purpose, so must eat muesli and keep body fit.'

His body is long past fit. Although, actually, he was <u>very</u> fit at one time. His passion for all things rugby demanded it. In fact, I think rugby players have to be extra fit because they are most certainly going to test their fit bodies with lakes-full of Guinness in the bar after each and every match. They have to be in prime condition to fight off the effects. He did that very successfully for many years but now he sports the full Guinness look. The paunch, the jowls, the heaviness about the thighs. These are added to the rugby look – the broken nose, the thick neck and the relentless beard that is never EVER totally shaved, even the second after it's *been* shaved; it is always there, just under the skin ready to power through with testosterone as its fuel.

Unlike so many of his beefy cohorts though, Husband is a minor miracle because Husband still has hair on his head. Loads of it. Thick, steely, could-use-it-to-scrape-stubborn-dinner-off-pans grey hair. It is warrior hair, Spartan hair. It will not die, it will fight and kill first.

It's curious then, that with an ex-rugby-player's physique, a perpetual five o'clock shadow, a broad back, a thick neck and a hint of broken nose, that he isn't more imposing. His very greyness has swallowed him up and, like me, he has become neither attractive nor unattractive – just middle-aged. The years have stolen his features, and somehow returned them to him after too many boil washes. He still has the bearing of the man I knew, but in a kind of soft focus.

Oscar prefers to breakfast on Coco Pops or any brightly coloured toddlers' cereal, followed by huge doorsteps of bread toasted and dripping with butter and jam. But the jam must be scooped out with the small silver spoon he received on his christening. Dora was genuinely addicted to Pop Tarts for five years and refused to try anything else but since the whitefood-stuffsonly regime has begun, she too is scoffing the white bread. With white marshmallow spread. Yeuch. The dog dined this morning on a bowl of croissant with bread and jam and had Coco Pops for afters. I wish they would all understand that Poo is a dog, not a bin.

Anyway, after a banana, which is *my* breakfast of choice, I drove to work. I am never bored at work, quite the opposite, but sometimes the habits of my life – the breakfasts, the squabbles, the same faces around the table, the same old journey – left, right, left, second right – past the same old places – shops, school, cricket pitch, war memorial – just exasperate me.

I had hoped that writing my book would wake me up but even that seems to be an exercise in churning out the same information I've been thinking about for years. I suppose we all get a bit weary of ourselves from time to time. Don't we?

SO – it was at least a little bit different to arrive at

163

work to discover that George had planned a surprise. We were due to have a share and support session in the afternoon. None of us had clients booked in, so George had decided that since the warm weather was now upon us, we should take a picnic down to the river and have our session in the open air. I found myself resisting with pathetic reasons like:

I'm not in the right clothes.

What if the weather changes, do we have brollies?

A mosquito might bite one of us, and it might go septic.

We might get grass cuts.

There could be adders . . . or worse . . . voles.

The look of disappointment on Noel and Lisa's faces was enough to jolt me out of my doldrums and when I saw the effort Jess had put in to prepare a splendid picnic for her husband's workmates, all her home-cooked hard work, I felt ashamed to have even questioned it.

Off we went, all squishing into George's estate car. I had a momentary pang of irritation and yes, I admit it, jealousy when Veronica climbed in the front with George. In the front. Where the parents go. George and I are the parents, aren't we? Then I realized how preposterous it was to think like this and, anyway, huddled up between Lisa and Noel in the back wasn't so bad.

Oh give me someone funny any day. You can't help but love them in the end. They will laugh you in towards them and you are helpless to resist. I can't remember the last time I've laughed so much. It's intoxicating. I remember that quote my father always used to repeat – it's J. M. Barrie, I think – 'Those who bring sunshine to the lives of others cannot keep it from themselves.' That's right. Lisa is sunny. She assumed the role of a tank commander, issuing loud navigational orders to the lowly, dim and blind tank driver, George. She guided us to the site where the picnic was to be with some pretty impressive map reading.

We tramped over a huge field 'til we found the spot George wanted on the riverbank, and we laid out the picnic. It felt strange and wonderful to be sharing advice and listening to each other whilst drinking cava and eating Jess's delicious tomato-bread and pro-sciutto. I wouldn't have imagined that an open-air clinic could possibly work but it did. Thank God George didn't include me in the planning of the surprise, I would certainly have tried to talk him out of it.

Surprisingly, I even nearly liked Veronica when she showed a vulnerability and admitted to a lack of confidence in her experience with one particular family. As she explained the case, I noted that she kept well inside all the restrictions of confidentiality, which is my particular bugbear – that confidentiality ring just <u>has</u> to be protected, especially in a small-town community like ours. Too many people know each other, it doesn't bear thinking how easily we could lose the trust of clients with just one careless mistake. Veronica gets that and was correctly circumspect. I even liked her analysis – she's astute, uses lyrical and literary metaphor to help clarify difficult theory. Yes, she's creative, I'll give her that, but she is still fogging up George's glasses and that is tiresome, especially when he's driving – so to speak.

After an hour or so, the work was done and we sat about chatting. Lisa regaled us with more funny stories of her crazy family in Brighton and Noel told us about how he used to earn extra cash by being a tour guide in New Zealand where he took carloads of wide-eyed *Lord of the Rings* fans on bumpy adventures to see various filming locations.

'I got so fed up, driving them up all the same old tracks, alongside all the other tours. Sometimes there'd be a dozen hobbit jeeps on the same road all shouting at the same time. So much for fantasy. In the end, I just took 'em anywhere I fancied and made up stories about the filming. Better stories than the real ones, mind you! I got quite good at it, actually, and worked in a few bogus characters, y'know, invented a few names to pep things up a bit. Sometimes I'd chuck in a curse word or something, for my own amusement, like "Boromuff, King of the Dorks" and "Gandarse the Wizard" and "Sam Ganga". One time, I just went all out and blatantly invented an entire character I named "Quim". Not one person questioned it! Bloody idiots . . . asking me to describe Quim, what did Quim sound like . . . on and on.'

I laughed so much at this thought that I started to snort unattractively. I know people say you can laugh 'til your sides hurt and it's true, my sides were actually hurting, and I was begging for my own mercy. It was exhilarating, exhausting.

I used to laugh a lot. Husband used to make me laugh all the time. I think he still could. If he tried. I think he might have stopped trying. Why?

Well, anyway, no one was trying today, they just were funny. That was the biggest surprise of all really, how easy it is to relax when you're not feeling old or invisible. It's lovely, really lovely.

THIRTY-NINE

Oscar

Ordinarily at the weekend, I am content to seek out the solitude of my own company. I am often ravaged with exhaustion due to my heavy academic workload. The work itself is not exacting, if anything I find the standard at my school laughably doddlesome, but the <u>quantities</u> of homework are demanding, sometimes requiring four hours of my time each evening.

I am not a fellow who wishes to waste away my life in pursuit of hedonistic folly BUT occasionally I should be permitted the opportunity to relax. Life is not all beer and skittles, I know, but a healthy interest in leisure time must form a part of every young Englishman's education, surely? It was in this spirit that I made an exception to my typical weekend routine of hermit-like withdrawal, and accepted an invitation to Rowe's sixteenth birthday celebration at his home this past Saturday.

What to wear? If only I actually owned the smoking jacket I yearn for. A properly tailored good jacket with plush collar, paisley satin, and three chunky Chinese toggles as fastenings down the front, perhaps in a rich forest green, a gentleman's green. Oh yes, that would be ideal. Until then, I have to settle for the Pater's old dressing gown, which I have customized. It does for now, but lord knows, it is severely lacking. I have indicated to both of my parents repeatedly that a quality smoking jacket would be a far preferable gift to any trifling item of the I-phone, I-player, I-don't-care-for-it-a-jot variety. Perhaps my birthday will bring me smoking-jacket joy? Who knows?

Meantime, I must make do with the cut-off dressing gown and my trademark silk slacks at any jolly social event. On this occasion I decided to complete the outfit with an amusing cluster of pearls and chains wound around one of Mama's scarves, worn cheekily at the sternum. From time to time, I impress even myself with my ingenuity.

This was certainly one of those times. There was something of the decadent roué about me as I stepped out. Rowe lives on a private housing estate built around a golf course. A location which fancies it is far posher than it really is. For me, the whole estate reeks of the desperate endeavouring to impress the deluded. A merry social dance that leads all the way to nowhere. Still, Rowe cannot be responsible for the misguided aspirations of his hopelessly lower-middle-class parents, just as I cannot be responsible for mine. Mine at least display a modicum of taste and choose not to live beyond their means, an attribute I have long admired in them both. They are honest, dull people and do not pretend to be otherwise, which is commendable, and we share a mutual understanding of my personal inexorable need to shine my own light in my own special way. And that's just dandy.

The Pater dropped me at Rowe's house and attempted the usual badinage about drugs and alcohol etc. which, although entirely unnecessary, is très endearing. Rowe's parents had sensibly decided not to trust Rowe to host the party without their presence so they had decamped to a small summer house in the garden and were waving wildly at each new guest. Rowe was painfully embarrassed and drew the curtains, plunging their drawing room into an unexpected dimness conducive to instant sexual behaviour, and since the party had been in full swing for a good hour by the time I arrived at nine, the sexual tension was palpable.

Most of the chaps from St Thomas's are sclerotic with fear when confronted with the prospect of living breathing females. They are perfectly prepared to brag or believe the bragging about their numerous fantasy conquests, but when in the company of genuine maidens, they are hopelessly incompetent. I have scant respect for any of them. Not one of them could beguile a girl or woo her with any aplomb. Have none of them *ever* whiled away a lazy Saturday watching *Breakfast at Tiffany's* or *Brief Encounter* or *Pillow Talk*?

It seems, sadly, no wooing techniques are necessary since the brand of female that most often attends this sort of ghastly affair is a filly all too quick for the off. Before the curtains met in the middle, the girls had leapt upon their prey like ants on jam. Their manoeuvres had evidently been intricately plotted for days, so efficient were their tactics. The chaps were powerless to resist and, for the most part, sat back and happily received the attention they so supremely didn't deserve.

I am so very disappointed with these wretched gals, teaching the moronic boys that no effort is required. They then proceed to behave like the most boorish of oafs, like the type of chaps who should be avoided at all costs.

Ah well, none of it concerned me other than to observe, with increasing chagrin, the decidedly Roman-esque orgy taking place under my very nose. I decided to remove myself from the writhing masses and take a seat on the swing in the garden to reflect on the paucity of pride amongst today's youth, and bask in the glow of the sunset. Rowe's parents continued to wave frantically at me and I waved back, but we all respected the division of boundaries, and neither actually approached.

What happened next shouldn't have shocked me quite as much as it did. One by one, the more attractive and popular of the gals came out on to the lawn. It seems they tire very easily of these licentious entertainments. No wonder. There is no thrill in it, no chase, no conquest. It's all too easy for them, and thus not at all diverting. The boys are hapless, passive submissives. There is no triumph in their capture, one might as well celebrate the capture of a slug. It ain't difficult. So, bored by it all, they tumbled out into the garden and, of course, in search of treats more challenging and, frankly, less dowdy, they buzzed around me like bees to an exotic bloom. Something about my distinct lack of interest in them beckons them on. I am the siren that calls them on to my rocks. Indeed I am rocks, for I have nothing here to offer them save a brief uncomfortable sojourn on the jagged nibs of my rapier wit. Undeterred by my dangerous cragginess, they flock to me and throw themselves willingly upon my sword.

I confess that one of my greatest pleasures is to perform for a hungry audience. These girls are not just hungry, they are ravenous, emaciated. They <u>long</u> for any tiny morsel of amusement. My mode of frank and free discourse is majorly pleasing to them, and they fall about in a chirruping cacophony of girlish giggles whenever I utter the vaguest of witticisms. They especially adore a heated bout of malicious gossip, and this I can provide in heapfuls, with pleasure.

I was not entirely impervious to their charms, they were as fine a litter of dazzling poppets as one could hope to meet. Fire these girls up with enchantment and they will respond accordingly with many juicy morsels of both fashion and beauty tips. We swapped countless trinkets of information, recommendations for the latest eye-liners and accessories, discussed the merits of the wide belt and condemned the inventors of Spanx to a life in purgatory.

It was a bountiful exchange of populist nosegays and frou-frou culminating in a heated debate about which camp we were pledged to: Team Andre or Team Pricey? Oh joy. Everyone was agog at the sheer depth of my encyclopaedic knowledge of the Adonal phenomenon that is Peter Andre. I urged all traitors to defect back to Team Andre and to eschew their cruel, inconstant mistress. Deny her, reject her, SPURN HER!! She is Beelzebub's right-hand goblin and must not be permitted to triumph. Over my dead but still undeniably dashing body.

The gals and I babbled on in this pleasant manner for aeons, while the moon glistened on their shampooed and shiny hair. The army of rejected chaps spectated from the stands, jealous and frustrated. After several hours, and completely spent from chattering, we all made moves to go home.

It was then that in the gloaming, in the garden, I was firmly tugged into a bush and suddenly found myself the recipient of several attempts to connect at the mouth by two of the more fair damsels. It has never been my style to appear rude, so I submitted to a frenzied forty minutes of fervent embraces, livid love bites and a pretty thorough tonguing. It was all very hot and high-pitched and breathy, and I found the clawing and snatching of their tiny hands at my clothes irritating, but overall it wasn't unpleasant.

Fortunately it didn't get out of hand, and so my disinterest remained fully trousered. I would hate for these delicious dames to find me mannerless or to think me ungrateful. It's just that, oh dear, they simply don't float my boat. They couldn't hold a candle to my beloved, I'm afraid. I couldn't possibly join them on the road to their Shangri-La because I'm using an entirely different map. I'm taking the scenic route, it will be more treacherous and take much longer but, my dears, I will be amply rewarded for my toil the day I wrap my arms around my darling Noel. He is my only paradise, and I am solely intent upon him. There are those who will think I'm looking for the moon at midday but I truly believe I will only be completely happy when I am in his keeping and he is in mine.

In the meantime I suspect I must put up with many more of these unsolicited attentions from females of every order. Today my mouth is twisted from kissing and so I will rest and soak my lips in milk. I may well add drinking chocolate powder to make it more sufferable. I pray that one day, my lips may yet be swollen from the vigorous and urgent kisses of my one and only. To even think of it makes me shudder.

FORTY

Dora

Still a virgin.

My big Food Tech practical exam is next week and surprise surprise, Mum has bought a copy of my textbook and plonked it on my bed so's I have like 'no excuse' not to revise. Yeah, all right, I geddit, thanks. I'm not a total idiot. I do *know* I've got stuff to study. That's why I'm on study leave, you dweeb. It's *my* bloody life, why doesn't she just like butt out?!! She's downstairs right now and she thinks I'm working. Whatever.

So, anyway, I've been thinking about my birthday and like, all the arrangements and stuff? I am now told by my cheapskate parents that apparently it will cost *too much* to hire a room in a hotel. Mum says it will be like five hundred quid or something plus at least ten quid per person for the food? I already <u>SAID</u> bring in KFC but apparently the hotel won't let you do that, for some bizarre reason. So now, it looks like we have to use the room above the pub where Dad goes, which is sooo rank but it's better than nothing.

Other things I <u>can't</u> have apparently, are The Hummer Limo (too expensive), the film all about me (apparently it's wrong to ask for this upfront … ?) and The Boy Band (also too expensive). The rest is OK and Dad's doing some prices and has already booked the room. There's some huge bloody fuss about the alcohol as well, because some of the people who are invited are under eighteen, and they're not allowed to drink apparently. Yeah, even though they get people to buy bottles of cider from that exact same pub and drink it on the bloody benches right out bloody side every Saturbloodyday night. Wassat all bout?!

Been thinking about being eighteen. Got a leaflet from Dad with like, all the stuff I'll be able to do but it's so like random:

I can: vote – Yeah. But like, do I want to?
Because I so don't believe in politics coz
they're all liars who nick our money to
buy castles 'n' stuff? So like do I <u>have</u> to
vote? Maybe it's against the law not
to – ask Mum. If it's not against the law
not to, then I'm not going to.

I can: get married – Yeah, like, to who? And
where? And when? And who would want
me? And why? And what for? I don't

think I'm ever going to get married. I will prob go to hundreds of my friends' weddings and cry and then be all alone and really ancient like thirty-seven or something, when some dork with no teeth will ask me coz we're the last two left and I will say yes coz loneliness will have eaten me away 'til I'm only half there. Great! Here comes the bride, all fat and wide, Married a mega twat, Happiness denied.

I can: join the armed forces with parents' consent –Yeah, and what, get shot? Thanks a lot queen and prime minister for sending me to Alfganistan to sweat and die for no reason. I know, the soldiers look quite fit in the uniforms 'n' stuff but that's not enough.

I can: buy cigarettes and alcohol –Yeah, thanks, been doing that for three years now, no bother. Actually, I really hate smoking but I buy the cigs for other girls at school coz I def look the oldest. Mind you, I think a baby could buy cigarettes at that corner shop – they honestly serve

anyone. Smoking is disgusting though.
Lottie smokes and her breath is like
really minging sometimes. And yellow
teeth. Urgh. I luurve alcohol though and
I'm so going to like drink so much,
especially on my birthday. I'm going to
get so lashed, it'll be a total blast. Karen
Burton got so pissed on her birthday that
one of her eyes popped out apparently.
That is <u>so</u> gross but maybe I'll get drunk
enough to like, sing out loud or something. Sing my Christina song. That
would be good.

I can: open a bank account without parents'
signature – Yeah, and put what in there?
Like, buttons or something?!! I already
have an account and got into trouble
twice for letting it go over. Then I had to
bloody pay for that! It's so unfair, how
was I supposed to know how much was
left in it for God's sake? I will open a
new one though, when I get my first ever
cheque for my first ever record deal. I
will like, put the money in there and say

to everyone, 'Hey – let's get champagne all round and loads of posh small food! It's all on me darlings!' That's going to be a big day. And it's comin' soon baby.

I can: change my name. Actually, that's the first really good one. I'm not going to go my whole life being Dora Battle. No hon, I'm here to tell ya – that ain't happenin'. I've always wanted a really sophisticated name like Susan or Terri – spelled like that with an i on the end. Yeah. Terri Trent. Something like that, where the last name is short and quick and has the same first letter. Hi, I'm Terri Trent. Yeah, I'm a singer. Yeah. My autograph would be like,

TERRi TRENT

Terri Trent

Teri Trent

I can: be called to serve on a jury – Yeah, but why? It would be good to hear all the juicy details of a murder or something

but I wouldn't listen if like, some kids
got hurt or something. I would like
totally refuse or whatever. Plus you do
get to stay in a hotel I think, and get
like really good room service. And
sometimes you can get really fit guys
on there who you can scribble notes
to during the boring bits. That would
be like, so hot. Especially if you're
staying at the same hotel. Oh yeah baby.
Gimme some o dat jury jiggy action . . .

I can: buy a house – Yeah. Why? Got everything
I want at home. Except Mum's there.
And anyway, I'm not even going to be
there much coz a singer's life is so full of
travelling and gigs and sleeping and
stuff? Don't need one.

I can: sue or be sued – Yeah. But I don't want to
be sued? So I'm going to pass on that
one because I'm not sure what it really
is. Don't you sue someone if they do a
like totally wrong thing to you or say
you're too short or something? Not sure.
Ask Dad.

I can: make a will – Yeah, like, why? I'm not
dead yet am I? Anyway, everyone can
have what they like to remember me
by – just come in my bedroom and take
what you like that reminds you of all our
good times. Lottie will def go for my
iPod and speakers. Peter will take all my
clothes to chop up and sew on his own
clothes. Mum will . . . Don't think she'd
want anything of mine. She's got pictures of me as a baby and that's when
she liked me best. I've def been a total
bloody disappointment since then.
Maybe she could have my box with all
my badges from Brownies and my
swimming certificates and stuff. That
might remind her there were some
things I was good at once. Poo will prob
just want my duvet. Which will smell of
me. A lot. Poo doesn't mind that, she
loves smelling me. She's the one I'll miss
most when I die. And she'll miss me the
most because I love her the most out of
the whole family. Besides Nana Pamela.

Dad will just cry for ages. He's hopeless
like that.

I can: place a bet – Yeah but like, someone
needs to explain how it works coz I don't
get it. What is evens? What is each way?
Does the horse run each way? <u>Both</u>
ways? What is twenty to one? Is that the
time of the race? I don't get it but I really
want to do it. Dad will explain.

I can: buy fireworks – Oh my actual God. I <u>so</u>
didn't know that! I'm going to buy
fireworks for my party then. You can get
these indoor ones. That will make such a
great ending. Not going to tell anyone,
just going to get them. As a surprise.
Wayhay!

Oh God, elephant-steps of approaching mother on
stairs, get books out – look busy . . . Why doesn't she
just bloody LEAVE ME ALONE!

FORTY-ONE

Mo

After my panic about Dora's possible pregnancy I realized it was time to get her along to see the nurse about some decent contraception. She yells at me that she is still a virgin but I have no idea what she's really up to during this time of total communication break-down. She will only speak in monosyllabic grunts and snorts and cannot look me in the eye. Consequently all information between us is conveyed in bulletin form. If spoken it is understood that it will be short, precise and instructive data. For instance, when she wants her allowance, she stands near me, looking away but holding her hand out saying:

'Pocket money necessary . . . please . . . immediately.' Or 'Shampoo required . . .' or 'Dog sick behind kitchen door. Action needed.'

If written, it's usually on Post-its left on the fridge or by the phone, again, concise and to the point. One particular Post-it simply urged me to 'Butt out you wonk!'

Charming. Absolutely no incidental conversation is happening, no discussion. Occasionally, if there are other people in the house, friends and wotnot, she will engage in a kind of fake functional relationship to ease the tension and to appear sociable. Dora is caught in the unenviable limbo between her own self-interest and what she knows is socially acceptable. It's classic 'Sturm und Drang'. We, the family, are simply obstacles the storm must batter in its path, in order to blow itself out.

I know this to be the relevant psychology but, frankly, what the cocking hell is wrong with her?! I'm sorry she is undergoing so much, but I have made it quite clear that I understand the process, for two reasons:

1. It is my job to understand, as a shrink.
2. I once was a teenager myself, thank you very much.

I know what's going on and so would she, if only she stopped raging for a moment to realize that I'm right. If she would just stop being so obnoxious, listen to me and take my advice she might even be able to skip the worst of this frenetic teenage turmoil. I could give her hints on how to sidestep it. For God's sake, she has exactly the resources she needs right under her nose at home.

I know Dora isn't the brightest spark academically, and I honestly don't care about that, but I *did* think she had a pretty good sense of self-preservation, so why doesn't she swim towards the light, towards me? I can't force her. All I can do is organize stuff around the periphery of her chaos.

That's what I did today, I made an appointment for her to see the nurse about sex. The sex-nurse. Oh God my daughter is going to/may already be having sex. I did sex and consequently had a daughter and now that same daughter is ready to do sex herself. But in my head she's only twelve. I have lost all concept of Dora time and while I've been busy, she has raced past me. Unbelievably, she will be EIGHTEEN in a minute. Actually I did my first bit of sex at sixteen but I shan't be telling her that . . .

I suppose it's only natural that I would be thinking about such a thing on the day I have my breast examination and smear test. I do panic about these appointments. I purposely book them for first thing, so that when I wake up there isn't too much time to do the dreadful dreading. I have been through it many times before. I know the routine. I know it doesn't kill you. Why, then, do I go stone cold at the very thought of it? I physically quake. I can't camouflage that, however hard I try. I've even heard myself say 'oo, it's cold in here, isn't it?' to try and excuse my pathetic shivering.

The nurse always agrees that it's cold, in her feeble attempt to comfort me, but she's the same sadistic witch who is about to clamp my tits in a vice and penetrate my frightened, frozen fanny with a metal boot-stretcher. All the while regaling me with tales of local council problems and the progress on the M4 bypass at junction eleven. That's her dirty chatter whilst she violates me, and of course I join in, keeping it as chirrupy as possible to minimize the awfulness of it all.

Occasionally during the humiliating probe, she requests that I should 'relax'. I agree. I *should* relax, yes. It would help, yes. But how can I relax when I am being entered by a woman I otherwise only ever see occasionally wandering around the biscuit aisle in Sainsbury's where we exchange pleasantries, all the while trying to ignore the fact that she has regularly peeked inside me and seen private areas of my body even I have never witnessed? I always imagine I see ghastly traces of screaming horror under the mask of affability she wears on her Sainsbury's face. As if looking at me takes her mind immediately to my nether regions. Is mine worse or better than others? Does she fleetingly think, 'Oh there's that woman with the lovely, healthy, tidy fanny'? Or does she think, 'Oh there's that old wreck with the monstrous mutant minge – the one I've taken pictures of to send to medical magazines as an example of a lopsided freak, or perhaps just to hand round at jovial nursey dinner parties as an amusing ice-breaker'? Which?!

Yes, Mrs Nurse woman, I would <u>LOVE</u> to relax, but I can't, can I, because I must remain tense at all times in case you breach our gynaecological contract, and go a step too far. You might perforate me or pinch me or lance something whilst you are burrowing around clumsily in my flue. Should something like that happen, I need to be braced for it like a coiled spring, taut enough to instantly expel you with the superhuman power of my mighty vulvic muscles of steel, catapulting you backwards like a Trident missile 'til you slam into the brightly coloured communicable diseases poster on your wall. And that's why I won't be 'relaxing' laydeee . . . OK?

Actually, it wasn't too bad today, even the breast-scanning machine didn't bite me too hard. Mrs Nurse's foot is on the pedal and she decides just how flat the bosoms will be pressed. Today the setting was 'flat as an omelette', whereas in the past, when she was particularly peeved, I swear she has set it to 'flat as a crêpe'.

Whatever the horrors of the examinations, they are

nothing compared to the worry whilst waiting for the results. The only happy moment is when the letter that plops on to the doormat reveals a negative result on all counts. I remember getting one result that announced 'subtle cell changes' which sent me spiralling into despair until the following examination, when the result indicated all was, thankfully, back to normal. Since then I am certainly jumpier, I admit.

On arriving home, I have informed Miss Dora via Post-it on her bedroom door that she has an appointment to keep with the sex-nurse. I will certainly sleep easier knowing she is fully contracepted.

I popped in on Pamela on the way home. It was an impromptu visit, no particular reason. When she opened the door, she greeted me with huge usual warm surprise and I followed her into her cluttered living room. She was mid-*Emmerdale* as usual, but she turned it off and put the kettle on.

'Why didn't you call to say you were coming, Mo? – I could have made you a beetroot cake to go with your tea, you twit.' She was right, I should have told her. That's my favourite cake of all the ones she makes. She's made it for me for years. I love that cake.

We made do with digestives and tea. I told her about the day I'd had and as always she sympathized. These soft moments with Mum, when she's not telling me off, are so nourishing, why don't I make more time for them? However much we disagree, and we often do, she still has a calming effect on me. She still grows me. I am always her daughter, however old we both are. Sometimes I forget how much I need that whilst I am busy scurrying about trying to harness the chaos of four people's turbulent lives.

Yes, she is kind and good and generous, <u>BUT</u>, yes she is also an interfering old bat. Just as I was settling into comfortable loved daughterliness, she spoiled it by steering the conversation away from my stresses to talk about Dora.

'It's just that, listen, love, I don't want to interfere, but I am a bit worried about her, to be honest. I think she's feeling sort of ... distanced from you, and while she's so untethered I truly believe she is quite vulnerable actually. Don't you? She needs to feel more, kind of ... anchored, that's the right word. Or she could really drift off, Mo. Permanently. And we don't want that. Have a think about it, love, I'm just ... frightened ... that she's heading for trouble. That's all. 'Nother biscuit?'

What a cheek! Firstly, Dora's feelings are completely typical of her age, and secondly, she is in no real 'danger' whatsoever. I wonder whether, at some stage,

ANYONE in my family might bother to notice that I AM A TRAINED CHILD PSYCHOLOGIST. If anyone knows how to deal with these developmental difficulties, it's ME. I would be the first to notice anything seriously wrong with my own daughter, for God's sake. As I said to Mum, Dora is going through a classic phase of bewilderment that occurs when an adolescent attempts to separate whilst still far too immature. She is living in a bubble of misguided self-belief punctured only by her confusion. She and I are actively engaged in a dance of such complex proportions, Mum, you couldn't possibly understand ... and it ain't the Excuse-me Waltz.

In the end, she was irritating me so much I had to drink up, make my excuses and go. Why couldn't she just leave well alone? I was enjoying our rare moment of intimate time and suddenly, out of nowhere, she's gone and bloody hijacked it, to address something she has no idea about whatsoever. Why doesn't she just bloody leave me alone, and BUTT OUT!

FORTY-TWO

Dora

How bloody insensitive to book a bloody thing with a bloody nurse about sex when you haven't even got a bloody boyfriend and you are still a bloody virgin? That's harsh. Yeah ... why don't you just like, punch me in the face or something Mum, you wanker!

Anyway, I'm not going. She's the one saying I've got to concentrate on my bloody exams for God's sakes. Well let me do that then. I don't need this right now.

JUST LEAVE ME ALONE, AND GO AWAY!! AND BLOODY DIE!!

FORTY-THREE

Oscar

Slowly slowly catchee monkey. Fortunately, I have been very badly brought up and consequently I have no regrets about the guile I am bound to employ to win my prize.

Mama has been psychobabbling on for months now about how she feels I need some therapy to 'explore' why I feel such an affinity with Oscar Wilde. Oh, but she does go on, jibber jabber, yak yak. Such pointless verbiage couldn't impress me less; <u>BUT</u> lo, an opportunity has been born out of this very same drivel. I have conceded that I may indeed need some guidance, but I have agreed only on the proviso that my practitioner should not be the eminent George as she suggests, but rather, the eminently *more suitable* Noel. I pointed out to her that he is closer to my age and we share no history, and that's why I claimed I would prefer him.

Mama, bless her, has not an inkling of my intentions nor my lusts and thus she has willingly agreed to organize it post haste. I couldn't be a more cunning cad if I tried and frankly, I don't really try. I simply am.

I am all smoke and mirrors, my dear. Watch me while I vanish, why don't you?

Thus, my own mother is the unknowing architect of my destiny. She even offered a surprisingly positive account of his prowess in the decidedly dubious world of teenage analysis. She thinks he has 'potential'. She thinks he is 'bold' and 'forward-thinking'. I fully intend to thrust his thinking very far forward and boldly display to him the entire landscape of my own particular potential . . .

The appointment is in two days' time. Just the correct duration. In the interim I intend to moisturize myself incessantly until I achieve the radiant glow I will need to blind him with my irresistible enchantingness. I know for sure I have it, but I'm a tad dry presently and am spotted here and there about my body with tell-tale blemishes of the flaky eczema variety. I have no doubt whatsoever that by the appointed hour on Thursday, I will be thoroughly moist.

I am delighted to announce that my bedchamber is now to be the chosen sanctuary for the increasingly expanding Poo. Why should anyone doubt that she should choose the nearness of me rather than any of the considerably lesser others in this family? It's perfectly clear to all that I am her obvious protector, I am

Lord Bountiful. That the dog has recognized this comes as no surprise to me. I am delighted to be able to host her confinement. She has appropriated my sock drawer which remains open at all times and is now a dog nest of sorts, where she has installed herself among the assorted hosiery, suspenders and garters. With the exception of an occasional visit to the garden for the purpose of ablutions, I expect her to remain settled therein until the happy event.

I am going to be a father. How thrilling.

FORTY-FOUR

Mo

I am reeling.

What's happened?

Has anything *actually* happened, or am I just a silly menopausal twerp? I don't know. All I do know is that I feel entirely unruddered. Shaky. I'm shaking. I'm not even breathing properly . . . Calm down. Calm down.

I'm so glad of this little study. I'm grateful to be able to hide here. I have to lie low while I think. Come on, Mo, think. Isn't it funny how when you need to really focus, you suddenly notice random unimportant things in great close-up detail? I think it's to avoid concentrating on the momentous all-consuming attention-command-ing thing in the extreme foreground. We sort of look straight through that, and find everything on the shelf behind supremely interesting.

So I look around this study and see that, in truth, I have acquired it for myself. I have occupied a good nine tenths of it for my book research and all my inci-dental jumble. I have in effect seized it from Husband who, I now notice, has only one small corner he's val-iantly stuffed to the gills with his own things. The computer is in his corner. He uses it. The children use it. I hate it. I begrudge it, actually. I begrudge the time it pilfers from us as a family. I am noticing how very dusty it is – the screen, the keypad. And there's a sort of rainbow effect ghosted on the black screen. Where's that coming from? The light must be spilling in somewhere, through something prism-ish? The curtains are open but the light isn't very strong. It's a cloudy day. No direct shafts of sunlight at all. Hmn. Maybe the screen is made of mercury or something? Something that reacts with light like this. I'm very fond of these curtains. We brought them with us from the last house. They were in the kitchen there. I suppose they <u>are</u> a bit more kitchen-y than study-y. Study-ish? Study-like? Huge bold red roses on a pale blue background. Quite retro. Very Cath Kidston. But not. Very female. For a female study, really. Yes, I was marking my territory right from the start, wasn't I? Oh and there's that little wooden angel Dora made when she was at Coombes Infants School. They made them every year for Christmas to hang on the tree. She was supposed to paint her own name on it as they always did, but that year she painted a very wobbly 'Mummy' instead. Insisted on it, her teacher said. No other kid did that. She could only have been ... what? ... six? I was disproportionately, uncontrollably touched by it, and wept openly. Dora was scared I was upset. I wasn't upset. I was surprised by how moved I was. Her little heart to my big one. A direct line. Not there now. No line at the moment. None. My books are so untidy, I must try to straighten them up, I can't read the titles properly. There's psychology theory, case studies, grand autobiographies of the great and good I always get for Christmas and never have time to read, there's the new Annie Proulx and Andrea Levy and Lionel Shriver and Marian Keyes. There's a book of quotations and copious atlases and what's that on the end? Something in tin foil? Oh God, it's an unopened copy of Madonna's God-awful sex book. Never even looked at it. Husband said to keep it in the wrapper – be worth something one day. I wanted to look at her naked body. But no. There's that lovely ink drawing in the style of Aubrey Beardsley, by a nine-year-old Peter. Extraordinary really. A precociously talented child. A good office chair. Husband found it on eBay, and got it because of my sore back. A red futon. Christ. Haven't used that since . . . well, never, really. Poo likes it. Got her hair on it. Smells. She's not using it at the mo. Sleep-ing in Oscar's sock drawer in readiness . . . double

Christ – the puppies will be here soon. How's that going to work out? It's all chaos –

STOP IT MO!

Come on.

Think.

What happened?

How did it go?

Go back over the whole thing . . .

Right. I had breakfast. Normal. I went to work as normal. Same old route. Left, right, left, second right. Same old shops, same old school, cricket field, memorial. Nothing peculiar there. All familiar, life as normal. Parked, went into the practice, said hi to Lisa. Lisa shows me she is wearing a gun belt, but with her mobile phone where a gun should be. Thus far, all is normal, very normal. The car is the car I know, Lisa is the Lisa I know, I am the Mo I know.

Noel comes into my office and we go through his cases for the day. Normal. At the end of that catch-up he explains to me that his own shrink has recently retired and would it be possible for him to do his supervised therapy with me? Now, I know it's good practice for all therapists to continue their own personal therapy, especially the less experienced ones, we actively encourage it. I was heartened that he should be so dedicated, and yes, I was flattered that he should seek my counsel. I am not related to him, and he is already halfway through his internship with us, and has proven to be both professional and enthusiastic. There is no hard and fast protocol that would prevent me from conducting a few supervising sessions with him. That is entirely valid, and completely legitimate. It's a <u>bit</u> unusual to have therapy with a practitioner at the same practice, but it's certainly not unheard of. Again: normal. A quick peek at the respective diaries and we asked Lisa to block out the last hour of the day. Normal. Saw my clients. Normal. Well, they're not that normal, but normal for us to be there together. Had lunch. Normal. Found a sardine in my tuna sandwich from the sandwich shop. Not normal. Revolting, actually, but nothing to knock me off-kilter. Clients in the afternoon. Relatively normal.

Four o'clock and time for the session with Noel.

He came in and sat down.

He looked too tall for the chair. And as he tugged his trousers up at the knee to sit comfortably, I noticed he wasn't wearing any socks. Brown ankles. It was pretty routine to begin with. I didn't say much, just invited him to voice whatever he felt he needed to. He explained to me that most of his therapy so far had been the exploration of his severe loss in early childhood. His mother had died and his father hadn't been able to cope and so handed him over to his maternal grandmother for safekeeping. He was an only child. The grandmother was not unkind, but she was emotionally chilly, and had always been so. She was also elderly and fairly infirm, so not much fun. He looked away as he told me how abandoned he had felt. How responsible. Responsible for his gran, responsible for his mother's death and responsible for his father's ineptitude. A whole bunch of misguided culpability.

He seemed to have investigated it pretty thoroughly, as a Kleinian practitioner should, and spoke of learning not to beat himself up. He also spoke of an awareness of his propensity to extol women, genuinely being inspired by certain women and less so, if ever, by *any* man. I was interested to note that he acknowledged there *are* remarkable praiseworthy men, but possibly because of his need for his absent mother, he finds himself less critical of women and even pathologically eulogistic.

This was all quite compelling for me since, working with adolescents the majority of the time, I come across very few idolatrous complexes of this nature.

Then I remembered that he had indeed told *me* that he 'admired' *me*, and I suggested this might be symptomatic of what he was referring to. He went very quiet, and for a long minute he didn't speak and kept his head bowed. I thought he was contemplating the session and all we had just discussed.

Then he looked up, sighed and began:

> *The dawn was apple-green,*
> *The sky was green wine held up*
>> *under the sun,*
> *The moon was a golden petal*
>> *between.*

> *She opened her eyes, and green*
> *They shone, clear like flowers*
>> *undone*
> *For the first time, now for the*
>> *first time seen.*

He just kept looking at me, holding my gaze. Daring me to look away. Neither of us spoke. I felt as if I had been tipped out of my life. What was taking place? I had no tools, no equipment, no idea how to deal with this moment. Then he said,

'D. H. Lawrence. It's true, Mo. For the first time seen . . .'

He left the room. Left me sitting there alone with *that* still hanging in the air. I was stock-still but my mind was fizzing. I tried to rewind it in my head and play it again to understand it. What? WHAT? I felt like I'd been punched. Then I felt like I wanted to be punched again immediately. Come back and punch me again so I can try to understand it. What did he mean? Are they *my* green eyes?

How many minutes passed? Could have been three, could have been three hundred, before Lisa knocked on my door to chase me out. Then, somehow, I drove home, feeling as if I was starring in my own foreign film. It was all so shocking and strange. Perhaps my life from now on will have subtitles and be permanently incomprehensible. I arrived home and I came in here, into my lair, to sit and stare. So here I am.

My family are gathering out there, in my home. Is everything different?

What now?

FORTY-FIVE

Dora

Eating only meringues and butter beans. Still fat.

I am so going on Facebook for ages tonight.

I know I'm supposed to like be revising 'n' shizz but it's not my fault Mum took me to see the nurse just before exams. It was like so major. I need to talk about it.

Mum drove me there in silence, then sat outside coz I didn't want her in, so she sulked. I didn't know there were so many options. Oh my like bloody actual God – the nurse like showed me EVERYTHING. She was the cutest loveliest lady, and I couldn't believe how young she was. It was so cool because she was talking to me like I was an adult 'n' stuff. We had a big laugh when I was a twat and got in a muddle . . . She said that she wanted to go through everything to do with birth control. I said I didn't need that. She said how come. I said because I'm not controlling any birth. She said that 'birth control' is just another name for contraception and we both agreed that was a stupid name.

Anyway then she got all the stuff out and laid it on a table. Omitriplegod! There was a patch you put on your bum (huge plaster), the pill (makes you fatter), condom (old balloon), women's condom (bin bag), cap (midget speed skater's helmet), natural family planning (calendar and thermometer – need Maths), injection (an actual injection, with an actual needle), implant (microchip), IUS/IUD (tiny metal anchors that go all the way up inside, ow), sterilization (cut tubes).

Everything looked pretty rank except the pill which looks just like pills. I said I wanted that, twelve packets please, and she said, since I'm not having sex at the moment, I should go home and take time to think through my options. She was so kind and cool. She said *she* didn't have sex 'til she was twenty and that no one should force me into it. She sounded just like Nana Pamela.

Then she told me that whatever method I choose I always need to use a condom because boys can carry diseases and stuff. God, boys are like so disgusting sometimes. Then she opened a condom packet and we practised putting one on a banana. It was sooo hilarious. She was really good at it, she must be really experienced. Not like a slut or anything but she really knows her way round a banana.

She got a *bit* serious when she was telling me all the bad sides of everything, like terrible periods, getting fat, headaches, sore tits, pain, being sick, blood clots, bruising, sore fanny, pain and more pain. On top of that, none of the choices are 110% safe and you can still catch herpes. Bloody hell. She asked me, coz I said I wanted the pill, if I was the kind of person who would remember to take a pill at exactly the same time every day. I said that yes, I was, and I heard a loud cough from Mum outside the door, who was obviously listening in all the bloody time! Sooo embarrassing. I was proper livid with her in the car on the way back but she just said the walls are made of cardboard at the doctors' and you can hear everything. Yeah thanks, I really wanna go back there. Not.

It's gonna be great on Facebook tho, I've told all my friends to look out for my status which I'm going to update in like fifteen minutes to: STATUS: OWNER OF 20 NEW CONDOMS. She gave me twenty for God's sake! Couldn't believe it! Think I might invite Lottie over to open a few (<u>never</u> with your teeth, she told me that really clearly . . . and never with scissors . . .) and do some practice. It would be sooo funny coz Mum has a banana like every morning for breakfast, and she would like be eating the one we put all the condoms on. That would be well wak. Serves her right for being the nosiest parker that ever parked her nose in nosey parker town centre.

We hardly spoke a single word all the way home, which is how it is at the moment. She hates me. I hate her. So at least it's like equal. She asked two lame questions. Honestly. Oh my days. One was if I knew how Peter got all those love bites all over his neck and one even on his face? I said no comment. The second was so bloody sarcastic. She asked me if I knew that my A level exams are next week? Yes, o mentally disturbed mother, I <u>DO</u> know thank you very much . . .

FUCK! FUCK!! FUCK!!! My A level exams are next week!!!

FORTY-SIX

Mo

Several times today, I completely forgot to breathe. Luckily my body is remembering all the essential functions through sheer force of habit, otherwise I'm not sure I would be walking, talking, driving, working or anything. All my inner clocks have stopped, I'm in a time fermata, yet I appear to be continuing on. No one else has noticed, I don't think. They are all behaving towards me as if it were any old normal day. As if my circuit wasn't entirely rewired. As if I was the same Mo as before it happened. I'm not. I'm different and changed and awake. I've woken up. I'm wide awake.

I have seen him each day but not alone yet. He has no qualms about looking me in the eye. We discuss what needs to be discussed but there is undoubtedly something more that's unsaid. I feel as if there is something new showing on me and I think only he can see it. Perhaps it's that I am seeing myself reflected in him, as someone ... I don't know ... somehow more than I was.

And I see *him* completely differently. Well – I just <u>see</u> him. I like his crisp white shirts and his watch that has a proper leather strap and the shape of his square shoulders and the length of his legs and the crescent grooves at the corners of his mouth, so used to folding when he smiles, which he so often does. And the smile ... Why doesn't anybody see? Why don't they notice the meteor flash that occurs when he does that? Why doesn't it blind them? It floods the room. It floods me.

I have shamelessly curtailed several sessions mid-crisis in the hope of catching a moment near him, around him, in the kitchen or the hallway, or anywhere. Not a word has been said. Yet volumes are spoken. I am utterly aware of his presence all day long. I am tuned to him. I know which room he's in, I hear his footfall outside my door, I'm aware of wherever he is and I am drawn to that place.

I can't voice any of it yet to him. I mustn't, because I'm not entirely sure that I'm not insane and haven't wildly exaggerated some figment of my imagination. Is this some hideously cruel trick the menopause is playing on me? Have all my senses deserted me and in their place left a sugary Elizabeth Barrett Browning poem for me to reference as my only emotional landmark? Are the sentiments of cheesy greetings cards my sole measure?

I will be beside myself until our next private session in a few days. Maybe then, I will have some answers and be able to make sense of what is presently wholly unfathomable. And wholly intoxicating.

I wish I wasn't looking forward to it so much. I wish I could feel more sensible, more rational. I'm not either. Good God, I'm giddy.

FORTY-SEVEN

Oscar

Today was the Day of Days. I would dare even Larry to be as happy as I was first thing. Knowing that 4.30pm was going to usher in the golden moment, the rest of the day decided not to upstage it and to remain unshiny. School was simply school, odious, drab and functional. I received yet another uniform penalty when I resolutely refused to don an unsightly tabard with a huge ugly label displaying my 'team number' for rounders.

It is already a source of great ignominy to myself and my fellow sports outcasts that we are forced to take part in this joyless ritual each time there is a physical education class. We are a noble band of conscientious objectors who ought rightly to be hallowed for our courage in defying the evil Nazis who run the PE department. Instead, we are mocked and scolded and publicly shamed into running around in pointless circles sporting offensively gauche tabards. I am not, and never shall I be, a number. I am marvellous and enchanting, and they shall never diminish me with their childish games.

There followed a dreary lunch in the dreary cafeteria where the only surety is that one's lunch <u>must</u>, by order of the kitchen, be dreary. I could not distinguish between the meat and the vegetables in the sloppy offering, so slimy was the fare. The only tantalizing moment was when Wilson scuttled by, amongst a flock of squeaky young Year 9ers, and dropped a note into my lap. Quelle interesting. I read,

'I too, am enchanting. Notice it, whydoncha?'

Just as I suspected, and as is the natural order, Wilson has evidently fallen in love with me. I have to admit that I don't find him entirely displeasing either, and now that I know about his tragic background I feel drawn to the constant and beautiful pain of the tortured little mite. There are those who regard him as a puss and a wimp. I don't. I know him to be the survivor of immense sorrow and grief. Although small and delicate in stature, he is a lionheart. A clandestine lionheart. I wish I could reciprocate his advances, but it would be cruel to lead him on. He knows my heart is pledged to another, and thus, must accept his fate as the sole occupant of the reserve bench. On this throne, he is undoubtedly the prince ... but there is a king who yet awaits my attention ...

3.28 pm. 3.29 pm. 3.30 pm ... where is the infernal

bell? Why doesn't it ring to release me from the torment that is double chemistry with old Cock Cooper? 3.31pm. A minute that disguised itself as an hour ... and there at last it was. A short and clear peal of a bell to announce the birth of my happiness.

A quick grooming session, the exact same outfit as was intended before, some fleet footwork, and I was at the practice by 4.20pm. I briefly espied Mama hurriedly ushering out a 'troubled teen'. She was a tad brief with me and said that she might need to foreshorten my hour with Noel in order to have some obscure meeting with him. I quickly put her right and assured her *that* was not about to happen under any circumstances, that it was a monstrous suggestion, that I was in dire need of this therapy and that I was entitled to my full hour, thank you very much indeed. Wisely, she backed off.

I took a big gulp of peppermint mouth spray and sat on the chair outside his room. It occurred to me that these were to be my final moments. The last ticking minutes of my life BEFORE Noel. Pretty soon I would be referring to now as 'before'. 'Before' we were together, 'Before' we met, 'Before we knew our futures were bound together'. We will laugh and call these times 'Back then'. This is now, and now is as nothing compared to the bliss of what will be in a matter of minutes. The threshold of his door is the portal to my paradise. Once I cross it, I doubt I will ever return. This is it. The point of no return. The beginning. Hello, new start . . . Hello . . .

'Hello?'

Yes . . . 'Hello' . . .

'Hello, Peter, sorry, did you doze off? Come on in.'

He was there, all of a splendid sudden, speaking out loud, as if out of the ether. I followed him in, and took up my place on the sofa. I cursed myself as soon as I sat, realizing I still had my dratted dreadful school blazer on. I had fully intended to remove it at the outset, otherwise he might think me some kind of measly schoolkid. I felt it would be too fussy and draw attention should I struggle to remove it then, but I was secretly heartbroken to think he wouldn't witness my ruffled linen shirt, which I have introduced to some bleach since I last wore it, in an effort to return its luminosity. (Not an entirely successful enterprise, but it's marginally brighter than the tepid grey it had become.) I thanked God that at least I had snipped a bloom, a sassy orange gerbera, from the Headmaster's splendid front garden, to slip in my lapel, and it proudly sat there, defying my love to overlook me.

214

As I remember it, the next little while went something like this:

NOEL: So, Peter . . .

ME: Oscar, please. If you would be so kind.

NOEL: I would actually like to speak with Peter
initially.

ME: Sorry?

NOEL: Could I speak with Peter? Would Oscar
allow that?

ME: Well, yes of course, for they are both me.

NOEL: I realize that, but I would like Oscar to
leave us alone for a while. Could you ask him to
do that?

ME: Forgive me, I couldn't possibly do that.

NOEL: Who am I speaking to now?

ME: Why, my dear chap, to me of course.

NOEL: Which 'me' are you referring to?

ME: Me, Peter. And also me, Oscar. For we are one.

NOEL: I see. This is a more considerable situation
than I'd thought.

ME: How so?

NOEL: Peter, I will need you to push through so
that we can discuss Oscar. Come forward, Peter,
please.

ME: Darling one, you are addressing me as if I were dead. And you were Doris Stokes. Please desist, we have so much to say and nonsensical prattle of this sort just fritters away our precious time together. Now, pin yer shell-likes back and prepare to be flattered . . .

NOEL: I only want to speak with Peter, please.

ME: Sweetheart, understand that I _am_ Peter. That is my given name, but I beg you to try and comprehend the misery of a lifetime with such an inconsequential label. It's a kind of daily death. My parents are evidently sadists. So, you see, I decided to ring the changes and claim a more fitting moniker. Simple as that. Admittedly, I feel a certain affinity with the mighty Oscar Wilde. I am, let's say, a fan. That's all. I have always read him and always adored him, but, dearest, I don't imagine I am him. Not at all. _I_ should be so blessed! I simply offer a bounteous and elegant display of substantial and tempting passions for life and for love. I am what we English do best, sir – I am not a crackpot – I am an eccentric. All hail everything enchanting!

SILENCE

NOEL: Hmmm (puzzled frown on gorgeous

freckled forehead). I see . . . but could I speak to
Peter? . . .

Oh heavens, what a body blow. It would seem that
my New Zealand honeybaby might not be the brightest bulb in the chandelier. Why would I assume a
psychologist would be clever when I am armed with
the undeniable evidence to the contrary in the person
of my very own mother?

Our session went on in this tedious fashion for a good
half hour where my only sustenance was to remain
fixed on the frankly insolent green-ness of his naughty
naughty eyes, which were frantically searching mine
for the answers to pointless questions. He was seemingly hell-bent on his decidedly wobbly theory that I
must be hosting many personalities or worse – what? –
actually channelling Oscar Wilde? Oh dear. I'm not a
shrink, but, honestly, Noel poppet, do catch up.

However much I tried to steer our sinking ship
towards land where I could commence my wooing in
earnest, he pointed us firmly into the oncoming wind
of his wretchedly misguided assumptions. I know
how important it is to allow an alpha such as he a
measure of leadership and validation, so I played
along, all the while wishing we could dispense with

217

this silly distraction and move along to the important and essential part – the kissing.

I thought better of hurrying him along, and so our session finished rather disappointingly with the following:

NOEL: Thank you for your openness today, Peter.
ME: Oscar. To be candid is to be quite wonderful.
NOEL: Do you believe you have been truthful?
Or untruthful?
ME: Untruthful? Impossible. I am from
Pangbourne, sir.
NOEL: Well, that's good then. Would you be
comfortable if we play-acted at our next session?
ME: I would be delighted to oblige you in any
way you see fit. And some ways you don't.
NOEL: That is inappropriate.
ME: Oh, I do hope so.
NOEL: Goodbye, Peter.
ME: Oscar. So long. Farewell. Auf Wiedersehen.
Adieu.

I left, accompanied by an effective deal of flounce, leaving him agog and, I suspect, yearning for more.

And so it begins. This crazy love affair.

FORTY-EIGHT

Dora

Fifteen hours of Art over two whole days, that was just, like, a punishment or something, not an exam. You weren't allowed out of the room or anything except for lunch and breaks and toilet breaks and stuff. It was like, so harsh? I have decided that even if it ever turned out that I was quite a good artist, I really don't want an artist's actual life. Not a painter anyway. All you do all day is paint, and look at it and paint and look at it. By the end of these last two days I am so fed up of looking at it, I never want to see it ever again. I never want to see the Art room ever again, it feels like I've been in there my whole life since the day I was born. And it's all been leading up to this day, the day I can say that's the last Art day I will ever ever do. Even though the teacher was saying, 'Come on, Dora, stop talking and get painting, you can do it. Go Dora!' and stuff, I still feel like I've just spent fifteen hours working on something that's just going to be rubbish in the end. Nearly everything I do is rubbish. I know it is. I'm not dumb. I can see that other people are doing way better than me.

Anyway, it doesn't matter, it's done now and I've only got one more cookery theory exam before I finish school forever. Omigod, no more school! Bring it on baby, yeh. What's it gonna be like? Oh, is that the alarm ringing at 7AM? Is it for me to get up and put on a rank burgundy and grey disgusting school uniform with absolutely zero taste? No, it isn't – because Dora Battle doesn't go to school any more. Bye school! Seeya! Hasta La Vesta, school! Bon voyage!

Why is studying text books so effing hard? I tried to be dyslexic way back in Year 8, because they get extra time and wordsearch and spellcheck and stuff but apparently I'm not, which is really annoying. At least I did find out I need glasses, so that's something. Not sure that totally 125% explains why I hate reading though. It <u>could</u> be because I actually just hate reading, words and sentences and text books 'n' shizz. <u>BUT</u>. What's really interesting, and I think the government should like wake up and realize this about young people today, is that I really do love reading Facebook and MSN 'n' stuff, and that is, after all, reading isn't it? It's still words.

If I was allowed to, and if my prison warden mother would let me, I would stay on Facebook all night instead of sleeping. Well, not completely instead of, but I could so manage on like two hours of sleep instead of the eight hours she forces me to have.

I luuurve Facebook. I love it so much I would marry it. Darling Facebook, please marry me so's we can always be together and you can entertain me non stop and I will never be bored.

Wish I had more friends on there, though. Lottie's got three hundred or something but she's like really pretty and popular 'n' stuff. Even if I had, like, a hundred it would be like so great. I've got some new ones recently but mostly they are my cousin's friends from their school and they're so immature 'n' stuff. Lottie's brother is one of my friends. He's cool but he's crap at answering and he only talks about his girlfriend all the time. Yeah thanks I so get the hint.

Sam used to be quite good at talking on there, which was so cute because he's so bad at talking in person. God, I remember when we were out on our first date and he was so shy he was almost silent. We sat on a bench holding hands. We were both, like texting people 'n' stuff, then I received a text from him that just said, 'Can I kiss you?' It was sooo sweet. And so was the kiss.

Sometimes I thought he was more like his real self when he could write it down on Facebook than to my actual face. Which is why it's so weird that it's even called 'Face'book because the one thing you are actually <u>NOT</u> talking to is someone's face. Mum gets it so like wrong when she's always telling me that people invent a person to be on there that isn't like their true selves, and it gets everyone confused. Well, yeh maybe, sometimes, but I know, for me, I can be much more who I properly am on there than any other time, just like Sam. It's all right to pretend a bit Mother, coz you never know, one day we might actually get to be the person we wish we could be. Pretending's just the practice for that, I think.

Anyway I wish I had more people to pretend <u>with</u>, that's all. I'm going to update my profile and put on some better photos and I might even make a special offer on the Start Groups thing and send it global – something like:

'Free cupcakes for first twenty hot guys who sign up to be my friend! Must be fit and funny, no losers or uggos need apply. Guaranteed responses to all post.'

Something like that. Do guys like cupcakes? I've never made cupcakes but Peter's pretty good at them and he would like *so* like to see the responses I got if I did that. He's quite good on computer stuff, he completely unfroze ours when it went dead. Plus he doesn't go blabbing to Mum and Dad about my private stuff even though he can be a right little freak sometimes. That's one of the good things about having a mother from the Neanderthal ages is that she hasn't got the first clue how to even switch on a computer so she can't go snoopin' about, coz I so know she would if she could.

Omigod!! Lottie just posted a response to my message about our prom dresses 'n' stuff to say she thinks she might have an actual date for the prom, but she's too shy to talk about it on Facebook so she's going to tell me when she comes over. Her mum's being all moody about the exams at the moment so she's not allowed to come over for a few days.

Got to be honest, I'm a bit jealous if she's got a date because we were going as eachother's date and I was looking forward to getting ready together and saying, 'Yeh, so what everybody – we don't need a guy to have a great night. Watch us, suckers, we're bezzie friends and we're going to dance 'til we die!' That's what we said we were going to do, but we can't if she's got someone. I should be happy for her really. And maybe her date will have a brother for me! Or a mate or something? Or anything . . . ?

FORTY-NINE

Mo

The biggest difference is that I feel lighter. Physically, actually, lighter. I'm not of course. The effect of it is so convincing that I found myself taking stock in the mirror. I was even slightly surprised to find that, disappointingly, I appear to be exactly the same as the last time I looked. I thought, just for a tiny second, that it would show. How? A luminosity of the skin? A light in the eye? A more upright posture? Less heaviness on the thighs? I saw none of this, and yet I feel distinctly different.

Even the journey in was unlike before. I drove the same old route. Those roads, those houses, those shops, yes, but everything was curiously heightened. As if it had all been dipped in paint, or washed clean with a power jet. It was all a tad cleaner and sharper. Or perhaps I'm wearing new ears and new eyes and they see and hear every single thing afresh. Someone has cranked up the volume and the brightness settings on my life. I am utterly in the tinging crystal-clear nub of it all. Except it's not clear, there's no actual clarity. If anything, it's all blurred. So my senses are sharp but my perception is blunt. Talk about confused.

In the grip of this emotional maelstrom, we started Noel's second session this morning. I found myself ridiculous when I caught me in the mirror applying more mascara just before he was due. I nearly always wear make-up, that's not unusual, but every woman knows when she is applying those extra little touches. It's when the eye socket is a fraction darker and deeper, or the eye-liner has a sassy little feline flick at the outer edge, or when the blusher is blushier, or when the lips are more carefully outlined and the red is audaciously, no-doubt-about-it red. I did all of these things, and I knew I couldn't possibly deny it to myself when I realized my blusher brush was sweeping over my cleavage, revealed in my new top which was, I knew, too low. Far too low. What was I thinking? Fact is I *wasn't* thinking. I didn't want to <u>think</u>. I wanted to <u>feel</u>.

Rejecting any doubt or conscience, I ushered Noel in and he did that thing again, where he steadfastly holds my gaze – it's unnerving. I tried to start the session by asking if there was anything on his mind. He was silent for a moment. Then he said one word.

'No.'

Oh God. I'd been an idiot and imagined the whole ghastly, embarrassing episode. I felt a pall of humiliation creeping over me, and tugged up the front of my top so it wasn't so compromisingly low. My mouth went dry and I started to fidget with my pad, which then of course fell on the floor and as I reached down to get it my top fell forward, revealing even more bosom, a great quantity, a strumpet's amount. More frantic tugging, this time so obviously flummoxed. By the time I had regained any shred of composure and managed to look him in the eye again, he was smiling that confident winning smile.

He said, 'I mean NO, there isn't <u>any</u>thing on my mind, there is <u>some</u>thing. Someone. And only that someone. Nothing else. Please release me from this torture, cut the crap, and tell me you feel the same, Mo.'

That's when I knew I hadn't imagined it all, and that he was the most beautiful sight I'd ever seen. Exquisite. I was suddenly remarkably aware of where we were, sitting opposite each other in my room, at work, and it all felt supremely inappropriate. We ought to be by a fountain in Florence, surely? I am programmed to be professional at work, especially in my room, where so many secrets are told, where so much is entrusted to me. So, in a vain attempt to be normal, and evidently working on autopilot, I ploughed on with the therapy . . .

'I suggest, Noel, that what you are experiencing . . . is . . . in fact . . . transference . . . first described by

Freud . . . as you know, it means the unconscious redirection of feelings for one person to another . . . very commonly misdirected towards one's therapist . . . which is . . . er . . . possibly what's hap-happening here. I would suggest . . . maybe . . . ?'

'I see. Well, if that were the case – and, for the record, I am convinced otherwise – but if indeed that <u>were</u> the case, am I not, then, witnessing the sister phenomenon – that of "counter-transference", where, might *I* suggest, the patient's situation resonates with the therapist consciously . . . or not. Empathy can cause the therapist . . . to fall in love.'

He had said the word. Just like that. 'Love'.

Just like that.

Dropped it in there, a depth charge, which exploded me. In one stroke the equilibrium between my intellectual faculties and my undeniable animal propensities was shattered, and I was his.

I said, 'Look, Noel, we can't continue this here,' and he said, 'No. I know. Where then? Just say when and where. Please.'

Then I said, 'Let me think.'

And now I'm thinking.

FIFTY

Oscar

Hargreaves couldn't attend our meeting of The Enchantings today. He is away to Reading to have his foreskin removed. He claims to have a condition called phimosis, where he says it is too tight to retract correctly, but I am convinced otherwise. I clearly recall when we displayed our 'swords and medals' to each other at the inaugural meeting, that his foreskin was entirely functioning. I suspect he has fallen foul of Bollox Bailey's crazed pontifications on the merits of the helmet-less warrior. How Bailey ever succeeded in claiming the revered post of Head Boy is a mystery. It will take the school a decade of the fittest and finest minds as Head Boys to recover any kudos for that position.

The moron Bailey has attracted ill-repute to every move he has made thus far. His campaign last term, to banish all 'floppy' hair that reaches below one's collar, was barbaric, rendering many of the follicularly elite shorn to within an inch of their ears. I refused to play Samson to his Delilah and instead employed the services of an ingenious little gadget called a 'scrunchie' donated by Dandruff Dora, thus sporting the most impudent of swishy ponytails for the remainder of term, well above my collar, and escaping Bailey's infernal ire. I threatened him with a snood should he persist next term with this idiocy.

Oh Lord, what about the time Bailey decided we all had to refer to him as 'sir' as if he were a teacher? Blackguard. I had to be seen to capitulate, and so dreamed up a canny ruse. Instead of calling him 'sir' I called him 'cur'. If I spoke it fast enough he couldn't tell the difference, and thus I slandered him regularly, maybe twenty times a day. It was most satisfying. I can only hope that the despots who control the school will come to their senses in time for next year, and that *I* might be rightfully elected Head Boy. My first command shall be that I am referred to as 'Most Excellent Head Chap', and my second shall be that on any journey betwixt the Grand Hall and all classrooms, the only mode of forward motion acceptable is the skip. A double or single hop would be equally acceptable. Running or walking will be deemed abhorrent and be punishable by spanking. By hand. By me.

Whatever Hargreaves's reasons, and I reiterate that I am positive he is maiming himself purely to appease Bailey, or at the very least to find himself vaguely aesthetically sufficient, he was absent today, thus leaving the meeting to consist only of Wilson and myself. It was Wilson's turn to choose a password, and he chose 'Jacqueline Onassis', which was, I think, a sign of his renewed application to his studies and a quantum leap forward for him. I was touched by his efforts to win my approval.

We pretty much covered the agenda in a few minutes, making all kinds of decisions regarding matters of Enchantment. We added the esteemed Clooney to our 'Approved-List' although there was a heated debate concerning his sexuality, which is as yet uncategorized. Secondly we agreed that the unfortunate clog-like sandal, named 'Croc', cannot be permitted under any circumstance. Finally we Fêted and Elevated the word 'Dreamboat' and attached it to the divine John Barrowman in perpetuity.

Since there was no Any Other Business, Wilson and I sat together in the quiet for a snatched moment or two awaiting the 'end of lunch' bell. It was unusual to be in such close quarters with only each other, but it didn't feel in the least bit awkward. He complimented me on my choice of kerchief, which was peeking out of my blazer top-pocket. I explained that it was, in fact, faux. It was one of a swatch of fabrics Mama had been sent, from which to choose, to cover the ottoman in their boudoir. He correctly described it as an 'ingenious trick of the eye, a pocket-square trompe l'œil if you will, of the dandiest kind'. Well done, Wilson, dear boy. I rewarded him with a little demonstration of two different styles of folding – the Cagney, and my particular favourite, the Astaire.

He marvelled at my expertise, and seemed not a little moved. I felt tenderly towards him and told him so. His little bright eyes lit up and he asked whether I might reconsider the official rankings of my Beloveds, perhaps promoting him further? I assured him that his place was secure, that I could never be unkind to one who had survived such immense sorrow and that I thought him a corker of a chap, and a tiptop honey.

It was then that I realized I may have been a tad loose-lipped, for his quizzical frown told me so. He asked how I knew anything about his past? That if I did, how much did I know?

'Oh, Wilson,' I said, 'never fear, I will forever keep your counsel, dear dear boy. You have suffered so much . . .' and I reached out to him. But he upped and dashed away, and I fear I spied a tear in his beautiful eye. And indeed, another tear in his other one.

OOOPS!

FIFTY-ONE

Dora

Well, I'd like those three hours of my life back, please. That theory exam has told me for sure everything I know I <u>don't</u> want my life to ever be about. In fact I can't imagine how I ever like even thought Food Tech was going to be useful to me. I mean, come on, who <u>cooks</u>?!! I am never *ever* going to cook. Fact. So why do I need to know anything they have ever ever told me on that course?

One question was – describe the nutritional properties of egg white and egg yolk. Whassup wit dat? Duh. Hey Mr Examiner – ask yourself this – why do you need to know? Nobody ever needs to know that shit, so why you askin', you wonk? OK, let's see I <u>might</u> need to know the properties of an egg if I was:

a) A food professor
b) An omelette chef or
c) A chicken.

I am neither or all of the above, SO IT'S NOT IMPORTANT!! Check this out teachers and examiners,

I ain't never gonna cook a egg, you get me? So get off my back with all the bloody annoying questions. I ain't interested. No interest. Interest rate equals zero. Interested? <u>NOT</u>. Tell the egg info to the toe coz the foot ain't listenin'. Tell it to the foot coz the knee ain't listenin'. Tell it to the knee coz the thighs ain't listenin'. Tell it to the thighs coz the . . . torso ain't listenin'. Tell it to the torso coz the arm ain't listenin'. Tell it to the arm coz the hand ain't listenin'. Tell it to the hand coz the face ain't listenin'. Tell it to the face coz the ears ain't listenin'. Tell it to the ears coz the . . . cochlea in the inner ear ain't listenin'. And listen up suckers – Dora Battle ain't listenin' to *any* of it!

In the end, I put that 'a large egg yolk contains about 60 calories of energy plus vitamins A, B1, B2, D and E. The white has no fat and about 4g of protein.' And that's all I know. Debbie Gabb said that was the right answer and she's dead clever, so I think I've got two points at least. Not that I am one tiny bit bothered.

Soon as we came out of that exam, it was the end of official school for our group so we went bloody mad. There was like, Tango being poured all over you and loads of screaming and kissing and stuff, and we all signed each other's shirts with things like 'always be

233

you' and 'food tech sluts rule' 'n' shizz like that. It was so wild. I did my hair up in like a big pineapple ponytail on top with some tennis racquet tape. It was crazy. I never show my roots underneath like that, I felt like . . . so free. I can't believe I never have to go to another single lesson in my entire life. I will happily never ever learn another single thing ever again. Yippee!! Double smiley face.

Me and Lottie just hugged and hugged and then she did like this amazing thing? She gave me this small pink box with a ribbon on and asked me to open it. Inside there was like this gorgeous little mirror with all stuck-on beads 'n' stuff around it and on a dangly label attached to it, it says, 'Look in here to see my forever best friend, whatever happens.' I so couldn't believe it, it is so completely beautiful and I like instantly burst into complete tears.

All I had bought for her was a toe-ring she liked from when we went shopping at the Oracle in Reading on her birthday. I had to describe it to Dad and he went back to get it for me the week after (God, try describing a toe-ring to an ancient old man with no fashion or anything in him. But hey, he <u>did</u> get the right one and actually, he <u>did</u> pay for it so big props to him) but

what she gave me was so like thoughtful and meaningful – just like *her*. No wonder she is my best ever
friend, coz no one else even comes close. Nothing
compares. To her.

So, I came home and tried on my prom dress for
next week, which is like *so*. Radically. Gorgeous.

I ordered it online with Dad so Mum hasn't even
seen it, not that she cares. She hasn't even asked me
about this last exam AT ALL. Unbebloodylievable.
She's not even looking me in the face at the moment,
she obviously detests me so much. Fine by me. Keep
your distance, doesn't bother me one bit. Suits me, in
fact.

The dress is gorgeous but I am so going to have to
lose weight for it to look right, and I've only got a week.
So instead of only eating white food, I think I've got to
only eat no food. That's the only way to lose the big
lumps of fat bulging out over the top at the sides. I will,
of course, be drinking loads of water though, coz you
can really like die 'n' stuff if you don't? I will def need
tights coz got no time to tan but I've got all the other
stuff I need I think. What I *haven't* got is a limo. Parents refused to pay for one and everyone else's is full
so me 'n' Lottie still have to find a way to get there.

So, exams are over. YAY!

God, I'm actually missing Art. Wishing I had a bit of
Art coursework to be doing. I actually realize I actually quite like Art. Yeh . . .

Omigod. I'm like SOOOOOOOOOOOOOOOOOOOOOOO
OOOOOOOOOOOOOOOOOOOOOOOOOOOOOOOOOO
OOOOOOOOOOOOOOOOOOOOOOOOOOOOOOOOOO
OOOOOOOOOOOOOOOOOOOOOOOOOOOOOOOOOO
OOOOOOOOOOOOOOOOOOOOOOOOOOOOOOOOOO
OOOOOOOOOOOOOOOOOOOOOOOOOOOOOOOOOO
OOOOOOOOOOOOOOOOOOOOOOOOOOOOOOOOOO
OOOOOOOOOOOOOOOOOOOOOOOOOOOOOOOOOO
OOOOOOOOOOOOOOOOOOOOOOOOOOOOOOOOOO
OOOOOOOOOOOOOOOOOOOOOOOOOOOOOOOOOO
OOOOOOOOOOOOOOOOOOOOOOOOOOOOOOOOOO
OOOOOOOOOOOOOOOOOOOOOOOOOOOOOOOOOO
OOOOOOOOOOOOOOOOOOOOOOOOOOOOOOOOOO
OOOOOOOOOOOOOOOOOOOOOOOOOOOOOOOOOO
OOOOOOOOOOOOOOOOOOOOOOOOOOOOOOOOOO
OOOOOOOOOOOOOOOOOOOOOOOOOOOOOOOOOO
OOOOOOOOOOOOOOOOOOOOOOOOOOOOOOOOOO
OOOOOOOOOOOOOOOOOOOOOOOOOOOOOOOOOO
OOOOOOOOOOOOOOOOOOOOOOOOOOOOOOOOOO

OOOOOOOOOOOOOOOOOOOOOOOOOOOOOOOOOO
OOOOOOOOOOOOOOOOOOOOOOOOOOOOOOOOOO
OOOOOOOOOOOOOOOOOOOOOOOOOOOOOOOOOO
OOOOOOOOOOOOOOOOOOOOOOOOOOOOOOOOOO
OOOOOOOOOOOOOOOOOOOOOOOOOOOOOOOOOO
OOOOOOOOOOOOOOOOOOOOOOOOOOOOO bored.

Just gonna check if anyone's answered my Facebook
friends ad.

That's all I've got left to do in life.

FIFTY-TWO

Mo

Hello, you have reached Mo. If you would like to speak to psychologist Mo, press 1. If you would like to speak with author Mo, press 2. If you would like to speak with mother Mo, press 3. If you would like to speak with wife Mo, press 4. If you would like to speak with wanton amoral fast harlot potentially adulterous lunatic Mo, just whisper, because she is very close by. Thank you. You have selected crazy Mo. Unfortunately the person you wish to reach is otherwise engaged with all-consuming thoughts of frivolous fancy and is dangerously teetering on the brink of shameless folly, and so is perilously out of control and presently unreachable. The remainder of your call will cost you dearly and do you no end of unsalvageable damage. Please seek the permission of an adult before you proceed and thank you again for using our service. Don't forget – we can also provide you with train times, cinema listings and bereavement counselling.

FIFTY-THREE

Dora

Why the wank does she do it?! My exams are finished, Mother, I'm allowed some time to *chillax*, for God's sakes. My way of relaxing is talking to my friends on Facebook. I'VE TOLD YOU THAT NINE MILLION TIMES, YOU IDIOT!! I am not a car-jacker or a joy-rider, or a shoplifter, or a happyslapper, or a pisshead or a crack whore. It's not against the bloody law to use the internet, even if it <u>is</u> for 'two hours and it blocks everyone else's time'. Dad is watching bloody rugby and Peter's in his room making fur leg-warmers out of Granny Pam's old coat.

Listen Mum, you don't even know how to switch it on you cockhead, so why are you so stressed out? What has it got to do with you who I'm contacting and why? People who are seventeen and about to be eight-een in a couple of weeks are *meant* to be talking to each other on Facebook. It's the law. Go and talk to all the other mothers and bloody find out that actually, I am hardly on it at all, compared to some of them. Talk to Rachael Faulkner's mother – she is bloody like addicted to it! *And* she has her own laptop. *And* she has an iPhone. *With* a *Twilight* cover. *Which* they pay the contract for. So actually I think you'll find I am a breeze. You should be grateful to have someone so bloody generous as your bloody daughter you bloody cow. GO AWAY!!!!!

Anyway, during the twenty-seven tiny minutes I was actually allowed to be on there, I was glad to see that my cupcake offer has brought in three really quality new friends. One is a friend of Lottie's brother called 'Cupboard'. One is a guy from a party last year who I can't really remember if he's fit or not called 'Not Robert Pattinson'. And one is a guy who says he knows Peter and has seen me and thinks I'm hot, called 'X-Man'.

Oh my actual God. Three guys! That's more than I expected. Three more, actually. It was like, so cool talking to them although I think Cupboard might be called that for a good reason coz he was nice and everything, but he seems mainly interested in the cakes. I'm going to ask Lottie all about him when she comes over to get ready for the prom next Friday.

OMFG! I'm so excited about the prom. Peter wants me to watch a film called *Carrie* with him tonight coz he says it's all about an American prom and what normally happens at them. He's being quite nice at the moment. Maybe he realizes that his big sister is, like, a woman at last and he ought to like really respect me or something? Looking forward to the film – I love films with loads of floaty dresses and buff guys in.

So does he.

FIFTY-FOUR

Oscar

What a perfectly ridiculous day. I was already somewhat exhausted due to the rantings of Disgruntled
Dora, who was abominably ignorant of the content of
one of modern history's finest motion pictures, *Carrie*,
directed by the charmingly suspect Brian De Palma.
She found it 'horrific' and 'disturbing'. How can Desperate Dora be so deeply brainless?

Perhaps the more pertinent question should be 'How
on earth can she be genetically related to me in any
way?' I must take time to sit Mama and the Pater down
in order to posit the difficult unavoidable questions
regarding Dingy Dora's true parentage. The only
possible solution I can offer with reference to her bird-
wittedness is that, if she is my genuine sibling, then
surely in a cruel twist of DNA mutancy, I somehow
imbibed all of the many brain cells she left behind in
her haste to exit Mama's womb, some two years prior
to my entrance. Typical of her to leave the place untidy.
Whatever the process, the result is staggering. She is a
freakish marvel. My sister, the empty-headed lady.

Despite her absence of quantifiable intellect, I still

find the creature to be endearingly amusing, and I can't help liking her. Upon discovering the true depth of her ignorance about this particular film, I couldn't resist watching her very closely as the full and frightening nature of it dawned upon her. Her mouth fell open in staggered stages too funny to ignore. She frowned repeatedly as she tried to wrap her understanding around the concept of such a masterful piece of terror theatre. I witnessed the gradual creeping-on of the collywobbles and the dawning of the heebie-jeebies. I failed to predict that she might be awake half the night, blubbering on about how haunting the imagery was. This constant whimpering, along with regular visits to my bedchamber throughout the night to thwack me soundly about the head as punishment for frightening her, resulted in a day-long fatigue on my part.

Today was specifically the day I least of all wanted to be deadbeat. Today was my all-important second session with my Beloved. Today was to be the clincher, the bells and whistles moment. I did not require anything haggard or droopy upon me, on this most propitious of days. Thanks to Dotty Dora, I was most definitely wilting where I ought to have been perky. Damn her to a thousand screaming hells. I needed my

243

wits about me to play my Kleinian wizard at his own game, to dazzle him with my virtuoso display of wicked wisdom.

Ocean blue was the order of the day, wardrobe-wise. I was to be azure from head to toe. I wanted my garments to say 'Come on in, the water's lovely. Go on, Noel. I am your ocean. I dare you. Dive in.' Regrettably, I don't have any blue slacks but my mossy green stripy boot-legs sufficed. I suppose I was still saying 'dive in', but also, what with the virescence of the trousers, 'watch out for the rocks and indeed any floating algae'. I wondered why I had bothered when Noel beckoned me into his room in the most displeasingly perfunctory manner. As if I were simply the next client. In out, in out. Don't treat me like that, mister, and you'd better get ready to shake it all about.

We sat and he sighed and smiled. Ordinarily his smile is breathtaking and reduces me to jelly, but today I detected in it the briefest whiff of contrivance. It was somewhat forced, I thought, but I was prepared to overlook it, considering that it may well be a symptom of nerves. Could it be that Noel was suffering the initial misgivings of inchoate longing? Could it be that he was barely able to stifle his fears of expressing the love that dare not speak its name? Possibly. There is something about his demeanour that proclaims self-confidence, and yet ... Hmn.

He started our session with a fair amount of bumbling, stating that he had 'thought very long and hard about our last meeting' which he had found 'challenging and fascinating'. Oh yes, my dear. You have me there, pinned in glorious amber. I am delighted to recognize myself as challenging and there is not a soul who knows me would deny that I am most certainly fascinating. *I* might have chosen 'dazzling' in the stead of 'fascinating' as a more accurately nuanced description myself, but no matter.

He then proposed that I think back in time to when I was about three years old, in order to investigate my relationship with Mama and the Pater. It's a potent tribute to my contented childhood that I could remember only rather lovely things, mainly to do with Mama's wardrobe and having wonderful stories told nightly by the Pater. I regaled Noel with gloriously amusing anecdotes concerning my panoramic journey from childhood to teenagehood via a vast motley panoply of marvellous shoes. At this point he assumed I wasn't taking the session very seriously. Perhaps he was right, but my stories were far more entertaining than anything he was desperately trying to elicit, and I have

245

no desire to bore him. How would that be in the slightest bit enchanting? It simply wouldn't.

He then started a confusing diatribe about how my 'posing' might be my way to arrest my own personality, to tear myself from the clutches of the parents, that I possibly deem myself as so completely different to them that my opposition might be referred to as 'murderous aggression'. 'I beg your pardon, dear darling deluded boy?' I said. He replied, 'I don't suggest that you want to <u>actually</u> murder them, but that you may be murdering or sabotaging something in yourself in order to stand apart. It's purely provocative, and it's a stage.'

Well, honestly, talk about the Depressive Position, I could easily have fallen into a black hole of disappointed despair on the spot if I didn't have my eyes so keenly focused on the prize. A prize which, with every word he was speaking, was becoming less beguiling and rapidly turning from gloss to matt. I held up my hand to his mouth to halt this off-putting torrent of nonsense. He seemed surprised. I had to seize the day, I couldn't be part of this charade one single moment further.

I said, rather gallantly I thought, 'Poppet, you must shush now because you are babbling. I understand that you are nervous, darling, because believe it or not, so am I. See how I quiver? Let us not protract this masque a nanosecond more. Let us admit the magic between us. I can no longer continue prospecting for romance in this elliptical manner. Let us be bold. Tumble into my labyrinth of love. Kiss me, Noel, I implore you. Kiss me hard, dammit man, and mean it!'

Noel shot up out of his chair looking not a little surprised and said, 'Peter – Oscar – whatever your name is, this is entirely wrong, mate. You have utterly misunderstood. You are sixteen, for God's sake!'

To which I replied, loudly, possibly *too* loudly, 'I AM NOT A CHILD. I AM A FUNCTIONING ENCHANTING GENTLEMAN WHO JUST HAPPENS TO UTTERLY ADORE YOU, YOU SILLY NAUGHTY FOOL!'

At which moment, Mama barged in. She has always taught me that it's rude and wrong to do so when a client is in session, but nevertheless, she did it. It was most impertinent. She caught me mid-opine and, as so often is her wont, she immediately punctured the delicate moment with her brusque manner.

She said, 'Oscar, you are ranting. Stop it immediately, this isn't clever or funny. I know you have a schoolboy (*ouch*) crush (*ouch*) on Noel, but this is just

247

ridiculous. He has no interest in you whatsoever (*ouch*).'

I looked to my darling, who was looking in turn at the carpet. (The awful claret carpet. I keep telling Mama to sort out the ghastly soft furnishings in that place, they are not conducive to harmonic thinking in any way.) 'Noel,' I said, 'is this true? After everything we've been through?'

The look on his face told me he didn't think we had been through *anything*. Oh dear, he is so very superficial, and actually I realize now that I could never truly love one so shallow. I require a chap to have depth. Buckets of it.

He eventually spoke. 'Peter, there is, was, and never will be, anything going on between us, mate, never. I'm just not . . . that way.'

What 'way' could he possibly be referring to?! He's just not . . . splendid? Is that it? Not . . . fascinating? Not . . . intriguing? Not . . . clever? Not . . . ENCHANT-ING? If that weren't insulting enough, he called me '*mate*'. Twice! He dares to suggest I am his *mate*?! AAARGH. How very low.

'I am not your "mate", sir, and never shall I be,' I retorted. 'You should away to your lodgings to consider the enormity of your loss, and pray never darken

248

any of my portals ever again, you insufficient unchivalrous lout. Return you to Mordor, you Kiwi ... fruit!'

Mother hurriedly frogmarched me from that hideous place and sat me in her room. Which also has claret carpet. (The rot is irretrievably throughout, the sheer lack of taste has spread like anthrax.) I was breathing heavily, and felt faint. It had all been so heinously excruciatingly embarrassing.

She spoke in her terrifying soft voice. 'You are making a complete arse of yourself, Oscar, please stop or the humiliation will drown you. Put it all behind you this instant, you are barking up completely the wrong tree with Noel. There will be no more therapy with him, do you understand? I know you will be temporarily heartbroken, but you will recover from this, for the simple reason that I suspect your ego will have broken your very great fall. Now. Much more importantly, I am cocking furious with you. Luke Wilson has just been on the phone wanting to know how come you seem to know so much about him? You know how important confidentiality is. Care to explain yourself? And care to prepare yourself for an old-fashioned thrashing, you blethering idiot?!'

Discovered. Revealed. Terrible. All is terrible.

FIFTY-FIVE

Mo

Everything is fractured. I'm not sure how to measure anything. All of my usual criteria are utterly skewed. I should have known that it would be difficult to behave normally around Husband. He is, after all, potentially the most directly affected. Ironically, he seems to be the most constant of all and is just being normal. Of course he's being normal, Mo, you idiot, he doesn't know anything is amiss. How *doesn't* he know? Are we so disconnected that he can't read the dilemma written so clearly just behind my eyes? If he looked a tiny bit deeper, wouldn't he see?

Mind you, I am continually avoiding eye contact with him, so he hasn't really had a chance to read me. That in itself ought to be signal enough. I can't believe he doesn't sense anything is up. Nearly twenty-seven years of marriage. Might he not have learned to notice and evaluate my behaviour by now? I certainly feel as if I can judge his. Is this an example of one of those awful trite Men are from the North, Women are from the South arguments? Men are the Sun, Women are the Moon. Men are Red, Women are Blue. Men are

Coffee, Women are Tea. Men Have Cocks ... Women Don't Have Cocks. What does it actually mean?! Of course men are different, but aren't we supposed to be properly connected inside this marriage, and shouldn't we be frequently tending and maintaining it, so that no weeds get the chance to grow?

I thought we were quite good at that, vigilant even. Every wedding anniversary we sit together and assess what's happening and how we feel about each other, our lives and it, the marriage. I have always thought we investigate it quite well. I have never felt restricted when it comes to airing any grievances. I have regularly done that, quite voraciously on occasion.

In fact, I recall, with a certain amount of cringe, an anniversary trip to Paris, when I thought it might save time to list my complaints, as a sort of aide-mémoire, on a small card, which read something like:

1) Sweaty gym towels left on bedroom floor
2) Honking up phlegm whilst in shower
3) Scratching of balls when in company
4) Old, ill-fitting rugby shirts worn as regular shirts
5) Overuse of term 'wassup' in silly growly voice
6) Referring to me as 'my first wife' as a regular
   joke followed by guffaws of laughter

7) Regularly waking up kids to kiss them goodnight

8) Guinness-fuelled farting. Endless.

He grabbed it from me and read the list aloud, adding comments such as, 'I agree, appalling' and 'unacceptable behaviour' and 'Divorce this monster immediately' after each complaint. Eventually he leaned across the table in the gorgeous restaurant in the Marais, and said, in a faux French accent, 'Madame. I now see ze error of my evil ways. You <u>must</u> dump me immédiatement. You have not option. But be warned, if you do. I will immediately commence my irresistible seduction tactics on my all-time number-two favourite woman, ze divine Coleen Nolan. And I will succeed. Of zat zer is no doubt. Can you live wis zat?' Silly man. Funny man. But silly man.

Come to think of it, he doesn't ever complain about *me* – or about anything. He listens and digests and always problem-solves, just like he would, but he doesn't hurl any mud at me. He wouldn't. I think he actually really loves me. Warts and all. Unquestionably. Always has.

I remember he once said to me, in the middle of a Friday night shop in Sainsbury's, 'You see, this is what I love the most, this stuff, where we operate as a team.

I know which pasta sauce you like and you know which ham I like. We both know what the kids like. We know when they don't like that any more and like something else instead. We even know what it is we buy each week to make us feel healthier, but which we rarely eat. We know we just like seeing it in the fridge. It comforts us, that raw spinach, that melon, that low-fat no-fat fat. I love it. I love it all. The splendour is in the detail. The big is in the small. Spaghetti hoops? I think so! Salad cream? Bring it on! . . .'

Yes, he loves me and he loves our family. We work well together, he's right. We are a good team. I relish the organizing, the action, the busy forward motion, and he enjoys the hiccups, the difficult stuff, the stopping. He is unafraid of that, of the ugly and the tricky. Which is just as well, because I am fit to burst with both.

I know I'm not thinking straight. I'm not properly thinking at all. I have no will of my own. Except I do, because if I am honest with myself, I am also choosing. Choosing not to stop. Choosing the chaos.

In the midst of this whirlwind, I am desperately trying to go about normal life, but I can see I am getting it very badly wrong. I thought by mirroring Husband's calm but inquisitive demeanour, I might appear normal, like him. What a mistake. I am obviously not usually calm or inquisitive in quite this way. I'm obviously faking it quite badly – I seem to have disturbed them and rubbed them all up the wrong way. I simply asked how Dora's exams were going, and she was instantly apoplectic with rage, claiming I was a 'selfish, useless wonk who hasn't bothered to notice that her own daughter had actually done her last exam and finished school for ever, thanks very much for no support whatsoever'. Husband looked away in embarrassed agreement. Oscar doesn't want to communicate at all, claiming that I humiliated him in front of Noel. I had to, he was behaving abominably, using his sessions to fulfil his pathetic little fantasies. With Noel. Of all people. *My* Noel.

On top of which, unbelievably, he has been nosing around in my files and has virtually sabotaged a very intimate and fragile trust I have with Luke Wilson and his mother. I am only just beginning to unravel this poor boy and Oscar has gone and clumped all over it in big concrete boots, the twit. He <u>had</u> to be reprimanded for that. It was totally unacceptable, and he knows it. Honestly, what a meddler. He is simultaneously so clever and so bloody thick. It's terrifying. Both of my kids are terrifying at the moment. They are loose cannons, out of my reach. They have drifted off and I'm not sure I like either of them much. They certainly don't like me.

Dora marched off in a huff and is now in intense congress with Lottie in her bedroom. It's their prom tomorrow night, another thing I am not included in. I haven't even seen the dress she was so excited about only a few months ago. I can't help finding the whole thing preposterous though. A prom? How ridiculous. We live in Pangbourne, not Ohio.

I absolutely flatly refused the request for a 'limo' ... !! To take her the half a mile it is to her school. Really. Dora is Dora. Dora is not Elton John. Or Mariah Carey. Or Madonna, or anyone else she is fantasizing about being. She's a girl who is leaving school. That's all. I know it's a rite of passage and it's important, blah blah ... yes, I remember myself how liberated I felt ... and that's why I went to the pub for a pint of cider and blackcurrant. And I walked there on shanks's pony, I did not get in a limo. I didn't get one and you're not having one. 'Cause it's just not fair. You think you're so special, Dora Battle. Well you're not, you're just a kid leaving school, just like everybody else. DEAL WITH IT! I've got more important stuff to sort out. Like my bloody mess of a life.

FIFTY-SIX

Dora

Oh my God, I can't believe it. Lottie is going to the prom with Sam. My Sam. Sam Tyler. I so can't go now. How could she do this to me? She said he was a twat. She said he gave her the creeps. And now she's like going out with him, he's her bloody actual boyfriend. I bet I'm the only person in the world who didn't know. I bet I'm the last one to find out. As usual.

This is proper wrong. I actually feel actually sick. I thought we were going to have a great evening getting everything ready for the prom and everything. Instead, I'm well devastated. I can't go. I can't. I can't believe Lottie would betray me like this. With him, of all people. Why can't she go out with ANYONE ELSE IN THE WHOLE BLOODY UNIVERSE?! Not him. I hate him. I hate her. I hate them.

OMG. They are 'them'. They're together.

Can't stop crying. I am such a loser. Why does everything always go so wrong for me? Loser. Loser. Fugly loser.

FIFTY-SEVEN

Oscar

One must always get one's priorities right. It is of paramount importance, <u>vital</u>, in fact, to have a surfeit of banoffee pie at a hellish time like this. I have fallen into a dolorous state of wretched misery. I know where I am bid at such a desolate juncture.

Pamela responded magnificently to my plight and prepared quite the most splendid dish, her best yet. She encouraged me to sit and eat and talk and eat, until there were only crumbs remaining. The entire ten-inch-in-diameter pie lay deep in my stomach after meting out its culinary comfort with every bite. There could be no doubt that my purgatory was significantly alleviated by the very banana and cream and mushed-up deliciousness of it. The salve for my poor battered aching heart.

I retold the entire sorry Noel episode to Pamela in great detail. We spoke in low and hushed tones. She was compelled, I suspect, to show respect for what had thus far been the greatest love of my life. She said that she understood the momentous and dramatic effect of first love, and she appreciated that this cruel

257

rejection has knocked the stuffing out of me. She also reminded me, quite rightly, that I am a fellow of great fortitude and courage and that I would eventually prevail.

I agreed that, with time, I could possibly imagine healing somewhat, but as of this moment, I live on echoes, I appear to have very little music of my own. I am an empty bagpipe. A dried-up, spent and useless old scrotum of a chap, with the heaviest of hearts. I explained that my colossal love for the Kiwi dream-boat had been so achingly spurned that I wasn't sure I could climb out of my lonely and bleak pit of des-pair. We who toil in the heated quarries of life, we who feel and taste and sense and smell so very much more than the average mortal are in real peril at emotion-ally raw times like these.

Pamela, who it transpires, has a streak of the school-marm in her, then suggested that I might, 'Butch up a bit, Master Oscar, come on. This fellow obviously didn't get it, didn't want it. You did. He didn't. He's an idiot with no taste and it's his loss, but you can't force someone to fancy you. Unless you're Donald Trump.'

I didn't warm to the cut of her jib initially but I knew she had a point. I suppose I ought to think about the difference between a caprice and a lifelong passion.

Was it possible that Noel could have been a mere fancy? A whim? A crush? I must confess to a seismic withdrawal of my affections during my supposed 'therapy', wherein he proved himself to be the most amateur and misguided of quacks, relentlessly barking up someone else's tree. He really couldn't have misjudged me more if he'd been a misjudger at the county misjudging fair. In fact, his diagnosis was hopelessly awry. What a serious fellow he proved himself to be, so very grave. As I always say, seriousness is the only refuge of the shallow, and I suspect Master Noel might never ever ever splash about in the deep end of life, so to speak.

'What of my future?' I lamented to Pamela. 'How shall I move forward carrying this heavy burden of my savaged feelings?'

To which Pamela replied, 'Perhaps, love, you might stop being a selfish wuss for a sec and think about someone else? Isn't there a <u>certain</u> someone else near by who would relish the chance of having his heart broken by you?'

I knew instantly to whom she was referring. I had indeed overlooked a chance at real happiness. I had leapfrogged it entirely. What was I thinking? Perhaps this was to be the year of hope and enlightenment after all. Perhaps I have been seeking my sugar in the wrong sweetie jar altogether.

It is at seminal moments like these, moments of epiphany, that one is helpless to do nothing but that which one's conscience dictates.

I had no hesitation in kissing Pamela full on the lips with gratitude. She may be frightfully dowdy, yes, she may be awash with uncultivated taste, no doubt. She may have an unhealthy addiction to all things viscose, and true, her closet is a tragedy of bad shoes, but she's as sharp as a Pointer dog for directing one to the right path. The old crone has an uncanny nose for it.

I am utterly and completely over Noel. Just like that. So it ends.

Pucker up, Wilson, I'm comin' atcha!

FIFTY-EIGHT

Dora

It's all laid out on the bed, and I can't bring myself to put it on. The purple dress is gorgeous. I know it looks better on the bed than it does on me though. Even after all the bloody endless white food I've been scoffing, I haven't like lost a single gram. That diet is pants. What I really can't believe is that I haven't lost any weight through crying, coz I haven't stopped for twenty-four hours and that is like so much water and water usually weighs a lot. Not my water apparently. It's the only part of me that doesn't weigh a lot.

It's all there. Dress, bag, shoes, tights, everything. Dad knocked on my door and handed me a box of Mum's jewellery, some of her really best stuff – I bet she doesn't know – but what's the point? It will be so awful. Bloody bloody awful. I'd have to walk in on my own and everyone will know that my best friend has chosen my ex over me.

My best friend disses me so much – hates me, she <u>must</u> do, why else would she do this to me? I thought we were forevers. That's what we said. I meant it. She didn't. She lied. You shouldn't lie about love. That is like so wrong. If you say you love someone you should so mean it or just don't bloody say it. Sam, Lottie, Mum, bloody all of them are big fat liars. I've got no one. No one.

FIFTY-NINE

Mo

I was supposed to spend the evening writing. The first draft of the book is due in this month. Why the hell did I agree to such a stupidly early deadline? I agreed because I didn't know I would be upside down. By now I should have slogged away steadily at it and have a decent handle on the first draft. I should be editing and tweaking at this point, instead of faffing about with a superfluous chapter about how to ask your teen open questions in order to elicit answers. Who bloody cares?

What I ought to write is a chapter about how to refuse to speak to them until they can find it in themselves to address you with some civility. About how *we* didn't have to be 'negotiated with' when I was a teen, we got a clip round the ear and no sweets on Saturday if we were rude. And even if we <u>were</u> rude, we weren't that rude. Pamela used to give me a thwack simply for mumbling or eating in the street. I wouldn't have dreamed of open retaliation, that would have been unthinkable and it would have meant certain death as a punishment.

Dora has retreated to her room in a foul mood, refusing to speak to anyone. She yelled in my face, 'Don't even look at me! Every time you do, I see how disappointed you are with your minging sket of a daughter. Go to Lottie's house and look at her instead, she's much more your type, you're both liars. The two of you belong together! In hell!!' Then she slammed the door so hard it broke the handle, which caused her to utter a stream of obscenities a Marine would be proud of. I'm assuming she has had some sort of fall-out with Lottie, which is a shame. Lottie is Dora's only friend. Dora must have done something spectacularly stupid to scupper it. I won't know, of course, because I am not informed, not in the loop.

I would like to have helped out with the prom outfit, not least because I suspect it is massively sluttish, far too revealing, and I might have been able to sew her into it so that she doesn't flop out. In less war-torn times, when the battles were fewer, I have enjoyed being part of the chummy business of her getting ready. However old she is, it's still dress-up and I am, after all, a woman. I used to love it when she asked my opinion.

Which shoes?

Which bag?

I might be much older but the joys of girlish pleasures still live in me, are not yet extinct. In fact, they were substantially reignited when a daughter, when <u>Dora</u>, came along. She was my chance to revisit pink and net and angels' wings in a way it is hard to admit to liking when you are a grown-up. There is a latent fairy in all women, but look how carefully we have to secrete her in order to be taken seriously. And fairies come in all shapes, colours, sizes and types, they don't have to be fluffy. They <u>can</u> be demanding and furious if they like. They <u>do</u>, however, have to wear a tiara. That much is compulsory. I even have one in a box somewhere in the wardrobe. I would love to have given it to Dora for this evening but we are hunkering down in our separate bunkers at present and the journey across no woman's land to deliver it is a potentially fatal one. She can have it for her eighteenth instead. *If* we are speaking by then.

Funny how women are ashamed to own up to their inner fairy whereas men are forever proudly displaying their inner cowboy or fireman. They're not even slightly inner, they are outer. There's Oscar, of course, who has always unashamedly furnished us with <u>his</u> fairy, from the word go. What a fabulous boy.

Anyway, I can't write. I can't write because I can't

think. I don't want to write. I hate writing this bloody book. It's like an albatross around my neck. It's all stuff I know perfectly well, it's not difficult. Maybe that's the problem. I should be trying to write something more challenging, something I am less certain about. I know about teenagers, I know how to communicate with them and I understand them. I should write instead about women on the cusp of their fifties and on the verge of insanity. However, if I were to write that book, I would have to do it whilst being spun around wildly in one of those giant tea cups because that's how I am experiencing it.

I have the most precarious hold on reality at the moment. Reason and logic, two familiar friends, have deserted me and left me with frivolity and lunacy as my trusted guides. It's as if I have mercury instead of a brain. Madness mercury, which repeatedly rises and falls continuously, depending on the extent of my instability.

One moment I am grounded and the next I am floating.

One moment it's all ridiculous then it's all destiny.

It's simple, it's complex.

It's right, it's wrong.

It's right.

He's a magnet. I am bafflingly helpless to resist. I don't stop thinking about him. I am exhilarated. I am alive. I am desired and alive.

Look at me right now. I have it all laid out on the bed, my outfit for tomorrow, and I can't wait to put it on. I know that black top with the soft edging looks good on me, it shows my neck. It's extremely well cut with darts in exactly the right places. It follows the curve of my waist and it outlines my bust. I even have exactly the right underwear ready. The bra is a miracle and raises my breasts on to a sort of shelf. The plum lace and threaded blue ribbon are beautiful and it's the only bra I own with matching pants.

Last time I wore this was on our anniversary ... don't think about that.

Bias-cut skirt. Purple. Oh God, stay-up stockings. Never been out of the packet. New on tomorrow. How <u>do</u> they stay up? Black heels. Good jacket. Tapered. Sharp. I think I might just look a bit fab in this. Dare I say, sexy?

Sexy at work?

Oh fuck, I've become Veronica.

SIXTY

Oscar

On the odd occasion, the Pater really does prove himself to be a crackingly excellent chap. He has a wonderfully primitive instinct for exactly the right gesture at exactly the right moment. Usually in the nick of time. Apposite to the nth degree. That's precisely what happened last night.

Devastated Dora was in a terrible state owing to her inglorious dumping by Lazy Lottie. An untimely cull, considering the fact that their end-of-school celebration was the very next evening. How very rude of her. And cruel. Desperate Dora fell into a sour temper and was stomping about threatening to remain at home, which would have been a catastrophe since the Pater and I had agreed we would settle down together to watch *All About Eve*. Bette Davis was to be my next subject of discussion at The Enchantings. On reflection, I'm not sure she is entirely enchanting. She is quite frightening. I may rethink.

The Pater turned to me on the sofa, and simply said, 'How do you think Dora is? I'm worried.' I didn't venture too detailed an opinion, but I did have to agree that the silly sausage wasn't her usual self. So, the Pater sprang into action. Initially, I was reluctant to take part in his plan, thereby forfeiting an evening of potential enchantingness, but he was quick to remind me of the importance of family duty, especially since Mama is locked away in pursuit of her muse. Or, in other words, escaping from all three of us, to whom she is so clearly allergic at present. The Pater located a tuxedo for me and a dark business suit for himself, complete with his father's own RAF service dress cap. Very fine he looked, too.

'Will I do, son?' What a sweet man.

The tuxedo was a tad roomy but with a few added touches of panache (fur leg-warmers, beaded cummerbund, pearls, fringed turban, etc.) I was pretty much remarkable.

'Will I do, Father?'

At this point, he rather over-laughed until he fell on to the bed clutching his sides. It wasn't <u>that</u> funny. I snipped a particularly luscious bloom from one of Mama's orchids – she won't be pleased – and, with that in hand, the Pater and I approached Depressed Dora's bedroom door. Pater tugged his jacket down and tentatively knocked.

'Go Away!' came the charming response.

'We're here for Miss Dora Battle,' he said in a silly, formal tone.

'Dad, really, go away, I can't deal with it right now.'

I had to intervene. 'Dora Battle, beloved daughter of Mr and Mrs Battle of Pangbourne, and cherished sister of the Esteemed Oscar Earnest Battle, please honour us with your attention . . .' Silence . . .

'In your own time, obviously.'

'Oh God!' she mumbled through gritted teeth.

We heard her pad towards the door, and she eventually opened it after much fiddling with what seems to be a broken handle. Poor, poor Distraught Dora. Her face was flushed and bloated from crying and her black eye make-up was streaked everywhere. She had the appearance of a deranged chimney sweep.

The Pater tipped his hat and said, 'Miss Battle, your chauffeur awaits, and here is your escort for the evening,' at which point he shoved me quite firmly forward.

I was overtaken with the unexpected urge to bow and kiss her hand, something I'd never done before and am unlikely to ever do again. 'At your service, m'lady.'

She burst into tears and fell heavily into the arms of the Pater, who I noticed was also a tad moist about the eye. 'Oh Dad, it's horrible . . .'

'Come on, puddin', get yer glad rags on, you can't let a couple of class-A twankers like those two ruin your evening, you're better than that. You are better than all the buggers put together. Didn't you know? You're <u>the</u> Dora Battle, the most beautiful girl in the known universe? I can't believe you didn't know that, it's been on the *Ten O'Clock News* and everything ... "Today, in Pangbourne, Royal Berkshire, a well-fit babe called Dora Battle, seventeen, was voted Most Beautiful Girl in the Known Universe and Beyond."' At this, she snorted a laugh, which unfortunately unleashed a stream of snot so she rushed off to compose and ready herself whilst the Pater and I waited at the kitchen table.

Her outfit when she finally emerged was sublimely Dora. Wrong colour, too tight, inappropriate accessories, etc. Plus she was alarmingly orange, but we had to admit she had scrubbed up rather well in her own brassy fashion. The Pater ushered us into the back seat of the car with bowing, scraping and doffing aplenty.

The queen o' the night turned to me and said, 'Thanks, Pete, I appreciate what you're doing ...' I patted her hand to reassure her, and she continued, 'but if you embarrass me in any way, I will razor your balls off and feed them to Poo, understand?'

I understood.

Thus, I spent quite one of the dullest evenings I've had in my entire sixteen years of an otherwise colourful life. I watched whilst Daffy Dora uncarefully avoided the dreaded couple, who were brazenly seated at a table à deux. She made the monumental error of drinking excess alcohol within the first eight and a half minutes of arriving. This didn't help her to comport herself in any elegant manner whatsoever. My sister and alcohol do not good bedfellows make, and certainly the cooking brandy she had secreted in her handbag wasn't the most prudent foundation on which to build an evening of dignity. Pretty early on it was clear her gown was surrendering, until eventually her staggeringly huge white bosoms shook off the restraint altogether and they too attended the prom entirely unfettered.

It was at this opportune point I decided to emerge from the dark corner whence I had retreated (might I add that however dark, I yet again attracted the unsolicited attention of a good many unchaste young fillies. What an immodest and bawdy troupe they are) in order to escort Debauched Dora away and home to safety. She was stupendously offended by my offer of help and violently lashed out.

272

'Get off me, you bloody prickhead! I'll go home as and if and when and with who I want! You shit ... cocker ... head! Go away!'

Really, the silly girl pushes ingratitude to the point of indecency. She lurched towards Sam and Lottie and misguidedly decided that giving an astonished and petrified Sam an exclusive lap dance would be just perfect. Lottie understandably took umbrage and a frenzied squabble ensued. It was far from pretty, though I couldn't help noticing with no little pride that Diesel Dora was actually pretty nifty with the old fisticuffs.

With the assistance of the burly (and not unattractive) phys. ed. teacher Craig, I was able to extract her and herd her towards the exit. I did not, however, waste the opportunity to whisper a few words in the young and poisonous Master Sam's ear. 'It would be well, sir, for you and your disloyal floozy of a companion to keep your distance from my darling sister. You make a powerful enemy in me, you errant cad.'

I fancy he cowered.

SIXTY-ONE

Dora

Please, I beg you God, be merciful. Everything on me, in me, and around me hurts. It's so like bloody awful. I woke up next to a neat little hill of sick on my pillow. In a way it's good it's there, because if I hadn't got that out, I would have so choked on it. That's exactly how that giant lady in that band from the old days died. What were they called? Mum bloody loves them. The Mums and Dads, or something. Anyway that's how she died, that lady.

I woke up because I could hear Poo slurping, and when I turned over, she was just starting to eat the sick. Disgusting, totally gross. That dog will eat any bloody thing, cheese, bananas, space dust, gum, horse poo, shoes. Once I saw her eat the bottom half of a rotten old rat out in the field. I was gobsmacked, I couldn't take my eyes off it. She just munched and crunched 'til it was all gone. Then we walked home and she threw the whole lot up in front of the telly when Dad was watching Jeremy Clarkson. Mum said at least the regurgitated rat was 'highly appropriate'. Didn't know what she was talking about. Never know what she's talking about. Don't know who she is any more. Don't care.

Lost one of her earrings last night. I'll get killed for that, probably. Dad said it's made of real diamonique or something? Shit. I'm in so much shitting shit. I cleared away the sick, but there's still a stain, can't get it out. What is sick made of? Why has it got yellow paint in it? I didn't eat anything bloody yellow. I only ate white stuff. In fact I didn't eat anything atall yesterday. That was the bloody problem. Then I had the brandy. All of it. Then apparently I had some vodka and Red Bull which I hate normally. I think it was the no-food and mega-fear mixture that worked out so badly.

I remember seeing 'them' as soon as I walked in. I went over to the bar and they looked away. It felt so weird to see Lottie and not to run up to her and give her like the hugest big hug, especially coz that prom was supposed to be the sign that we were finally finished with school. We've dreamed about this for ages. Her and me together. Not her and him.

Luckily, no one said too much about it but I honestly can't remember much that happened, I remember the first ten minutes or so, but nothing else after that. Peter says he will tell me all about it when he's up. Hope nothing too bad happened. Don't think it did. Like, I would so know if it had . . . I think. Yeah.

All of my whole head is thumping. My legs are itching. My back is sore. My skin isn't on my face right. My stomach is full of acid and my throat is croaky. I can't see properly, even with my glasses on. I can only just see my screen. Which tells me that, omigod, I was talking on Facebook at three this morning. God. Who to? Oh, once to Not Robert Pattinson who told me to shut up and go to bed. Then for omigod forty minutes to X-Man. God, it's such a long chat. I am rambling on about Sam and Lottie mostly, how embarrassing. He is kind about it though. God he must be so patient letting me go on and on.

I tell him at one point that I am crying and can't type for a minute and all through that he has kept saying, 'Don't worry Dodo. Calm down. It's cool,' 'til I feel better. He's given me a nickname. Dodo. That's lovely. Then he tells me he 'gets nervous at parties too'. Ah, sweet. He says he is 'sooo shy and will probably never get the courage up to actually meet in person'. I say, 'Course you will babe, don't be scared, this bitch don't bite.' Oh God, that's a bit embarrassing. Then he asks what I wore to the party so I describe it. Hmmn, it sounds a bit more sexy than I really looked.

He says, 'Stop coz it's getting me hot.'

Omigod. I make him hot. No one's ever said that before.

Then he asks me to 'Post a pic of you in your prom dress.'

I say, 'You first.'

He says, 'I haven't got a prom dress.'

I say, 'Ha ha. U know wot I mean. Let me see wot u look like.'

He says, 'No way. You'll never want to talk again, I'm a proper geek.'

I say, 'No u ain't. U silly boy.'

He says, 'I bet u look fit. Dunno wot Sam thinking . . . his loss.'

I say, 'OK will post pic. Feast ur eyes. Tell me wot u think!' Omigod. What did the picture look like?

OH. MY. ACTUAL. GOD!

I have sent a picture of me with my boobs out. It's bloody hideous. OMIGOD. What did he reply? Nothing. Omigod. Nothing. Silence. Now I've lost X-Man too. I never even met him. I am 130% idiot. With shit tits.

SIXTY-TWO

Mo

He walked in purposefully this morning and sat down. It was now our third session, and not one of them had been what they are supposed to be. Far from it.

I started. 'I said last time, that I needed to think. Since then, I've done nothing but. Well, I say "think", but actually my brain doesn't seem to be functioning correctly at all. Anyway, sorry, what I need to say is this – much as I ... I don't think we can take all this any further ...'

He stood up. 'Please get up.'

It was such a simple and odd request. I stood. He was looking at my mouth. Oh God, was there something there? I automatically touched it to see. Was I wearing the remnants of my breakfast as a jam moustache or something? There was nothing there. But he was still intensely staring at it.

Then he looked up into my eyes. 'Mo. I have to know what it's like to kiss you. I'm not asking your permission, I'm just warning you that I am going to take that kiss. Right now.'

With that, he moved towards me a good three big steps. I was paralysed. It was definitely about to happen, and the anticipation was so charged, I couldn't breathe. I suddenly realized I still had my pad and my pen in my hand. My pad in its lovely old leather holder. That Husband gave me. Lovely old leather Husband. Gave me that holder. He's not here though, is he, at this exact moment when I am about to be kissed by a handsome young man in his thirties?

I turned and put the pad down. This brief perfunctory distraction was my chance to escape, but I dismissed that option immediately, and turned back. I'm tall but not as tall as him, so I had to tilt my face to look at him properly. He didn't grab me or gather me up in his arms in a frenzied embrace. I sort of hoped he would. I thought that was definitely what happened at moments like this. What do I mean by moments like this? I've never had a moment like this. I've seen them in films. I've never lived one in my own real life. Is this my own <u>REAL</u> life?

He perched my chin gently on the crook of his index finger and leaned in very close. I could feel his breath. I could smell his citrussy aftershave. I could see the texture of his lovely young skin. So close, so close.

279

Now both of his hands were cupping my face. He was looking right into me. He whispered, 'What will you do? Let's see . . .'

The lightness of his touch. The softness of his mouth. The heaviness of his breath. The taste of his tongue. The life in him. Breathing it into me. He was claiming this kiss. Taking it from me. Then he pulled me closer, and put his arms around me, and it was a different embrace altogether. Then, he was giving me the kiss, testing if I was going to return it. It was impossible to do anything else, it was so utterly wonderful. Every thought of everything and anything else lapsed into temporary oblivion. The allowing of it was such a release that once I had crossed that line, I was unleashed. I was transported back to a more beautiful time, way before being married, before kids and jobs and uni. An irresponsible unguarded carefree time, when, if you want to, you could kiss like this for hours on end. In fact you were convinced you would die of sorrow if you had to be apart at the lips.

So that's what we did today, Noel and I. Whilst my friends and colleagues were barely ten foot away, in sessions in other rooms or at reception or in the kitchen or on the loo or feeding the fish, I was kissing

Noel, sighing and moaning in gorgeous raptures of juicy delight for fifty-five minutes.

Fifty-five minutes!

And we only separated then because we heard George's door opening as he was finishing his session with his client. Otherwise I think it might have continued for days. Days and days of perfect kissing. Even then, he remained close. I felt smooch-drunk. I was dizzy. I wanted him to shut up and start it again, but he was speaking clearly. 'You can't lie in a kiss, Mo, I've seen the truth now. Thank you. God, your face – your face looks different. You look about eighteen. Please say there can be more.'

To which I replied the fabulously eloquent, 'Yes please more now soon please thank you.'

He laughed and left. I heard him greet his waiting client in the hallway. He switched just like that. Turned on a sixpence. Abracadabra. He was gone.

I couldn't go to collect my next client immediately. I had to compose myself. I felt I would surely be struck off if anyone saw me like this. Drunk on duty. Inebriated with kissing. Pissed with pleasure. I looked in the mirror. He was right, I did look different. I was lit up. I was decorated. All because I know I am kissable. Still.

SIXTY-THREE

Dora

If I wasn't actually me, I wouldn't bother with me at all. I am so bloody useless. I wouldn't be my friend, I wouldn't go out with me, I wouldn't be my brother or my parent, or my doctor or my dog or anything. I'd be one of those other people sitting about like calling each other and saying, 'Did you hear what Dora Battle did at the prom? When she did that like disgusting lap dance on Sam Tyler and had a scrap with Lottie Evans? And you could like so see her pants and everything? What a slapper.' That's who I'd rather be than me. If a human is, like say 100% then I am, like 22% or something. Well, for body: I'm 6%, clothes: I'm about 12%, hair: I'm 2%, personality: I'm 23%, friends: I'm 0%.

I went to see Nana Pamela, coz she's the only one that doesn't know about what I did. Well, <u>didn't</u> know. She knows now coz I told her. She made hot chocolate for me to drink while she was making me a pineapple upside-down cake. How has she always got the ingredients? Even when she doesn't know you're coming? Mum is so not like that. If someone is coming round they have to be invited on a gold-edged card and the

282

shopping has to be done eight weeks ahead so she can practise and like really pretend she knocks up these like fabulous meals so casually, or something. If anyone just drops in she totally freaks coz she hasn't got the right food to show off with. Why didn't she learn from Nana Pamela? That is her mother after all. Her actual mother. You would think she would respect her and learn from her. I would if I was her daughter. God.

Anyway, I told Nana Pamela all about what happened and she was like sooo funny about it, doing impressions of Sam and Lottie getting ready for the prom and saying about how Lottie would have to take Sam there in her handbag coz he's so small 'n' stuff? Maybe even she'd have to like keep him in a matchbox and let him out at mealtimes and parties. She said it would be such hard work being his girlfriend coz you have to like spend all the time making sure people don't step on him.

Then she said, 'And that little missy Lottie had better watch out. Doesn't she know that dating your best friend's ex-boyfriend is the height of bad manners and betrayal? It's reprehensible. The patron saint of Amity, Saint Jonathan of the Immaculate Holy Friendship Bracelets, will send his invisible demon revengers to enter her nostrils and eat out her brains from the inside and gradually work their way down through

283

her body, munching and chewing her up until they exit painfully through her bum hole to remind her of the agony she caused you. Yep, that's what the Saint will do, God bless him in his mercy and benevolence.'

She is like, so on my team when like no one else is. Well, Dad is but he doesn't count coz he's just Dad. She asked me if there had been any developments on the contraception front, if I had decided what to go for, but I told her I don't think I'll be needing any contraception for like the next twenty years because everyone can't wait to get away from me. Especially boys. I expect my fanny will just mould over or something, like seal up, and if I do get the chance to make sex with someone, anyone, in the future, I'll just have to like call up the council or something to get them to open it up. Nana Pamela said a van will arrive with four guys in overalls and reflective yellow jackets and they will have all this equipment just for that purpose. They'll have protective headgear with hard hats with like torches on and stuff, and they'll have to be tied together for safety! She is sooo funny. That's the first time I've laughed in ages.

I told her that I had a secret that I wanted to tell her but that she like so had to keep it secret. She promised and so I told her about the *X-Factor* auditions and how they're in a couple of weeks' time, after my birthday and how coz I'll be eighteen then, I don't have to get anybody's permission or anything.

She asked if I wanted her to come with me. That was so sweet but I think now that I haven't got Lotts to go with, I'll probably be better off on my own, and anyway we'd have to queue for hours and she's got bad knees. She totally understood and asked if I would sing her my song. So I did. I started singing and got to the 'I am beautiful, no matter what they say' bit and Nana said, 'Oh I know this one, hang on!' And she went over to the piano and started trying to play it but she so doesn't really know it so it sounded so like abysmal, and just like wrong.

In the end she started playing that Eva Cassidy song 'Somewhere Over the Rainbow' which she loves when I sing it. At least she sort of knows that one, so we could sing it together. She thinks it would be better if I did that one at the audition, but everyone does that one, and I need to really stand out. I'm sticking to my choice. I would so kill myself if I did her choice and then didn't get through to the next round. This is my dream, after all. I've got to live the dream. My own dream. There is no point to my life if I don't get through. If I don't win really. It's all I'm living for. It's the only good thing I've got to look forward to.

Oscar

This evening was a revelation. The Parents' Association Quiz Evening at school. It was school versus teachers. Fatal. How singularly disappointing it is to witness the deepest depths, the widest widths, the highest heights and the densest densities of the shocking levels of ignorance of the staff.

I suppose I shouldn't condemn them <u>all</u>. There are those who deserve some respect. Shitehouse Shelley is all right, if one can tolerate his toxic halitosis. At least he is curious enough to read a book or two about something outside the parameters of his own subject. If I taught German as he does, I would read incessantly about absolutely anything else. A man whose job it is to splutter gutturally all day shouldn't have poison for breath. Mrs Gibson, the chemistry teacher, is the other one I appreciate, although I fully realize that one shouldn't need to be quite so grateful for the simple fact that she is a woman, a gentle and intelligent flame flickering in the inky darkness which is the tar-pit of woeful male unenlightenment that pervades our school. These are the inglorious fellows who make me feel ashamed to occupy the same gender. I savour opportune moments like these, when they are clearly adversaries and, even more clearly, philistines.

The Pater and I were representatives of my year along with a gallant few at our table. I spied Wilson with his mother, such a tiny pale woman, at a less well-positioned table some distance hence. His mother is terribly sweetly shy and I could see that this evening was her idea of purgatory, so singularly uncomfortable was she. I excused myself and made my way to their table. En route, I felt the guilt of my indiscreet transgression creep up on me. I was walking as if through a treacle of shame. I nearly stopped and turned back, too embarrassed to confront them, but something urged me on. Contrition, perhaps?

I leaned in between the two of them, and whispered, 'I hope you will forgive me, but I can't help noticing you are surrounded by rascals and knaves at this table, in whose unsophisticated company you are unlikely to lay claim to a rightful victory by the end of the evening. It is vital that we outflank these wretched thieves, the teachers, in order to reclaim the coveted Dimbleby Quiz Cup which they stole so dishonourably from us last year. To this end, it would suit us well to extend an invitation to you, Mrs Wilson, and your dazzling son to join us at our table there. Two such prize additions would be nothing short of marvellous, your support would be invaluable. Might you honour us . . . ?'

Luckily, the two of them acquiesced and followed me to our far superior table. The Pater was charming and rose to his feet to greet them. They installed themselves comfortably, and I dispatched the Pater to the 'bar' for a jug of orange squash and an assortment of Family Circle Biscuits to sustain us.

The competition was fairly fierce, but had its moments of levity, my favourite being when Cock Cooper displayed his towering heathenism by thinking an 'autocrat' was an 'aristocrat'. As Wilson observed, he actually almost said 'aristo<u>cat</u>'. Which, on reflection, would have been miles better, much more amusing at any rate. Our table proved to be infinitely more savvy than almost any other.

Some strong competition came from the Headmaster's table. He had illegally recruited his own two sons, who were neither teacher nor school. Both are postgrads and fairly well equipped in the brain department. Needless to say, neither actually attended our school, a fact which certainly proved to their advantage. Their mere presence was proof enough to me of the Head's familiarity with underhand dealing. It is no surprise

that our leader is widely known as the Hegiveshead-
master. He commands utter disrespect from one and
all who meet him, quite appropriately so, but alarmingly his table were surging ahead with precious and
ill-gotten points. I couldn't quite believe the luck they
had with their questions, one of which was the bafflingly simple: name the prime minister. Yegods! Talk
about a fix. Mind you, I suppose that could be catego-
rized as a challenging question when one considers
the turnover of late.

The Pater showed some expertise in the sports sec-
tion, and Wilson's mother was fabulously handy for
cookery and history. Actually, she and the Pater
seemed to be getting on famously, I haven't seen
him laugh so much for ages. I've never seen Wilson's
mother laugh at all 'til now. I suppose one wouldn't, if
one lived inside the grip of such debilitating sadness.
She seemed resuscitated, for a while at least. I watched
as the Pater and she made such heroic efforts to be
sociable, and obviously found surprising pleasure in
it. I wished that perhaps Mama could sometimes make
a little bit more effort to bring smiles like these to the
Pater's kindly face. He is so very willing to be happy.
And she seems so very reluctant of late . . .

Suddenly I felt Wilson squeeze my knee under the

table. 'They're really getting on, aren't they? We could be the Brady Bunch!'

It was shocking to realize that Wilson believes my father to be so available. Is he?! I do hope not. There's nothing more humiliating than a caddish Pater.

'No, no,' I assured him, 'he's just pleased to be out; overexcited, that's all.'

'Right,' he said, not convinced.

'Wilson ... Luke,' I whispered, 'I must apologize to you for my reckless indiscretion. I am as sorry as a sorry thing for doing what I did. Your personal history is none of my nosey business. I hope you know how very ashamed I am. Can you find it in your heart to forgive me, my dear boy? You have every right to be piqued as hell. I know that.'

'It's impossible for me to resent you,' he said, 'I am altogether in your thrall and I know you will keep my counsel. And have me in your safe keeping.'

'I will, Luke, I surely will. Need I extend my apology to your darling ma?'

'She knows nothing of it, so no call for that. And anyway, see how happy she is here tonight, let's not ruin it. For anyone.' With that, he twinkled at me and I caught it, and, in turn, lit up a little bit myself. Yes, he's a tad special is young Luke Wilson. 'Pon my word, his staggering strength and capacity for kindness has caught me napping, I have to admit he is a tiny bit marvellous, now that I come to stop and properly notice.

He then went on to answer three very difficult questions in a row. A hat-trick, by Jove, which triumphantly brought the Dimbleby Cup back to our table, and to school, where it rightly belongs. Victory. Needless to say, the Head was seething. Livid. Foaming at the mouth. Wilson caught his eye and stood up, and bowed to him in an astonishingly impressive act of defiance and excellent manners in equal measure. The Head was forced to acknowledge him and smile.

Wilson is a contender. In all senses. I immediately invited him as my date to Dame Dora's eighteenth birthday party.

SIXTY-FIVE

Mo

Do I have some kind of announcement branded on my face? Am I wearing a sandwich board with all my personal info on it? How does my mother always know? I didn't relish the thought of this week's visit for exactly that reason. I have tried more and more, recently, to make my visits about <u>HER</u>, but she reads me instantly and is pretty much surgical with her questioning. She knows I have come bearing emotional weight and she wants me to empty out my knapsack. I have resisted this for the last few years. I find her interest intrusive and I somehow can't bear that she knows me so well. Her concern can be claustrophobic.

I thought for a while that she was simply being nosey, needing to hear all the gen on my life because her life had become so much smaller since Dad died, and she might be living vicariously through me. I didn't mind that really, in fact I would sometimes embellish in order to make the telling more interesting and give her something to get her teeth into. I'd exaggerate to make my life seem more elaborate than it is. How pathetic is that? I don't really mind the deceit in itself but to your own mum? For what purpose? To impress her? I don't need Mum's approval for anything. Obviously it oils the wheels if she is proud of my achievements and thinks I'm an OK person, which I know she does, but I'm not seeking her validation. I have it.

I went there to connect, that's all. We certainly did that. This time I gave her plenty of warning that I was coming, so she had made me a beetroot cake. No second-rate biscuit substitutes today. The icing was bliss – bright pink and utterly delish.

Mid-chew, when I was on the web and disadvantaged by cake, she pounced.

'So, what's going on?' A seemingly innocent, harmless enquiry, but I know Pamela, and she wanted to prise the lid off me and root about in all my private stuff.

'Nothing much, Mum, we're all fine.'

'Are we now?'

'Yes.'

'OK, if you want to hide that's fine, but I can see you from here, young lady m'girl, and I'm happy to wait 'til you're ready to come out.'

'Til now, this momentous event in my life has only been known by two people, him and me. It was very hard to imagine sharing it, but I did long to. I was completely torn. On the one hand, of course I wanted to tell her, to include her in the dizzying mix of it all. I was longing for a confidante, someone to know the sheer delight I feel at the idea someone so wonderful wants me so much. I wanted to endlessly mull it over in detail, and gossip and giggle, that's the fun of a new relationship, the marvelling about it. I wanted us to be amazed together, to tell her details of what had happened and watch her eyes get wider and wider. To keep repeating 'I know, I know'. But I couldn't, it's not that easy. It meant letting her into a very private place where she didn't belong, and where it would be dangerous for her to be. In the betrayal place. Where I am wilfully ignoring my real life.

We ate cake and drank tea in an awkward silence. The cake and tea were divine. The silence was not. I tried a few feeble enquiries about her life, but she was perfunctory in her answers, she didn't want to be diverted.

I said, 'So, how's Janice?'

She said, 'Like Janice always is, thanks.'

'Right. You been busy?'

'Yes thanks, Mo, very busy.'

'Been into town this week?'

294

'Yes, right into town, thanks.'

Then, she stunned me with, 'Your old man was here yesterday, Mo. I don't think he came just to eat whisky cake. He didn't say much but what he did say broke my heart.'

'Oh?' I tried to remain impassive.

'Yes, he said he feels loss and lost.'

'Right. Interesting.'

'Care to elaborate? Or just another slice of denial for you?'

She ought to be dunked in the pond for a witch. She knew. She knew something. Why would Husband be round here on his own? I know they have a close friendship, the two of them, but isn't your mother supposed to be in your team, no question? I found to my shame that feelings of jealousy about Husband and Mum's collusion were rising up my gullet. It was highly uncomfortable.

'Mum . . . I wouldn't exclude you from anything unless there was reason. It's not that simple.'

'I understand, Mo, but what you really need to know right now is that it most certainly IS that simple. You either still love your husband or you don't. Simple as that. Which is it, love?'

It crossed my mind to keep the fraudulence going

but my emotions took over and forced my face to cry. Only a slight welling to begin with, partially controllable with coughing and blinking, but less so with every passing second that she was looking at me, until it wasn't possible to rein it in any more. With crying, I find that once the tipping point has been reached, it is pointless to resist it. My God, I didn't know I contained that much water! The release was almost orgasmic, it was so good to feel the tension subsiding.

'Come on, love, let's be having it. Get it out, get it all out. You can trust me.'

'Oh, Mum ...' I started jabbering about what had happened, what had not happened, about my confusion, my awakening, my greyness, all of it. On and on, throughout which she held my hand and patiently sat and listened. I said much more than I should, but I was unable to stem the flow. I needed it all to be out, to be said, to be in the open air, like a cat sicking up a fur ball. I started to feel better.

Pamela sat patiently and, eventually, after I spluttered out the last few sentences of the story, she responded in her inimitable, succinct way. 'You had need of a knight, and you think he's arrived, don't you, Mo? To save you.'

'From what, though?'

'From thinking that you don't matter to anyone any more.'

That was a slamming body blow. It hurt. It really hurt. Because it might be true.

She went on, 'Here's a fact to put in your handbag and think on later. You matter to me.'

That was it, I was suddenly at her chest, sobbing and sobbing. 'It's unbearable, Mum, I'm unbearable.'

We sat like that for some time, with her smoothing my hair and patting me. Well, I'm not quite sure how long exactly because, unbelievably, I nodded off with my head on her shoulder, feeling gratefully safe and wishing her quiet strength would seep into me, and steer me through this shocking storm.

SIXTY-SIX

Dora

Sometimes things just crash together for a reason, even if you like don't know it at the time. It all looked so bad for a couple of days, the Mum stuff, the Sam and Lottie thing, then the prom thing and THEN realizing that virtually everyone is away for my birthday or hasn't even responded to my email invite so it's down to like only three girls in my year who can come, and they are Emos.

So then I spoke to Dad about it and he said let's not spend the money on the room at the pub, and he agreed to give me that £200 instead, plus he would get some drinks and stuff so we could have it at home. That means we can have KFC buckets, so actually I prefer that. The food part, anyway. Trust me to get born right in the middle of the school holidays so no one is around. It sucks big time. Except, like Dad said, I really love sleepovers so that's what it will be now.

Three sad Emos and me. Great. Not.

Then none of my new Facebook guys were talking to me, and I thought I'd lost them for ever. I'm not speaking to Peter coz he invited his new friend to my party without even bloody asking me. I'm not speaking to Mum coz I hate her. So all in all it looked pretty wak. Then luckily, a really like amazing thing happened? I got post on my Facebook and it was X-man. Yay! He's back,

X-MAN: Sorry haven't been in touch. Felt bit awkward after you sent pic.

ME: OMG. Soooo sorry re pic. Was pissed. Shouldn't have. Just for record – my chest normally looks tons better than that. No bronzer. Was weird angle. Sorry.

X-MAN: No prob. Don't want u to think I'm a perv.

ME: Ha. Ha. Def don't think that. Think I am!

X-MAN: Have deleted pic immediately, so you know.

ME: Thanks.

X-MAN: U shld b more careful. Weirdos everywhere.

ME: R u my mum?! Sound just like her!

X-MAN: Def not.

ME: U OK?

X-MAN: Yeh. Bit stressed re exams.

ME: Me too. Mine finished now.

X-MAN: 2 more 2 go. AAAARGH! Then freedom.

ME: YAY! Which 2?

X-MAN: Both music. Fav subject.

ME: Me 2!! You play instrument?

X-MAN: Yeh. Piano and guitar. U?

ME: I tried. Pants.

X-MAN: Don't believe u.

ME: I can sing a bit.

X-MAN: Really?

ME: Yeh. A bit. Tiny bit.

X-MAN: Wot type music u like?

ME: Loads of diff. stuff. Love pop, dance, musicals. Loads. Bring it on, baby! Wooo! Party!

X-MAN: U crazy chick.

ME: U ain't seen nuffink yet. Might sing at my 18th Birthday Party . . .

X-MAN: Wow. Sounds great.

ME: U wanna come?

X-MAN: UMMM . . . if sure?

ME: Be great if you came. Will forward details and time.

X-MAN: Great. I'll be there.

ME: YAY! Hey . . . wanna know a secret? . . .

X-MAN: Go on then.

ME: Won't tell?

X-MAN: Promise. On dog's life (important).

ME: Yeh, I love my dog too. Havin' puppies any minute.

X-MAN: Aw. Wot name?

ME: Poo.

X-MAN: LOL.

ME: I know. Shut up. No. Tell u secret coz trust u.

X-MAN: U can. Always.

ME: Yeh. Guess what? – I am going for *X-Factor* audition in 2 wks.

X-MAN: Cool! Wot singin'?

ME: Beautiful. C. Aguilera.

X-MAN: Good choice. U singing that at party too?

ME: Yeh.

X-MAN: Cool. Had a thought.

ME: Yeh?

X-MAN: Part of my music A level is singing training. U want help?

ME: OMG so can't believe.

X-MAN: Tis true dat.

ME: Booyakasha!

X-MAN: Bet u is skill wiv de singin', yeh?

ME: U get me?

X-MAN: Seriously, could help you. Get nervous?

ME: So badly.

X-MAN: Poor ol' Dora. Chill, coz I'm gonna help from now on. Will be the shizzle. Promise.

ME: Thanks. Glad we met. Not that we have. Yet.

X-MAN: Yeh. Talking of which. Want to? Meet up? Go out? Or tell me to piss off if I'm creepin' you out.

ME: Def not. Will make date at party. Will send details.

X-MAN: Ta, Dora. U is top human bean.

ME: No, u.

X-MAN: No, u.

ME: No, u.

SIXTY-SEVEN

Mo

I'm never going to get this bloody book written. Committing what I think to the page is somehow the death of it. And what am I writing that hasn't been written before or isn't perfectly obvious common sense? Whilst I am personally unravelling, maybe it's impossible to write something which aims to fix.

I think I was hoping the writing would prove easy but, of course, nothing that really counts is easy. I had hoped that I might impart something of use, that parents might find a few helpful nuggets in *Teenagers: The Manual* to assist them through the passion and the intensity of their children's adolescence. That they might come to understand the teenage mandate which compels the adolescent to shun their childhood, and which of course involves turning away from their parents. That parents are expected to let go at the precise time when the stakes are at their highest, and when mistakes could lead to harmful consequences. To point up how hard it is to stand by and let them make those mistakes, to not constantly rescue them.

Most of all, I wanted to point out that it's important

for us as parents to recognize that our children often provide the reason, the central meaning, to our lives, so it can be very hard to shift to a new gear and let them proceed on without us ... so ... perhaps it's at a vulnerable point like this, when the attachment to the key meanings in one's life is under scrutiny, that one might find oneself feeling lost?

Could this be seen as an all too obvious time to be seeking other options to attach oneself to? Other, more dangerous options that throw one's whole frame of reference off balance, perhaps? As a psychologist I can see how that might easily happen. As a woman, I don't know what I could possibly be referring to. Surely I am not replacing my ever-diminishing relationship with my own adolescents with an equally challenging injection of youth in the form of a young lover? The two can't possibly be related. Can they?

This morning, Lisa was in full camouflage gear on the front desk, flak jacket included. It's normal now, none of us question it. Not even the clients. She is our appointed leader. She's certainly our appointment leader, that's clear. She reminds me of the character Klinger in *MASH*, who wore increasing quantities of women's clothing in his overt attempt to be discharged from his army duties. Perhaps conversely,

Lisa is wearing increasing quantities of army gear in an attempt to remain in pole position at the front desk? She is not, like us, a trained practitioner, but I have come to realize she is every bit as important to the running of this practice. She understands that the people who validate us best are ones who see us as equals, and maybe she *wasn't* seen as equal in this job initially. Certainly not by me. She is now. And she is certainly 'seen', in every sense of the word. I just hope she doesn't incorporate a machine gun into the ensemble.

As I walked in, Lisa said, 'You look lovely today, Mo.'

'Oh, thanks.'

I think I <u>do</u> look . . . not exactly 'lovely' but certainly better than a few months ago, when I was dead. It's surprising how seeing yourself reflected so positively in someone else's eyes can lift your spirits so radically. Mum is right really. In Noel's eyes, I am of consequence. I'm more than that even. I'm desirable and kissable.

Am I just being greedy? After all, Husband still finds me desirable, and he is always kissing me. Too much, if anything. He thinks it's hilarious to kiss me at the most compromising moments. He's done it while I'm talking to teachers at Parents' Evening, he did it during a mortgage meeting at the bank, he does it at the checkout till in supermarkets. He has always found it hilarious to embarrass me, and, actually, it *is* quite funny.

It's not that I don't fancy him any more, it's just all . . . a bit . . . ossified. We've stopped growing somehow. We're a bit set. It's not unusual, I know that. It's not a crime but it is a killer. Familiarity and Security, two facets that parade as desirable, but, in truth, they are terrorists. Stealth bombers who creep in under cover of time to implode you. Add to that Need and Opportunity, the two greatest requirements for any betrayal, and the scene is set for a disaster.

I know it would be so wrong, so hurtful. I know it, but I am steadily swimming towards that chaos. I want it so badly, I choose not to control my desire. I choose to let it lead me anywhere, however unsafe. That's why I am going to lie so that I can be with Noel. I haven't done that yet, but I am about to, I can feel the tightening.

I am after all wearing a matching plum underwear set.

SIXTY-EIGHT

Dora

Dora Battle is eighteen! So can't believe I've actually got to this day. Mum made a chocolate cake, not as good as Nana Pamela's but still good, with sparklers, and they all piled on to my bed to eat it with champagne. All except Mum who was dressed up dead posh for work so she didn't want to get messy.

I got the money from Dad that we're not using on the hire of the room for the party. That's going in the bank. <u>But</u>, I might get it out again on Saturday coz I've seen some rad shoes in Top Shop that need to be mine. Mum says I should spend the money on something that really lasts. Duh. Yeah. What d'ya think shoes are, you wonk?! It was weird really coz Mum had to be nice coz it's my birthday but we both know we're not getting on very well at the moment, so it feels fake.

Still, not going to let *her* ruin my day. I've lived for this day. That's right. I actually have <u>LIVED</u> for this day. I've been on the planet for eighteen whole years. Dad got all teary and told me all about the day I was born and how he had to seem all butch but how scared he was. He'd never seen Mum like that before, apparently she made lots of loud animal noises and stuff, and he had brought along one of those cold boxes you get on picnics, but like for keeping ice packs cold to cool Mum down if she got too hot. But like, he had hidden a secret can of Guinness in there to drink for when I was actually born, so when Mum was shouting and swearing at him to 'give me something cold to put on my cocking boiling bloody head you twat, this is all your bloody fault!' he reached into the box and quick as a flash he put the can on her head by mistake. And then they laughed so much that she couldn't do her breathing and pushing and the nurse kept saying, 'I can see the head! No, it's gone back in. I can see the head again! Nope, it's gone.'

And that's how I arrived apparently, changing my mind, in the middle of laughter and screaming. Mum says that's how it's been ever since. Dad went on about how the world was when I was born. Something about Yugoslavia, and the Olympics and a fire in Windsor Castle where he said the queen went on telly and said she had a horrible anus or something? Then he and Mum were talking about the prime minister who looked like a milk bottle and ate peas all the time.

I had to interrupt them with, 'Excuse me, all focus on the Princess please. It is <u>my</u> birthday!'

Then Peter gave me a charm bracelet with, like the letter 'D' on it, and he said that it would 'charm the life of a charming young woman'. Sweet. Then Mum and Dad gave me my main present. Oh. My. Actual. God. I am now the proud owner of my very own iPhone. I so can't believe it because I so wanted one for so long. Plus they gave me fifty pounds credit. I spent all morning putting all my numbers on there. Def <u>not</u> putting Lottie and Sam on. Although it feels so weird not to have her number on there. It usually comes up top of the list of 'friends'. She's the top of my list. Yeah. Usually.

The middle part of the day was a bit normal really. Watched telly, opened cards 'n' stuff. Nana Pamela came round at five with a proper cake thank God. The whole bunny outfit thing had been ditched, so I didn't really even have to dress up much but I did my hair and put my new top on to feel a bit special. After all, I was going to meet X-Man for the first time tonight. Didn't tell Dad I only know him from Facebook, he would go mad and like not let him in, and anyway I thought when he got here Dad'll just think he's a friend's brother or something.

Mum called to say she had an emergency case and wouldn't be home 'til much later. Typical. Actually, it's better without her. Less stress. So me, Dad and Peter got the house ready with Nana Pamela ordering us about getting slowly sloshed on her own home-made sloe gin, 'til she was asleep by eight o'clock, in Dad's chair.

We set out all the cider and like, all the stuff for the soft drink cocktail, which is called a Shirley Temple, which I <u>so</u> love more than cider actually. It's lemonade and this red grenadine stuff. Mum used to make them for our parties when we were little, with umbrellas and cherries and stuff, and we really like thought we were dead grown up drinking such a posh thing in a tall glass.

We blew up balloons with 'Dora is 18' on and we had the badges with the same on, all ready. Dad set up the karaoke machine and we put my iPod into the big speakers and dimmed all the lights down. Just in time I remembered that I hadn't put any glitter bronzer on so I rushed upstairs and did that right when the door-bell went. I thought it might be X-Man but it was Luke Wilson being dropped off by his mother, who came in and had a cup of tea and chatted to Dad.

Glad Peter invited him, that kept him occupied so he wasn't bothering my friends. In the end, four of the Emos turned up plus one of them brought her pen pal from Croatia who was nice but ate like <u>all</u> of the popcorn immediately, plus Peter and Luke, and Dad and Nana Pamela (unconscious).

I kept listening out for the door in case it was X-Man. I was like, so excited to see what he looked like but he was like dead late so we started the food (KFC buckets – yay!) and some dancing. It was mainly me and Peter dancing. Emos don't dance much to our music. They actually hate Snow Patrol and Girls Aloud. How could anyone hate them? I haven't got any punk or metal stuff they would like but actually, when they'd had some cider they were dancing along happily to 'Mamma Mia' with us, no probs. Even though they're Emos, they're still like human.

I went outside to check if X-Man was too shy to come in or something, but no sign. That was about ten o'clock. We started the karaoke. I loved it when two of the Emos did 'I'm a Barbie Girl' and 'Reach For the Stars' and then like begged us not to tell anyone! Then Peter went all gay and sang that 'Mad About the Boy' song pretty much <u>all</u> to Luke, which was proper embarrassing.

Then it was my turn to sing my song. I was so sad that X-Man hadn't turned up, coz I was going to sing this for him, I'd told him that. Dad saw I was feeling a bit wobbly and he cheered me on. 'C'mon Dora. Gissa song!' So, I sang my audition song and like it was so beautiful coz they all joined in and Dad was waving his lighter and everything. And it was like so completely bloody ironic because at the end, one of the Emos shouted out, 'You should go on *X-Factor*, you'd bloody trounce them all you would!' and I was like thinking yeah, if only you knew.

And then it seemed even more ironic that my best best ever friend in the whole world wasn't at my party. It wasn't even ironic. It was just bloody sad. Then I couldn't stop crying for ages. Then I started again because I had to admit that X-Man was def <u>NOT</u> coming and like, where's my mum and everything? It was all too bloody horrific. 'I don't even want to be eighteen,' I was crying into Dad's shoulder.

He was so great then coz he just went straight into the cupboard in the living room and got my fav DVDs out and we made a huge bed of sleeping bags on the floor, put the lights out and watched *The Little Mermaid* and *Grease* and we all sang along with like, every single song whilst Dad brought us cocoa and crisps. I even saw one of the Emos sucking her thumb!

At about eleven-thirty, just when he was stranded at the drive-in, feelin'a fool, I suddenly remembered something. So I quickly ran into the garage and brought in my box of indoor fireworks I went out to get today, because I can, because I'm eighteen. I lit them all in the kitchen, on a tray, like it said, then carried them through to the front room where everyone was. From that moment on, it all went a bit quick. The fireworks were a bit jumpy and some of them whizzed off the tray. The Emos started screaming. One of the rockets got lodged in the like sofa, and like caught fire. Dad got the extinguisher and put it out but there was a big hole. One of the whizzers went straight up so fast it stuck in the ceiling with all the sparks raining down on everyone. One of the sparks must have got in Nana Pamela's hair and caught fire, coz she woke up and started jumping around shouting 'Bollocks! Bollocks!' and smacking her head.

Peter was the one who heard it first. He had pushed Luke to the floor and was lying on top of him to protect him from the sparks when he loudly told us all to shush. He was right, there <u>was</u> a noise. It sounded like a child crying, but it wasn't human. It was really like bloody creepy. 'Poo!' shouted Peter and he ran up the stairs. I'm sure the Emos thought he was having a sudden attack of explosive diarrhoea. We all followed into his bedroom and there she was, looking all shaky and shocked and happy to see us, lying right next to his sock drawer.

Dad pushed through and went right up to her on all fours. 'Hey, Poo, it's all right sweetheart, come on, calm down. What have we got here?' He put his hand into the sock drawer and pulled out a little brown furry thing all wet and weird with like mucus on it. 'Aw, Poo, I'm so sorry. What a shame.' Dad looked at us. 'This little one hasn't made it I'm afraid,' and he gently laid the limp little body inside one of Peter's socks. I could see its cute little face with a huge forehead and closed eyes. It looked more like a mole or something, not a puppy, it was so tiny. And so dead. 'Happy Birthday Dora,' I mumbled to myself. Then Dad said, 'Hang on, who's this?' He had his hand right in the back of the drawer and we could hear some scratching. As he pulled his hand out we saw he was holding a tail. A black tail. Then some back legs and slowly, as he pulled, we could see more and more of the new puppy who was huge and black and ... alive! Definitely alive. Unbelievably big. About half the size of Poo and four times the size of his dead brother. How did she push it out? No wonder she was yelping. Dad handed me the puppy and said, 'Happy Birthday Dora!' and it licked my face and sucked on my nose with its pinky new baby puppy gums. Yeah, HAPPY BIRTHDAY. Lovely.

SIXTY-NINE

Oscar

O for a Turkish bath. My life would be immensely improved if only I lived near one. One doesn't wish to cavil but, really, Pangbourne is nowhere. I might as well live on a lost kite, I am so disconnected. I would leave immediately if it weren't for my unfinished education, a sneaking affection for my family and the promise of a new beau. It's just that, damn it, I long for something suggestive and interesting, to wit, nothing Pangbourne will ever offer.

My desire for a rub-down is simple. The cleansing. I want to rid myself of any previous sordid desires and I want to prepare myself for the pure beauty that lies ahead. I want to be clean in thought, word and deed. Well. In thought and word at any rate. Well. In word.

I've always imagined a Turkish bath would go some way to bowdlerizing one's less savoury memories. Perhaps the folly of former misdeeds would in turn be steamed, rubbed and slapped out of every pore? Perhaps the vigorous scrubbing would purge one of improper imaginings? Perhaps. One would like the option to try it at least. And of that there is very little chance in these hereabouts.

I wanted to be squeaky and fragrant at Delinquent Dora's party, for what was in essence my first real date with Wilson. I simply can't conceive of how I have foolishly overlooked him in the past. My Noel goggles were an ill-fitting pair with utterly the wrong prescription.

In lieu of a Turkish bath, I chose instead to ablute in Mama's bathroom since she was conveniently absent and since she also has by far the most superior products in the house. I lit a fresh candle and soaked in something oily and jasminy and divine. I made use of her magnifying mirror with all its alarming revelations. I'd never fully realized just how errant my eyebrow hairs have become. They are positively cheeky. Some of them are presuming they are entitled to grow <u>between</u> the two brows. I think not. I attacked at once with tweezers. Back, sir! Back! Have at you, you varlet! With patience and a modicum of skill they were tamed. I can be quite appealingly assertive when required.

Suitable attire for a sister's Eighteenth Birthday Party? Quite frankly, the answer, surely, is the humble smoking jacket. Yet again. One simply cannot fail to impress with its classic timeless panache. They really do make ideal loungewear, smart daywear and stylish partywear, and I do believe they truly are synonymous with comfort.

Obviously, I don't own a couture model myself as yet but my custom-made gown must suffice for now. Black silk slacks, brocade slippers, a generous helping of the Pater's Brylcreem, a Jezebel of a brooch, and I was ready.

Darling Dora really was a peach all day, and everso grateful for the bracelet I gave her. I should co-co. That trinket cost me forty-five English pounds. Cash I was sorely tempted to spend instead on a big fat Havana cigar to go with my jacket. However, one only comes of age once apparently and, much as she bullies and annoys me, I can't help loving the silly creature. I think it's that I know she would always bat for my side if called upon, and likewise I would for hers. Lord only knows which team I'm batting for at present . . .

Wilson arrived, promptly, at the party, transported here by his doting mother, who came in for light refreshment with the Pater. I find it hard to refer to him as 'Luke' as he has requested, only because it seems so significantly intimate, and hell's bells, we haven't so much as held hands thus far. Although, of course, I anticipate that blissful scenario with bated breath. I acquiesced to his offer and called him by his Christian name, and what a very solid, biblical, good and true name it is. How well it suits him. It has air in it, suitable for an angel, but it also has profundity, suitable for a man. Truly, he is both.

I noticed immediately that he had taken much care with his appearance, and felt flattered that it might be on my account. He was sporting a cerise shirt with an oversized collar and a lilac tie with an oversized knot. The oversizing was promising, I felt . . . He wore drainpipe slacks of the black denim variety and a large studded belt. He had the look of a young Jarvis Cocker but with less geek, and much more tendril action about the golden hair. So much lovely curly blond hair. He must have been a cherub as a child. I noticed that he wore cowboy boots with a Cuban heel, and shamefully I pictured him in only those. So much for the cleansing bath . . .

We kept ourselves to ourselves for much of the evening since Desperate Dora had invited the oddest group. I think she is a little bit Directionless Dora since the split with Lottie. However, we did have a dance together to Girls Aloud's 'Sound of the Underground', she and I, during which I noticed Wilson . . . <u>Luke</u> . . . couldn't tear his eyes from me. I threw in a couple of my PlayStation dance mat moves for his benefit, and did my reputation as a smooth hoofer no harm whatsoever.

Later, when the karaoke began, I chose carefully and sung Eartha Kitt's version of 'Mad About the Boy'. I directed it to the whole room with the occasional sly glance tossed in his direction. It was oh so subtle, but I knew that boy could read me like a well-thumbed saucy book. He appreciated the sentiment, of that I was certain. I needed no further proof when we settled down next to each other on the sofa under a blanket to watch *The Little Mermaid* with all the gals. We were forced up against each other, shoulder to shoulder and thigh to thigh. It was completely thrilling.

He whispered to me, 'You know I think very highly of you, Oscar, you <u>do</u> know that, don't you?'

'I do indeed, my dear boy. You have in the past led me to believe you are not entirely indifferent to me.'

He continued, 'I'm fully determined to accept you, should you ask me to step out with you, you've certainly been long enough about it.'

I laughed. 'I feel bound to tell you, Luke, that I have conducted a lengthy meeting with my tempted self and, believe me . . .'

'Oh do shut up and ask me, Oscar.'

'Luke Wilson. Might you consider . . . ?'

Quick as a flash he interrupted with, 'Yes, I will. I do. I am. Whatever.'

We sat for a while saying nothing, just watching the mermaid learn how to use her legs in order to pursue her prince. He crept his hand into mine under the blanket. I ventured, 'Might I attempt a little wickedness?' to which he replied, 'Not here, Oscar, no. But know this, I will never forgive you if you should never try again.' What a gloriously sassy fellow. How delightfully fresh.

So, on my sister's eighteenth birthday it happened. At last, I am partnered. I took off my smoking jacket and wrapped it around his shoulders. 'I want you to have this, Luke. I can't bear for you to ever be alone or cold again.'

SEVENTY

Mo

Guilt. It's definitely lurking uncomfortably. It fills every waking thought to the brim. There's no more room for anything else. Especially more guilt. If my mind sprung a leak, and some of the giddy seeped out, leaving an inch at the top for new thoughts, I would only permit more lovely, frothy giddy to be poured in. I am suffused with it, full up with it the way a balloon is full of air, right to the very edge. There is no crevice or cranny where a shard of guilt can lodge. It tries to, but I am resolute. I am staunchly defending my right to be this much in denial. I know full well what I'm doing by deciding not to feel uncomfortable feelings. What I can't quite discern yet, is the line between this delicious adventure and my real life.

I went to work as per usual on Dora's eighteenth birthday, after a delightful start to the day where she grudgingly allowed me to participate in the well-wishes. She genuinely seemed to love her gift, the iPhone she has been coveting for the last year. It was Husband's idea to get it, against my better judgement. I thought she should have something more lasting, more memorable. Some important first piece of substantial jewellery, perhaps? But he was right, an iPhone was what she really wanted, her happiness at the sight of it was palpable, undeniable.

The day was just a day. An agonizingly slow day which seemed to have the brakes on. All of my concentration and energy was bound up in the tension of what was to follow. Honestly, I ought to give my clients a refund for the second-rate service I gave. I don't think they noticed, which, ironically, is disappointing, but nevertheless *I* know I wasn't entirely present, and that's not good. Not being there is bad, but not minding that is worse. That's what I don't: I don't care.

I ordinarily loathe people like me. Yes, I think I do genuinely loathe me at the moment, but it's hard to investigate that when I see myself reflected in his eyes as the opposite of loathsome. His eyes. My God. His eyes are the only place I want to look and the only place I want to be seen. I want to be held there in the strength of that irrefutably unflinching gaze, held in marvellous suspension. Held by him. I can't wait for that.

Lisa herded us out at the end of the day and I faked a kind of reluctance to go. I'm not sure why I did that, except perhaps as a feeble attempt to throw her off a trail I don't think she's even on. Maybe I have taken her hunting and scouting skills far too seriously. She is wearing a helmet now. A sort of safari hat customized to hold lots of tools and instruments, small knives, screwdrivers and corkscrews, along with what appears to be an assortment of medical or dental apparatus. I even spied a good-sized hammer. She ushered us out using a shepherd's whistle and we jostled along and obliged. I climbed into my car and drove off.

By the time I pulled into the empty car park of the cricket field, my breathing was fast and shallow, and I was continually repeating the mantra 'Oh my God, oh my God' under my breath, to try and keep my focus and excitement in check. I whipped out my make-up bag and hurriedly upgraded the daytime face into an evening one. A smokier, glossier face that just might get itself kissed again. Noel saw me only five minutes ago, wouldn't he notice the difference? Of course not. He's male. My hand was shaky, the rear-view mirror was too small, too dark, awkward. Breathe, Mo, breathe.

It was a forty-five-minute drive to the hotel, a sufficient distance from town to be safely anonymous. Husband and I have often passed comment on this particular hotel. How we'd like to go there for a 'special' occasion, y'know, treat ourselves sometime.

Oh dear. Banish him from all thoughts, quickly. If he is ensconced anywhere in this scenario, I won't be able to continue. Squeeze eyes tight (trying not to ruin new smoky make-up) and push all thought of him away. Go away, Husband. You won't want to see this. This will hurt you.

I sat still in the car for a few minutes. He's waiting inside. <u>Why</u> did I sit there? I didn't need to summon courage, I was definitely going in, no question. I was struck by the horrific thought that perhaps I was sitting there for effect? How dreadful. Was I sitting there because that's what people do when they're on the brink? For the first time in my life I slapped my own face. Quite violently.

Come on, Mo, if you are going to do this, to risk everything, at least have an authentic experience. <u>Feel</u> it. Smell it. Touch it. Know it. It might be the only time this ever happens, so be utterly in the present. Come on!!

With a stinging cheek I stepped out of the car and crunched across the gravel to the entrance of the hotel, a Gothic pile glowing red with warm welcome. In my hand I felt the straps of my handbag and the substantial leather handle of my small overnight tote bag. In that bag was the evidence of my intent. A new, strappy

324

silk nightgown and a washbag. Two items that said it all. All deceit was contained right there.

As I entered, I saw him immediately sitting by the fire in the small bar, in a high-backed armchair with another empty one opposite for me. There were only two other people there, an elderly couple sitting in the corner playing a round of cards, who gave me a cursory glance. That's all.

Noel stood up to greet me, and took me into an easy, familiar embrace. As he kissed my cheek and invited me to sit down, I wondered how we must appear? We were ... what? ... husband and wife? Lovers? Even in that tiny gesture of welcome, we had overstepped a very important line. We were pretending to be something we weren't. Yet. He remembered that I drink cider and he ordered me half a pint.

'You're here then,' he said, quietly.

'Yes, I'm here.'

'I'm so glad you came. I know it's not easy.'

Oh Noel, how wrong you are. It's actually very easy because I'm not connected to anything that would make it difficult. I am adrift from all that. I am only focused on you, nothing else. Thank you for wearing that crisp clean blue shirt and smelling of someone very recently shaved. Thank you for sitting in that chair where the firelight glows on your face and pronounces your lovely smile so softly. Thank you for being from New Zealand which is so far away that I have been able to make that part of the exoticism. The distance is the place I am operating in. I can be sufficiently lost there. And, especially, thanks for concentrating on only me, to the exclusion of everyone, everything else. You and me. That's all that matters. Us.

He leaned in. 'I didn't want you to feel compromised in any way, but I thought it would be easier if I booked the room, so it's all ready whenever we are . . . Might be more private there? Or not, if you'd rather stay here? No prob either way. Genuinely. No prob.'

This has been the case at every stage so far. Other than the forthright kiss, he has carefully, considerately let me take it all at my pace. Which is why it was 'no prob' to guzzle down the cider in one mannish gulp and be heading for the stairs, hand in his hand, within thirty seconds. I followed him to the room and into it. Over the threshold. Way over the threshold.

The room was ridiculously romantic. The decor was red and maroon, the colours of sex. It was almost too dark and I was glad the linen on the bed was such a crisp white so as to throw some illumination, some definition, on the scene. A huge bed (where do they find the sheets for this size? – it's bigger than a king-size – what is it? – a God-size bed?) with a harem's amount of pillows and cushions. There was one chair and a table, making the bed the only place to sit. On the table, though, was some champagne on ice and two tall glasses. I noticed a small vase of what looked like blue love-in-the-mist.

'That's nigella. Did you know it signifies fascination?'

I didn't. All around the room were little votive candles flickering away in glass holders, giving off heavenly scents. If I had been in my right mind that would have certainly put me off. Entirely. Men who know anything about good candles, never mind nigella, would ordinarily elicit buckets of scorn. But now, in this blind and blinding moment, he couldn't be more perfect. He must have taken considerable time to prepare it all. I was touched by his effort. All this attention to detail, just for me. I was half expecting, half hoping for a frantic scrabble to claw each other's clothes off and climb quickly into those cold white sheets. His young strong brown body inside that Daz-white linen, next to me . . . but instead he spoke softly.

'Sit down, Mo. Would you rather I sat on the chair?'

'No, please sit here, next to me. I'd like you to be ... next to me.'

'I'm not going to open that bubbly right now, I don't think. I don't want to presume ...'

'No,' I said, wishing the opposite.

'The thing is,' he continued, as he sat right next to me, very close to me, on the bed, our thighs touching, 'I don't want to bugger this up, y'know? I want it to be right, otherwise it won't mean enough and it won't last ...' He took my hand and clasped it in both of his, with the intensity of a man who has been lifelong touch-deprived. He kissed it and put it next to his cheek. He looked right at me and stayed quiet.

'You want this to last then?' I knew that was a high-yield, high-voltage question to ask him.

'Yes, don't you? I'm not here for a quick fix, Mo. Something has happened between us, I know it and I'm pretty sure you do too. When I think back, I absolutely know the exact moment, remember?'

I nodded but actually I couldn't be entirely sure I did. I thought perhaps, possibly, maybe ... it was on the picnic? I daren't say in case he was offended, so I simply cast my eyes to the floor. Nice floor. Parquet with a deep red Persian rug.

I was astonished when he said, 'It was the instant you walked into George's office when you came back to work after the flu. The first time I saw you. You looked all kinda puffy and wrung out and like you needed some serious TLC. Then, when you spoke, you were super efficient, quite bossy, no-nonsense. I liked the discrepancy. The space between.'

'Did you?'

'Yep, that's where I've wanted to be ever since. In that hinterland. I think it might be . . . sort of . . . unvisited and soft there . . .'

With that he leaned in and kissed me. Nothing urgent or demanding, only loving . . . and . . . slow. I disappeared into it, and somehow in the midst of it we progressed from sitting to lying on the bed, wrapped up in each other.

He murmured, 'I am here whenever and if ever you are ready, I would love that time to be now, but I will be happy to wait here for thousands of days if that's what it takes . . .'

I was speechless.

'If I calcify in the meantime, please forgive . . . ? Perhaps you could just give me a good shaking when you've decided . . . ? In your own time?'

He was laughing now. It was catching, and so I started to laugh too. 'You would be prepared to turn to stone?'

'Yep. I will be your personal statue.'

'You would be lying here, rigid, waiting for me? So to speak?'

'Yep.'

'A kind of rigor-vita?'

'Yep. And that's the point Mo, *vita est brevis*. It's later than you think. Jump in.'

'Oh God.'

'Be with me.'

'What has happened, Noel? I don't understand it.'

'Well don't try then. Stop controlling it.'

'You think I'd be lying here if I was controlling it?'

'Listen, I lost all reason and sense the moment I saw you, and I don't know why. But I don't care if it doesn't make sense, I'm following a deeper pull. I have to, no choice. I've never known anything like this, Mo.'

'Me neither.'

'It's fucking lovely. You are just ... fucking ... lovely.'

He kissed me again.

Suddenly there was a loud ping of a text message on my phone. Real life clamouring to be noticed. I wanted

to ignore it, and be this new person, the lover, the kis-
ser, the carefree spirit, the object of his desire. And
only that. But the simple ping catapulted my mind
back into Mrs Battle mode with a thumping jolt. I was
further grounded when, after a hundred years of
scrabbling about in the bottom of my bag, I finally
found the wretched phone and saw that the message
was from Dora. Yes, I am Mrs Battle – the mother. Dora
will have navigated the cursor on her phone 'til it indicated 'MUM', to send her short, curt, effective message
which read: 'Where U? It my 18 b.day. U selfish cow.
I h8 U'.

That was me then, a satellite wrenched from the
orbit of Noel. Spell broken. We sat up and straight-
ened ourselves out. He moved to sit in the chair. I went
into the bathroom and sipped water from my cupped
hands to stall for time and to ease me back into the
uncandled unblossomed world outside this room,
which I knew I reluctantly had to return to now.

When I went back into the bedroom, he took me in
a huge wrapped-up, arms-right-round Bear Grylls hug.
'Right. Listen. You need to go. I get it. Don't worry. This
is only the first of a thousand attempts, remember?
The second attempt takes place on Monday. Same
place, same time. And so on 'til ... well 'til for ever

actually, or 'til you are with me. Whichever comes first.'

'OK . . . OK.' I was at a loss.

What do you say when your daughter has unwittingly seized your joy?

I left quietly and climbed back into my car, tote bag unopened. Me, unopened. I felt completely deflated. As I started to drive home, my mind was a continual rewind, pause and play of all that had just occurred. I experienced it over and over again, feeling the same thrill each time. Multiple thrill. As I was about to pass the cricket club car park, I suddenly swerved and pulled in, stopped the engine and sat still to allow the choking build-up of sobs to escape. I had felt the thrum of it start in the pit of my stomach from the moment I read the text, but now that sinking sensation was rising and urgent. It stoked my eyes and I was immediately a shocking heap of uncontrollable shaking and tears.

I had been to the edge of the reef. I had stood on the brittle precipice, and seen the lovely dark deep chasm teeming with iridescent flashes of beauty and promise. I had been so very ready to jump, willing to free-fall in and risk it. And now, here I was in the bloody cricket club car park, back on the big thick reef. These were sorry-for-self tears. A waterfall of them, a lifetime's worth. The build-up of excitement and adrenalin during the day and, consequently, the enormous disappointment had taken their toll, and I was exhausted. I looked in the rear-view mirror and saw a blowfish staring back at me, my face was so puffy. I had to wait until it all went down before I could drive home. In the waiting, the tears would try to come again and the redness would return. And so on it went for over an hour, until I was composed enough to go home, by which time I was, of course, far too late for Dora's party.

I crept into the house to discover a scene of mystifying devastation. The kitchen was piled high with plates and glasses and stank of fast food. There was an enormous empty cake stand, covered in the detritus of gooey chocolate cake. What appeared to be eight or so bodies were snoring and snuffling away in the frowsty fug of the front room. The funk was revolting – a mixture of teenage body odour and farts and an ominous smell of burning. Some of the bodies scattered about were people I'd never seen before. Raven-haired manga teens with nose-studs and smudged thick black eye make-up. One of them had her arm and leg cocked over . . . my mother, in a bizarre mutant embrace. Luke Wilson had fallen asleep cradled on Oscar's lap and there was a huge smouldering hole in the back of my very expensive sofa. John Travolta was still skipping with his tongue hanging out after a tinier than humanly possible Olivia Newton-John wearing black cling-film leggings on the plasma screen. I turned it off and headed upstairs, away from the stinking carnage.

Dora's bed was empty and I found her asleep on the floor of Oscar's room next to his sock drawer with what on closer inspection appeared to be an unfamiliar giant black puppy sprawled across her face, also snortling loudly. Only Poo woke up and wagged her tail pathetically at me, in the half-light. I patted her head. 'Well done, ol' girl. That one must've made your eyes water.' She looked as wrung out as I felt. I crept into the bedroom and went to my dressing table drawer.

I placed my old and beloved and worn-only-once tiara on Dora's sleeping head. Neither she nor the puppy moved. I whispered, 'I'm sorry, Dora. I really am. Happy Birthday my gorgeous grumpy Infanta.'

As I snuck into bed, Husband automatically spooned up behind, and wrapped his arm around me, murmuring a 'Yes. Yes. That's right. Yes' from the depths of a conscience-free, satisfying dream. I envied him momentarily. I nodded off eventually, my heartbeat chiming in time with his breathing. Deeper and deeper we both sank, together.

SEVENTY-ONE

Dora

I just like so love my new puppy? I've decided to call him Elvis coz he's like so huge and black. Like the real Elvis was. Dad like laughed his head off when I told him that. Don't know why, I think it's the perfect name. He's not going to be a good handbag dog or anything but he's like way better than that. He so loves me. He loves me best, more than any of the others coz I was the first human to hold him properly and sleep with him, so he probably thinks I'm like his real mum or something? Ducks do that, don't they? Obviously Poo is doing all the actual feeding and stuff, that would be sick if I did that, but otherwise Elvis totally adores me. He will never betray me. That's what I know for sure.

We had to have a massive clean-up this morning after everyone eventually went home. Mum had to give the Emos some bus fare coz they're too cool to call their parents. The Croatian girl got her words a bit wrong and said to Dad, 'Thanking you for the lovely orgy,' which took a bit of explaining to Mum. I'm not speaking to Mum atall after she didn't bother coming last night.

She thinks giving me her old crown thing will make me love her. Well it won't. Caring about me is what will make me love her and that is so off her chart at the moment. Who misses their own daughter's eighteenth birthday for God's sakes?! I've never even heard of that much cruelty. If I wasn't eighteen, I could like call Childline or something, coz that is like so neglecting. I did call them once before when I was ill, after Mum shouted at me, but they said that they couldn't class 'tidy your cocking room up this instant young lady or I'll tan your hide' as life-threatening abuse. Yeah, but they didn't see all the veins standing out on her scary bright red face.

After the clearing up, I had to physically push Peter off the computer where he was Skyping Luke who he'd only just said goodbye to half an hour before or something. They were blabbing on about what they were going to wear back at school to break the uniform rules. I mean, please, get a life.

I went straight to Facebook and there were six messages from X-Man asking me to talk. I was going to make him wait but actually, I so needed to know why he didn't come.

It was sooo sweet . . .

ME: So dude. No show?

X-MAN: Thank God u talking wiv me. Thought u mite not.

ME: Explanation necessary b4 normal service returned.

X-MAN: God. So 200% sorry. Had big row wiv Mum who wouldn give me train money. Got no other dosh. Gave it all to *Children in Need* thing on telly. Swore bad at Mum. She locked me in b'room. Kept key.

ME: OMAG. I h8 my mum 2. Abuses me. U OK?

X-MAN: Yeah. Just got let out. Given 5 quid to get bkfast but am savin' it to C U.

ME: Aw. Sweet.

X-MAN: When can meet? I could do any eve nxt wk.

ME: How 'bout Mon?

X-MAN: Cool. Somewhere quiet.

ME: Am 18 now. Pub?

X-MAN: No. 2 loud. Jessop's Park? I'll bring cider.

ME: OK time?

X-MAN: 9pm?

ME: Yeh.

X-MAN: Sorry again.

ME: It's OK.

X-MAN: Bring music for *X-Factor* song? I will bring iPod. Can go thru it if u like?

ME: U so kind.

X-MAN: Course.

ME: Ta.

X-MAN: Can't wait.

ME: Me too.

X-MAN: Tell parents?

ME: No. Too stressy.

X-MAN: Yeh. Just us.

ME: Yeh. C-ya.

X-MAN: C-ya. And Dora?

ME: Yeh?

X-MAN: Happy birthday you bloody Adult!

ME: YAY!

Oh my actual God. He gave his last bit of money to *Children in Need*! I like <u>so</u> love him.

Oscar

Discourteous Dora's monstrous claim that I 'hog' the computer is utterly unfounded. The silly wretch employs a mode of exaggeration which is eight million leagues beyond tolerable. The impertinence of the hussy. How unconscionably unjust for the unctuous bovine to accuse me thus. To violently remove me from my seat afront said screen, by use of the swinging of her enormous unladylike udders, thereby unsaddling me from my perch, was unspeakably uncouth. For what purpose? To continue the endless mindless twittering nonsense with her supposed 'friends'? I have read her unceasing twaddle on occasion and it beggars belief. Their communications are an intellectual vortex, and a merciless time sump. Nothing vaguely enchanting passes there. All is shoddy and vulgar. Take, for instance, the following baffling arrangement of words I once espied when I hacked into her site (of course I know her password, only an imbecile wouldn't guess it – 'SEXYDORA'. A contradiction in terms I fear). It went as follows:

'Hv spent all morn. blowing Sam.'

Hell's teeth! She hadn't of course, she'd been out shopping with the mater at Marks & Spencer's for her particular brand of sizeable underpants. What a singularly uncivil and ugly configuration of fraudulent words. Why in the name of Cat Deeley would she wish to announce such an ungodly atrocity to the world? Could she possibly have thought, somewhere in her unicellular brain, that that would garner her some respect? From what quarter? Perhaps a troop of Marines returning from an unaccompanied tour of the bleakest outposts of Taliban desert? Yes, perchance *they*, the desperate and lonely, and starved of any female company, might be interested or impressed or fooled. Every other soul alive would surely gag with revulsion or do as I did, and laugh heartily at the unlikeliness of it well into the night and throughout the following day. I suppose one ought to admire the monumental gall of the gal.

Ah me. How tedious it all is. Fortunately, I had the succulent memories of the previous night's bliss-merger *avec* the divinely romantic Master Wilson to feast upon in his absence. I dream of Monday. Oh Monday, when we shall be united once more in our own heavenly thrall. How shall I last 'til then? Patience, dear boy, and a host of distractions. Indeed, I had the

DVD of *Zoolander* to amuse me, and thus I watched it from start to finish, rewinding at the crucial catwalk moments. I fancy young Ben Stiller might well be willing to follow Dorothy all the way to Oz should she be in need of a friend . . .

Replete with viewing, I returned to the now-vacated computer whence I noticed that Dizzy Dora had once again left her Facebook page open for all the world and her husband to see. I noticed thereupon that she had arranged a clandestine dalliance with one who parades under the moniker of 'X-Man'. I fetched the Pater in to witness it.

Now she's in for it.

SEVENTY-THREE

Mo

It's Sunday, and I've always savoured Sunday. It's a lovely, fat day. Full of the promise of rest. The household is quiet. Well, not 'quiet' actually, but relatively still and controlled. I sit at the kitchen table nursing a 'hippy' tea as Husband calls it. This one is a berry mixture. I'd love a sugary white PG Tips but this half-tea half-Ribena is better for me. I don't want any milk in me, it glues up my brain and I need to be sharp at the moment.

I can hear Oscar in the den. He's watching *My Fair Lady* again and singing along with Audrey, who, in turn, is mouthing along badly to someone else. I can hear muffled sounds of Dora thumping about in her bedroom with Radio 1 on. She too is spasmodically singing along, and doing that thing she does where she harmonizes with the songs and adds too many extra trills to experiment with her voice. I can hear Husband in the study talking to the computer. The wretched thing has crashed and he is trying to cajole it back to life. He thinks he can persuade it to operate by flirting with it.

So, these are the sounds of my family in my house on a Sunday morning. Added to which I can hear the washing machine chugging on in its endless effort to keep our pants zesty-fresh. I can also hear the slurping of Elvis sucking on Poo. (Now _that's_ a sentence I never thought I would write!)

Yes, the sounds of the Battles on a Sunday morning, just being normal. If I do what I know I am going to do, very soon all of this will change, and I won't ever hear it like this again. As of tomorrow, nothing will be the same, because I now know for sure that tomorrow I am going to jump off the reef.

SEVENTY-FOUR

Dad

It's something I think all men fear the most. The beast within. I don't often access it. Maybe sometimes on the rugby field. Somehow the sports beast is a considerably more containable fella. And a welcome oaf to boot. To literally <u>boot</u>. And the playing field, literal or otherwise, is even. There is nothing *even* about a creep who pretends to be nearly twenty years younger and arranges to meet my daughter in a dark park, unbeknown to her parents.

What did he think? That I am not awake? Even if I am asleep, chum, I always lie across the entrance so that no one should enter or exit the lair without me knowing. Did he think that perhaps I don't care? That I don't care about my first-born and most vulnerable cub? That I wouldn't have my eye fixed very firmly on <u>especially</u> her? She who is so innocent and colourful? She who attracts the eye so easily and who has so much to offer? The other cub is much more worldly, however eccentric. And he's a boy. This one needs my full concentration. Not least because she is touchingly grateful for the smallest crumb of attention. And that's what X-Man offered. The smallest crumb. That's what he is. The least. Did he for one second think it was OK for her to accept the least? I will never allow that as long as I have breath in my body. I would <u>give</u> my body rather than have her diminished by one so low. One so deceitful and conniving. Does he think I would stand by and watch while the purpose to my life skips into his waiting arms? One so naively trusting? So beautiful? In such a state of grace? Runs to <u>him</u> – a filthy liar? My eye was very firmly on *that* ball. It had my undivided attention. My full focus. Yes indeed.

I arrived at Jessop's Park before seven. I had altered the timing, posing as her. I had to follow my instinct. I hoped I was very wrong. That I would see a spotty young rascal in too much hair gel, a hoodie and trainers, waiting nervously. I even hoped he might be clutching a bar of chocolate for her. Or a can of cider at least. I sat at some distance from the swing park so I could observe without being seen. It was getting darker and quite cold. At seven on the dot, a figure sloped into the park. I was pleased to see he <u>was</u> wearing a hoodie pulled up over a baseball cap, and for a moment I relaxed a little bit, but I watched very closely. He sat hunched on the swing. His head was down and he was fiddling with what looked like an iPod or something with earphones. Promising. Convincing. For a moment . . .

Then I started to notice little details that alerted my suspicions. His jeans weren't right. They were too smart, too . . . ironed. His hands weren't right, they were too . . . elegant. His stance wasn't right, too . . . assured. I walked closer. He was looking about, scanning the park, but I couldn't see him well enough under his hat and tightly pulled-up hood. I had to make a bold move. It was the only way. I approached from behind. Remarkably, he didn't see me for longer than I anticipated. When I was quite shockingly close, he suddenly turned his head to the side to look at the entrance to the park and I glimpsed his face in profile.

This was no teenager. This was a grown man. The lines on his face and his weatherbeaten skin were at odds with his clothes. It was all wrong. I said, 'X-Man?' He jumped up suddenly and swung round. Before he had even fully turned, I lashed out and landed a good'un on his left cheek with my right fist. It was sudden and instinctive. I didn't want to speak, I wanted to act. I was shocked by how much it hurt, and by the sheer force and speed of it. I hadn't punched anyone like this since I was about five. He put his arms up to defend his face, to shield it. For some reason this cowardice infuriated me further and that was the moment it happened. Not before the first punch. Up 'til then it was partially controlled. I consciously only wanted to go so far. But when he did that pathetic, guilty defensive thing, and I saw the fear in his eyes, that's when something in me changed. I imagined how that could so easily be the fear in <u>her</u> eyes at the moment she discovered what he was, when she was alone and vulnerable, when he could hurt her.

In that second I couldn't forgive him his intent and I felt myself splitting. I separated from me the dad, the husband. *That* bloke stood back and I let my deepest red-rage break free. It tore out of me with brute force and thundered me towards him like a missile. Ignorant of any fear, I pummelled him with blow after blow. I wanted to tear him to shreds. I slammed into him with my full body weight and knocked him to the floor. It was easy – he was slighter than me, he was in shock and he wasn't possessed, as I was, by the boiling heat of an angry father bull. I kicked him and then kept on kicking him harder, 'til he curled up in a baby ball to protect himself. I grabbed him by the throat and pulled him up. His hat fell off and he was bleeding from the mouth, spitting and dribbling. His breathing was fast and heavy. I jolted his head sideways and slammed it into the wood of the bench. I heard his skull crack, and I saw his teeth loosen and wobble. It was enough. But I couldn't stop. I wanted to demolish him. To pulverize him 'til he was powder. To end him.

But I'm not young any more, and I started to tire and gasp for breath. I wanted to recover and rally, but I needed a few seconds to just breathe. Stupid old unfit man that I am. In the time it took me to stagger upright, he got up and stumbled away. I chased after him, but somehow he jumped over the fence and disappeared into the trees. I knew I couldn't catch him. He was fit, and I was winded. I collapsed down on to the swing and I could feel, then, a pain near my right eye and a throbbing in the knuckles of both hands. I tasted metal in my mouth and I felt my bleeding split lip with my tongue.

When had that happened? Somewhere in the scrapping I had actually lost all sense. How long had it all taken? Five minutes? Thirty minutes? Two days? I sat on the swing as the night crept in on me. I was hurting, just as I had hurt when I occasionally scrapped as a lad of five. And here I was, back again, sitting in a swing park. The same arena. Fifty years later. I was glad to be emerging from the fog of the blind rage. I've lived with the knowledge of it within me for a long time. I have feared it. Been ashamed of it. Of the ugly violence of it. But today, I'm glad it's there. To ward off any predators. Get away from my family. Get away or I will kill you. I have no control in the matter once the trigger is pulled.

My phone rang. I felt my trousers – not there. Where was it? I followed the ring to find it on the ground under the bench. It was Oscar. No, it was Dora. Furious. Hates me. I don't mind. Feel free to be angry, Dora. Because you are free. And that's how it should be. Beware anyone who attempts to take away your freedom, my little girl. They'll have to deal with me, yer ol' dad. And the beast in him. In me.

Then, the beast limped off to see his mother-in-law to get a plaster and some whisky cake, before returning to his cave.

SEVENTY-FIVE

Dora

Monday. Most embarrassing day of my bloody life. I now hate Dad even more than I hate Mum, which I thought would be impossible. I double hate them both and I'm just so bloody glad I'm eighteen now so I don't have to stay here in this prison house with either of them any more. I'm never going to have a life if they don't stop like bloody interfering!! I'm not a kid any more, why can't they see that? And leave me a bloody lone.

The first part of the day was fine. I slept in 'til like two o'clock or something? Then, when I got up, the whole house was empty coz everyone was at work or out and I love that when I am on my own. I put my iPod into the dock, and had my music like <u>really</u> loud. I found the Pop Tarts where Dad hides them for me behind his supplement drinks where he knows Mum will never look. Me and Poo and Elvis had one each and I laid on the floor with them so's we could eat all together, and like, play for ages.

I love pretending to be a dog, and they love it too. It makes Poo laugh. I can always tell when she's laughing. Why do people say dogs don't laugh, when they like, so def do? Well, she does. She got a bit confused when I was drinking water from their bowl. Both of them tipped their heads to the side trying to understand it. Even I didn't really understand why I did it except I got carried away and it seemed like a cool idea. It wasn't. It totally grossed me out. And I had to go and brush my teeth after.

Then I got dressed and went to my appointment at the hairdressers to get my extensions sorted out coz they're so like minging now. I was, like so devastated when the girl said I needed to cut them out coz they've gone all ragged and like mouldy an' stuff? I can't afford to put new ones in coz my bloody monster mother won't bloody pay for it so I just had to go back to my normal hair length which is like bloody pathetic. It only just reaches my shoulders now, I look like a bloody pageboy from olden times or something. At least I got my roots done so I'm still blonde thank God coz I was meeting up with X-Man later, and I've never met him before and I didn't want him to think I had brown hair or something. How would he ever fancy me then? He just wouldn't and that's a fact. It actually hurts quite a lot getting the blonde roots done coz the bleach sort of burns your scalp. I've even had blisters from it before but it's like so worth it.

Then I went home and had a cold bath coz I didn't want the steam to make my hair go frizzy. I only had two hours left then to get ready. I heard Pete come in and I shouted down to him to make me a cup of tea. He took bloody ages but he brought it upstairs and sat on my bed to chat while I was getting ready. He loves doing that, watching me do make-up. I think he would so love to wear some himself, and I have seen him try with a bit of Mum's tinted moisturizer and even some mascara but I just know he'd love to go further if school would let him. Is he a ladyboy or something? I don't really care actually so long as he doesn't nick any of my stuff.

Anyway, he was yapping away about Luke and Luke and more about Luke and really getting on my tits. I told him I was actually dying, because I haven't been able to get on the computer for like three days now coz it's broken, and on top of that, Dad has taken my iPhone coz apparently there is a fault on it so they have all been recalled or something so he's sorting it out for me? So I haven't been able to talk to any of my friends or anything or like anyone. It's just lucky I already made my date with X-Man.

Then Pete suddenly pipes up with 'Or so you think ...' which was well annoying. He tried to leave the room with like, a big dramatic toss of his scarf, well, Mum's scarf, but I got hold of him and threw him on the bed and like, sat on him. He got all pathetic, wriggling about and refusing to tell me what was up. I can't bear it when he does that, so I had to like dribble on to him to get him to explain. Eventually, just as the drool was about to land on his face, he yelled, 'OK, OK, get off me you oafish wretch and I'll tell you!' So I sucked it all back up again.

'The computer isn't broken, you hell-born change-ling. The Pater *said* it was because he doesn't want you on there, on Facebook. That's why he has also confiscated your phone. He doesn't want you to contact your friend X-Man. He is concerned that you are meeting someone you don't know. So he went on Facebook himself, pretending to be you, and changed the meeting time, to two hours earlier. He will have met your chum X-man by now.'

'Whaaaaat?!!'

'Yes. Deal with it, sister. After all, he's only making sure the chap isn't a scoundrel.'

'Whaaaaat?!!!?'

'Try to find an alternative reaction, there's a dear. That screechy one is becoming tiresomely repetitive now.'

I started racing around the room pulling on my clothes and grabbing my shoes.

'Give me your phone, Peter. Now!'

'I certainly will not. It contains my dearest information trinkets . . .'

'NOW!!'

He handed it over and I speed-dialled Dad, who answered immediately.

'Hello, Oscar.'

'No Dad, it's me. What the hell are you doing? Where are you? How could you?'

'Slow down, Dora.'

'No, _you_ bloody slow down! What's going on?'

'I came to meet your friend, Dora.'

'Yes, _MY_ friend. That's the whole bloody point, _MY_ friend!!'

'Steady on. Calm down.'

'No, _you_ bloody calm down.'

'Listen, I'm your dad. I had to check him out. And I'm glad I did.'

'Whaaaat?!!'

'He's not who you think he is, sweetheart. He's much older. It's not right. Trust me. I've had a word and he's pushed off now. You won't be hearing from him again.

Sorry, hon, but I had to check him out. I just had a hunch . . .'

I didn't know what to say.

'Dora? You OK?'

'How old? What do you mean? He told me he was eighteen, like me.'

'Exactly. Well, he isn't. He's closer to forty, love. He's not a nice man. Not honest.'

I sat down on the bed, completely stunned.

'Listen, Dora, I'm popping in on Nana Pamela for a while but I'll be back later, OK? Mum should be home soon. We'll have a proper chat then. I'm so sorry, princess. Let's order pizza, eh?'

'Yea . . . thanks Dad . . . thanks.'

'It's OK, Dora, I love you, puddin'. It's my job to look out for you. More than my job, to be honest, it's my, well, it's my . . . you know, whole purpose.'

'Er . . . OK.'

So. X-Man is a bloody perv or something! Some old man who goes around trying to meet up with eighteen-year-olds? Oh my actual God! How could I make such a bloody stupid mistake? Why do all the weirdos come to me? He was going to help me with my audition and everything. I told him things, secret things.

355

No wonder he didn't come to my party. Bloody twatting bloody perv. Oh my complete and utter actual God. He saw my tits! Oh bloody God. The shame. Not going to tell Dad that bit. How did Dad manage to get into my Facebook? Is he some kind of spy from the government or something? A hacker or something? He shouldn't really do that really – nose about in other people's stuff. But I'm glad he did. But I wish he hadn't. Did Dad see the pic of my tits too??! Oh God. Please not! Thank God Dad did what he did today tho. But, y'know, how dare he? I bloody hate him for that, nosing about in my private business. Not as much as I hate Mum. Where the cock is <u>she</u> when I really need her? She's never here. I hate them both equally. But her more. No, him. Oh God I don't know, I'm so confused.

Pete made me a big sugary (eight teaspoons) hot chocolate and we sat on my bed and he put his arm around me. That made me cry. All over his shoulder. It's even his favourite top and he really tried hard to pretend not to mind. Glad I've got *him* at least. Will I ever get my bloody life right?!

SEVENTY-SIX

Mo

I sat in the room, in the very red, overtly carnal room. It seemed remarkably different without him there. It was too ordinary and badly lit. I wondered whether he would have set up all the candles again, brought the nigella, and made it as sensual? Maybe I should have done that? I didn't think to. I imagined he would be there, waiting patiently, waiting for me to come to him.

I had indeed come to him. I was sitting on a seat in a room, in a hotel, all set to alter my life. Outside, in the boot of my car, was a suitcase, packed with everything I might need to flee. I couldn't be entirely sure it really contained what I might truly need to start up a new life with this fabulous exciting new person, because I had packed it in a frenetic blur of impetuosity. I knew it contained plenty of new underwear and three tubes of hair-removal cream along with perfume and Nurofen and toothpaste and tights. But that's all I thought I might need. Because love will plug all the gaps, won't it? Any oversights, big or small, important or trivial, will fade into insignificance because I will have the strength of my new exciting love wrapped around me, to ward off any shortcomings or any doubt. I will have romance as my protector against reality.

Yes, I <u>will</u> have . . . but at that precise moment, I was sitting in a . . . frankly rather tawdry small red room. On my OWN. He was late. I didn't expect that. After all, I am the one with a big, full hectic family life to organize and abandon. He is a single guy with absolutely <u>no</u> responsibilities whatsoever. He should, by rights, definitely be here first. I felt the distinct frustrated rumble of disappointment. I was starting to find him wanting, and I did <u>not</u> like it. I didn't want anything to hinder this remarkable night . . . and his tardiness was annoying.

I looked around. The room was still irrefutably cheerless, and growing more ordinary with every passing minute. Without the candlelight, I could see that the furniture was rather cheap reproduction and it was chipped and repainted badly. I could see unpleasant stains on the cushions that set my imagination wandering down sordid alleys I didn't want to travel. I could see how worn the rugs were and I could see scruffy handmarks on the paintwork of the walls. All of this, and the time I unexpectedly had to think, served to remind me what a hotel bedroom actually is. A rented space for countless people to taint with their various and sundry base needs. Far from being the magical place I remembered it as from only a few days ago, it was suddenly polluted, and such a disappointingly obvious choice for seduction. The thought of the many who had been there before was starting to defile its beauty for me. The gap between my memory, full of desire and fantasy, and this rather inferior reality, was beginning to widen. The lacunae were appearing, but if I stopped to acknowledge them, I knew that would be the end of it all. I didn't want it to end. It had only just begun, I had only just surrendered, I couldn't possibly entertain doubt at this crucial moment.

Besides which, in my handbag sitting on the table were the brochures for the cottages I was given weeks ago when I lied to the young estate liar about wanting to buy. I had brought them with me. Perhaps we might look at them, my lover and I, and dream? Or, even better, look at them and plan? Either way I knew that bringing them was a sure-fire signal. I am leaving my old life. I won't be that wife, that mother any more. I will be whatever I see myself to be, reflected in your eyes, Noel, my gorgeous, intoxicating, breathtaking young lover. In order for you to be my flattering mirror though, my darling ... you have to ... essentially ... TURN UP!

I waited over an hour and travelled through a litany of emotions ranging from excitement to despair, stopping at doubt and humiliation en route. Where <u>was</u> he? I was gripped by a terrible unfeasible fear that he might have been in a car crash or murdered by a psychotic patient. I couldn't pretend not to mind any longer. I called his mobile, which just kept ringing and ringing. No answer. I clung on to any possible reasons and rattled through them in my head.

He was trapped in a wrecked car?

He had fallen mysteriously unconscious?

Been hypnotized maybe?

Been arrested?

He was a top-class spy who had been called away on a vital mission? Yes, I investigated that more absurd one at length. Perhaps Mr Tracy had let him use Thunderbird 3 or 'Q' had given him a new car that turned into a gun and he had shot himself? ...

All of these increasingly ridiculous reasons were a small distraction from allowing myself to entertain the more likely reasons for his no-show. It was eminently more believable that he had simply got cold feet, or that he had met someone ravishing, his own age, and he had suddenly woken up to the ludicrous implications of a lifetime ahead with a middle-aged grey woman he hardly knew. Well, half a lifetime really, because she is already over halfway through hers. Isn't she? Aren't I?

I made a cup of tea using the ludicrously hobbit-sized kettle with water from the splashy tap in the lavender-toilet-duck-smelling bathroom. In with the tea bag. In with two sachets of white sugar. One is never enough, and it takes too much willpower to staunch the flow of the second. Dunk dunk. Out with the tea bag. In with the dreaded UHT milk from the tiny capsule with the reluctant lid. Stir. Sip. Disgusting.

As I sat there, clutching the tea cup with the revolting greasy tea in it, the hopelessness of the situation gradually began to fill me up. I didn't know why he wasn't there, but the fact that he wasn't, was the only vaguely right thing in a very definitely wrong situation. Everything about it was amiss. The tea, the room, the ill-packed bag, the cottage details, the whole silly, damaging, utterly ruinous thing. I felt stupid ... and I felt gutted. I caught sight of myself in the bathroom mirror as I emptied out the dregs of the undrinkable brew. I looked haunted and shaken, like a person

361

trapped in a hurricane. That was me at that moment, the storm-rider.

He was by then nearly two hours late. I felt the first stirring of scorned resolve start to build in the pit of my stomach. It was proper old-school Mo resolve. It wasn't fully formed yet, but even in this embryonic state, it was eloquent, and I heard it. I decided in that crashing moment that this whole thing was over. So over, as Dora would say.

Dora! Oh Dora. And Oscar . . . My kids. Why would I ever want to flee from my kids? They are what make my heart work. They are the point of me. They are where I start and end. However dysfunctional or irritating or plain bonkers, they are my family, and they are who I matter to. Not Noel. Who doesn't even turn up. They turn up every day. So does Husband. Every day. For years. They are there. Really there.

I suddenly and desperately wanted to get out. I went down to the reception where, to my huge embarrassment, I realized I had to pay since I was, to all intents and purposes, checking out.

'Everything all right with the room?' said little miss nosey.

'Yes. It was lovely. I've had a really good . . . nap.

Just what I ... (*fake yawning*) ... needed. I've been, y'know, working so hard ...'

Why did I bother to peddle bad excuses? The shame of it all was dripping off me on to the counter of the reception as I signed the bill and removed my credit card from the machine. 'Transaction complete,' it announced. Yes. That's right. It is.

I virtually ran to the car, and I raced home. Home. To my real life. Past those same houses and shops. Left, right, right again, left. All familiar, all normal. There it was, my house. My normal old unchanged house containing my normal old unchanged family. Normal. Correct. Right. Natural. Normal. Good.

As I approached the front door, I could hear loud sobbing coming from inside. I walked in to find no sign of Husband, and Dora crying uncontrollably in Oscar's arms.

Initially, she wouldn't tell me what had upset her so much, she just yelled at me, 'Thanks a lot for never bloody being here!'

'I'm sorry, Dora. You're right, I <u>haven't</u> been here, I know that. But I am here now, OK? Tell me what's wrong? What's happened?'

'None of your bloody business since you don't care

so much. Thank God there's Dad, at least he cares . . . even though I am really like, pissed off with him as well.'

I called Husband who was, apparently, round at Mum's. Again. He explained what had happened, and how the guy Dora had arranged to meet was not who he'd said he was. And not eighteen.

'Oh my God, poor Dora. Who was he then?'

'I . . . er . . . didn't really ask, to be honest. I . . . er . . . just made it clear that he should, y'know, go right away. Far away. Soon as.'

'Oh God.' I knew what that meant, I've always been aware he harbours a sort of volatile Neanderthal just beneath the skin. His mother told me when I first knew him that, 'He has the temper of a tethered Doberman, but more snappy.' I've never witnessed it in all these years, but I've had no doubt that it lurks there.

'Is he alive?' I was only half joking . . .

'Yeah . . . Sadly.'

'Are you OK?'

'Yeah, I've got a corker of a bruise and Pamela's put a stitch in my lip. Otherwise I'm fine.'

Typical Pamela. As long as I can remember, Mum has never let us get stitches elsewhere, she kept a kit from her nursing days and always does any tiny cuts for us. She is a better seamstress than any doctor, she claims, and she's right.

'Well ... come home soon then ...' I meant that. I wanted him home, I wanted him back. Back home ... where we both belong.

'Yep. Just having a big slice of –'

'Whisky fruit cake?' I interrupted.

'Yeah. S'delicious. Even with a split lip.'

'I know. Don't be long. Dora's in a right ol' state. Do you think we should call the police?'

'Not sure. We'll talk when I get back.'

I put the phone down and went to talk to Dora. The famously unforgiving Dora.

I took a deep breath. 'I know you are annoyed with me, Miss Dora, but let me say this in my defence as your mother – if you ever EVER agree to secretly meet someone you don't know ever again, I will kill you. 'Til you're dead, OK? 'Til you are like, SO dead? Coz I like, so love you and you've like SO pissed me off now. Coz you could of got hurt or something? Or you could of got dead or something? And if that had happened, I would of, like, so killed you. You twatty wonk!'

She couldn't help it. She laughed. She so didn't want to, but she so had to. Then she started to cry, and then she fell into my arms and blubbed about everything

365

bad in her life for about an hour and a half 'til Husband arrived. Dora, crying on <u>me</u>. It felt like home again, like I'd properly come back. I am among the lovely chaos again.

Later, in bed ... afterwards ... I whispered in Husband's ear.

'Thanks for being here. And for being there.'

SEVENTY-SEVEN

Oscar

Not every chap can claim a hero for a father, but, presently, I can. The Pater is, of course, rejecting all praise in his usual self-effacing manner. It requires a very fine nature, I think, to resist such overtures, especially when the plaudits emanate from such ordinarily sour gooses as one's own silly daughter and selfish wifelet, who so rarely bother to notice one's acts of honour. By all accounts – well, by <u>his</u> account, which was so strangulatedly wrought from him – he was more than a tiny bit marvellous in his defence of Droney Dora's safety.

Why the daffy wretch insists on putting herself in the path of danger so very often is beyond my ken. I think it might be prudent for Luke and I to be more actively involved in her love life in future. I'm certain that any chap who had to pass through our proposed rigorous audition and interview process would be a far superior candidate to any she might stumble upon in cyberspace ... Either that, or we could provide our services as chaperones, thereby weeding out and eliminating all unlikelies from the vantage point of companion and spy. Thus, the woeful flotsam and jetsam that is the bilious human soup of the internet shall be washed up on some far foreign shore, and be of no threat to my silly sibling.

Master Wilson and I are blessed with a curse. The curse of immaculate taste. We would, I'm sure, immediately identify all knaves or savages who might dare to come sniffing around her and we could speedily dispatch them with a sobering and sassy bon mot or two. Nothing trumps a chap's audacity so much as a witty rejoinder. If one is as fresh and nimble-witted as one might dare to presume one is, then it is surely one's duty to enter into a minty badinage of waggish banter as often as one possibly can. How else might one sharpen one's esprit?

This is the fundamental difference between the Pater and myself. Where he might unleash his brawn, I might rather unshackle my biting drollery as my chosen weapon. I would have certainly ridiculed that odious predator right out of that park with a barrage of smart, rapid-fire japes. There's many a slip twixt swing and quip. Whereas Papa always has to rely on and resort to his natural animal instincts, bless him.

I can't reiterate strongly enough, though, that if one finds oneself compromised in such a manner, one is grateful for the sheer physical courage of a simple shallow chap such as he. For that noble reason, I am suggesting the elevation of the Pater to the rank of premier corps of The Enchantings. I may even be persuaded to craft him a medal. Or ... no ... rather, a bijou little jewelled adornment of some sort, a decoration in the style of regalia, with perhaps an array of frills and furbelows, trinkets and baubles. It would certainly be dandy to fashion, as the centrepiece, a badge with an impressive crest upon it. A family motto perchance, or an acknowledgement of his heroic achievement. Something that tells us he is a king amongst men and the undisputed Head of the Battle family. *'Rex inter homines. Dux familius Battalius'* ... or some such thing. Yes! I shall set about it this instant so it will be ready for him to wear for work tomorrow.

SEVENTY-EIGHT

Dora

Dad looks proper mashed-up. He's got a big fat red lip with stitches in, and like, bruises all over. Mum says he will have a huge black eye by tomorrow. But he was obviously well the winner, I think. For the first time I looked at my dad and thought that, OK, he's not a buff dad or anything but come on, he's like so well fit for doing that. He proper ghetto-style beat up that creep.

I wanted to go straight back on Facebook and tell X-Man where to like shove it and everything, but then I remembered the computer was broken. But then Dad said actually it <u>wasn't</u> broken, he'd just disabled it or something and taken my phone which also <u>isn't</u> broken, <u>pacifically</u> so that I couldn't contact X-Man. That was well dodgy of Dad. But I can see why he did that now and I'm well glad he did. I'm so not going to talk to anyone hardly now on there, coz you really don't know who might be a total freak or something, or someone.

We all stayed up like really late and instead of getting pizza, Mum made toasted sandwiches, which was tons better. I had mine with bananas and Nutella. That is so my favourite meal which I would like so choose if I was being hanged the next day or something? I was glad Mum was here to tell it all to. For the first time in ages, we had a proper talk, with her listening and looking right at me 'n' everything. She just kept smoothing my hair and saying, 'I'm sorry Dotty, that must be hard' and 'that must be awful' and stuff like that, when I told her all my bad stuff.

'Fact is,' she said, 'you just made a mistake, that's all. Everyone does that. We all do. Even Poo made a mistake – but look what we got – Elvis! I make loads of mistakes all the time. LOADS.'

It was well weird to hear her say that coz she's normally the super-perfect one who like never gets it wrong. But she said some good stuff about how I must of been feeling lonely and stuff and how that would make me feel more like I could take a risk that I shouldn't, like agreeing to meet X-Man when I didn't know him. And that's true, I think. I didn't have anyone to talk to. And she said sorry again for that, and then I went and told her about the *X-Factor* auditions and it was, like well surprising because she said to go for it!! I never ever expected that! She even said she would come with me and stuff, or like, even just take me there if I wanted and stuff! That would be sooo good, because even though I fight with her a lot, I still like bloody need her to be there sometimes for the important stuff. Not like in the actual room with me, but like outside holding all my make-up and my glasses and my lunch and stuff. Everyone needs someone to do that, you know, be a mother slash servant type person.

She said not to worry, that we will always, no matter what, be 'connected at a profound level' whether I like it or not. Well. Actually. I do like it.

Just had a text from Lottie, it says, 'Have dumped Sam. Creep. Huge mistake. Sorry. Need You. Please?'

Yeah, we all make mistakes . . .

SEVENTY-NINE

Mo

I know it's over. I know that, but honestly, how rude to not even acknowledge it. No message, no call, no nothing. I feel completely dismissed and unbelievably foolish. Humiliated. Did it all really mean absolutely <u>NOTHING</u>? Am I so supremely disposable?

In the car, the same old journey, left, right, left, second right. The same shops, school, cricket ground, war memorial. Not as zingy bright as before, when I was in . . . what? 'love'? no, 'lust'? no, 'lost'? yes, maybe. Not as colourful as when I was in lost. I don't mind that it's not so bright, because <u>that</u> was clearly a trick of the light. My heart fooling my eyes. But now, today, my eyes are seeing all this familiar stuff again, flicking over it all, and finding comfort that it's still the same. Everything has remained the same except me. I have been somewhere different for a while and experimented with being someone different. Am I changed? Not sure.

As I drew up outside work, my mouth went suddenly dry, and I felt extremely anxious. I was about to see him. Should I ignore him? Pretend I hadn't gone to the hotel? Be cool? No, I had tried to call him, he would know that. Should we have a debrief of some kind? Schedule in a session so we could have the 'closure'? How clinical and cold is that? Should I smile? Frown? How was this going to play out?

Lisa was there, behind her reception desk on which was set up a strange contraption. A tin bowl, covered with a huge leaf from one of the big pot plants, all perched on top of a small gas camping cooker. A clear tube was poking through the leaf at one end and into Lisa's coffee mug ('Survive or Die' emblazoned on it) at the other.

Something in the tin bowl was boiling and dripping out of the tube into her cup. I stopped in my tracks to digest what I was seeing.

'It's a desert still. Turns the steam into fresh water. Never ever drink sea water or urine, Mo, unless distilled like this.'

'And that is . . . ?' Why did I ask? I knew.

'Urine. My own. Will be good drinking water within the hour. Care to join me?'

'Um. I would, but I've got a bottle of arsenic in my bag which I think I would prefer. No offence.'

'None taken.'

'Is George in?'

'Yep.'

'Veronica?'

'Yep.'

'. . . Noel?'

'Nope.'

'Oh . . . Right.'

'Haven't you heard?'

'Sorry?'

'He called in this morning to say he won't be coming back, which is a total pain since he has endless bloody clients, only halfway through their sessions . . . actually, that's a point, I need to reschedule some of those into your list, Mo –'

'Won't be coming back? What do you mean?!'

'Oh, he got a call from home and someone is v. ill – is it his mother? – I can't remember, but he has to leave immediately. He's not even collecting his bits 'n' bobs from his desk. He's on a flight to New Zealand at lunchtimeish I think.'

'Right. I see. Right.'

I started to walk towards my office in a daze. Just going? With no explanation? Just going . . .

I was nearly at my door, and I turned back to Lisa and heard myself say,

'Lisa, jot down his home address, will you? I'll drop

375

his stuff off for him, poor thing. I can, I've got an hour before my first client.' With that, I went straight into Noel's small back room, and started to gather up anything on his desk that looked personal. Some books, a photo of a younger him with a much older, sour-looking woman with grey hair and an apron. His grandmother I presumed? There were some pens and a notebook with a Maori fern design on the front and a few scribbled notes in it, but that was all. Very little.

I raced out, grabbed the Post-it with his address on from Lisa and headed for my car.

He lived in Station Road. I didn't exactly know it, but it must surely be near the station somewhere? Key in ignition, no seat belt, I sped out of the car park. What was I doing? This was mad ... but ... I <u>had</u> to know. Why had he not come? Was this ill relative real or not? It couldn't possibly be his mother – he had told me she was dead. Was he fleeing? From me? Oh God, if that were true, this was going to be awkward. I didn't care, I had to face it.

I drove to the station and up and down various roads in a semi-methodical attempt to find his road. No sign of a Station Road. I stopped by a corner shop where they told me that Station Road was the road leading up to the <u>old</u> station on the other side of town, behind where the new industrial estate is. Damn! Should have used the SATNAV, but I have a pathological allergy to its smug correctness. I headed towards the estate and saw it on the left – there – Station Road. Now, what number? Number 8, Lisa had written. It would be on the left at the other end. Quite a long way up, about where that car was ... that taxi. The driver was loading seemingly the last case into the boot and a man was locking his front door. The man, who was, yes, <u>was</u> Noel, but different – a kind of crunkled bald version of him, strangely stooped. He was about to leave. I beeped my horn and tried to park my car awkwardly in the only space I could find, which was too small. I leaped out of the car with its back end still sticking out into the road, and hurried towards him.

'Noel! Noel?'

He was shuffling towards the taxi. What was wrong with him? Where was his hair? As I came closer, I could see he was trying to shuffle faster but couldn't. He was walking on a crutch and had his other arm out of the sleeve of his jacket and bound up. His head was shaven with a long line of stitches over a livid red gash. He was bruised and broken. One eye was half closed and I could see he had some kind of vicious-looking wiring in his mouth.

'Oh my God, Noel. What's happened?'

'I'm sorry ...' It was hard to understand what he was saying through the metal hardware.

'Were you in a crash?'

'I have to go. I'm sorry ...'

He looked squarely at me for the first time.

'I'm sorry ... I'm ... just ... lost ... I didn't mean ... any real harm ... I wouldn't.'

He held my gaze. It had that same familiar intensity but this time contaminated with a kind of sinister shame. Each of his mumbled words hit me like a blow. In that enormous moment, I knew. He was X-Man. He had made sure I was out of the way, pitifully longing for him in a cheap red hotel room, and had been to meet Dora ... And met Husband instead.

I was instantly infected with his shame because it was mine also. I had so unforgivably, so easily bought the whole pathetic scenario, and had played right into his nasty little hands.

He tried to speak ...

'I do like you –'

I slapped him hard on his battered face.

The taxi driver was shocked ...

'Hey, Mrs! Steady on. He's hurt himself!'

'Yes. He has. And everyone else ... Fuck off. Fuck right off, right now!'

He climbed into the car and they drove off. I was shaking. With remorse, with fury, with disgrace.

EIGHTY

Mo

TWO MONTHS LATER . . .

So. October. The winter hasn't yet quite closed in but the trees are showing off their pre-winter coats. And I am showing off <u>my</u> new winter coat. Pamela and I went shopping in Bath as a treat and she wanted to know what I'd like for my fiftieth. I knew immediately . . .

'I'd like a new coat, I think, Mum. Nothing brown or grey. Something loud and optimistic.'

We found it in a small shop for tall people. Ironic really that the shop is so small that only one tall person at a time can fit into it alongside the gangly sales assistant. Pamela had to wait outside in the cold and give the thumbs up or down through the shop window as she peered in. However uncomfortable the experience, it certainly sped things up. I spotted a coat on a rail and knew by the first glimpse of just the sleeve of it that it was to be my winter companion. It has a pattern of huge red roses with bright green leaves on a background of black, which only serves to make the roses look more dramatic. It's the kind of pattern that can make you look like a walking sofa if it's wrong, but full of confidence if it's right. This one is right. I completely <u>love</u> it. It is made by someone called 'Ann-Louise Roswald' whose pretty label is hand sewn in at the back underneath a neat little chain to hang it with. That's a curious name. Just as chipper as the coat. I want to hug her, whoever she is, for making something so entirely cheerful, that fits me so well. Really, I should only wear this coat for 'best', but I'm not going to do that. I'm going to wear it <u>every</u> <u>day</u> so that I will never have to catch sight of myself again in a shop-front window as a gloomy spectre. If I see myself now, I will be instead a huge bunch of flowers. Infinitely preferable. When we finally sat down for tea and 'not-as-good-as-mine-you-can't-deny-it' cake, Pamela was as concise and sage as ever:

'You sorted now?'

'Yep, thanks, Mum.'

'Not out of your depth any more then?'

'No. Back on the reef, ta. Can feel it under my feet. Firm as ever.'

'That's good then, because there's sharks out in those deep waters.'

'Yes. There are.'

'They can take big chunks out of you. Huge jaws. Five rows of backward-facing teeth. Three thousand teeth.'

'I know. Don't worry. I got nibbled. That's all.'

'OK. So long as you're all right.'

'I am.'

'Best way to fend off a shark attack? – Punch them right in the nose.'

'Right. Well. Job done then.'

'Yes, or jab their eyes out with a sharp stick.'

On the way home, she asked me to stop by Dad's grave with her, and we stood quietly arm-in-arm for a while, remembering him.

'Bet he can't believe you're fifty, Mo.'

'Not sure I can.'

'He wanted a little girl so much. Dead chuffed when you turned up. Chest expanded by a foot, I'd say.'

'Nice. Good men really love their daughters, I find.'

'Yes. We both love you very much. All six foot and fifty years of you.'

'I know, Mum. Thanks. For everything. For . . . you know . . . the cake . . . and everything.'

'Oh do shut up, you sentimental twerp.'

I dropped her off at home and she wouldn't let me go until she had furtled around in her 'special' box

382

under the bed, and found Dad's old wristwatch. She thrust it into my hand and said, 'Find the right home for that, would you? Somewhere safe.'

We talked a bit about how Dora's audition for *X Factor* had gone the week before. I explained that I had taken her there and that she was extremely nervous. She took off her specs, went into the room and came out two minutes later, explaining that she'd got through to the next round, which meant singing in front of Simon Cowell and co. She was delighted, streaming with tears.

On the way home in the car she suddenly shouted out, 'Not going any further!'

I went to pull over, a bit shocked.

'No, don't stop! I don't like, mean <u>now</u>, in the car, do I? I mean on *X-Factor*. I'm not going to go any further because if I like stop now, I'll always think I <u>could</u> have made it but if I keep going I'll probably get rejected and just feel ordinary like everyone else. I'd rather stop now and dream about it, but still be me ... d'you get me?'

It was typical of her convoluted, pessimistic logic, but it was also magnificent. She was preserving her aspirations and honing her survival technique and finally being realistic. Attagirl Dora! All the way home, she yabbered on about how fantastic it was going to be at Manchester Metropolitan on the Food Tech course and how fit she'd heard the guys were there. My baby seems to have growed up quite a bit.

My birthday itself was low-key, exactly how I'd asked for it to be. I am fifty. And I <u>can</u> believe it, because it's true.

The kids and Pamela brought me champagne and beetroot cake with clotted cream all over it, in bed. We stuffed our faces and felt sick. Excellent. Then came the gifts. The remarkable, beautiful gifts. Pamela finally gave me the splendid coat, which I put on immediately and wore <u>all</u> day, indoors and out. Oscar gave me a poem he'd written, very much after Shakespeare, extolling the virtues of my everything. My mouth, 'item: two thin lips in mocha red, item: two green eyes with lids to them, one neck, eight chins and so forth . . .' Cheeky bugger.

Dora totally floored me by presenting me with her A level art final piece, which was a triptych of three drawings she described as 'Beauty Across the Age Divide'. There was a charcoal portrait of Pamela, one of me and, finally, one of herself, which pleased me the most since she had included herself under a title which contained the word 'Beauty'. At last, she has given in. Surrendered to the truth. There we were. Three generations of our family, all women, all connected in such a profound way. She had drawn all three with such love, such attention to detail. All the flaws I had seen before in Mum's face and in the mirror were here, but interpreted as lovely, by Dora. These are the faces that made her and that love her, so she was showing her appreciation like this in return. I was deeply, sincerely touched by this beautiful thing and wept like a silly baby. As did Mum, then Dora, then Oscar. Husband was the only one with a dry eye and then . . . It was his turn to give.

He handed me a small box. Inside it was a simple gold ring.

'It's a ring.'

'Well spotted.'

'Is it an eternity ring?' I asked.

'Yes, s'pose so . . . but read what's engraved on it.'

I did. It said simply, 'REMEMBER'. I looked at him, at his lovely nervous, broken face.

'It's a remember-ring so you always remember . . . that you mean everything to us . . .'

And that was it, now <u>he</u> was blubbing too! It was hilarious, all of us pathetically out of control. Laughing and crying together. I sprang out of bed. Well, I creaked out of bed in as springy a fashion as a newly fifty-year-old woman <u>can</u>:

'Right. Come on. This birthday signifies all sorts of wonderful things – like – for instance, I am halfway through my life or thereabouts, so if I am going to make changes, I'd better buck up and do it now, eh? So today, my darlin' family, I wish to shake it up, and give <u>YOU</u> presents, so please step forward to collect your giftage as your name is called, in an orderly fashion, please. First. Nanny Pamela. To you, I give this cake tin, containing the fruits of my labours yesterday, a coffee and walnut cake, made from Granny Marjorie's own recipe. I know it won't be as good as hers, but it's made with the love of your mum passed through you, to me. I hope you like it. I love you.

'Next, Oscar Battle, step up. This box is for you. It contains the very finest smoking jacket or rather, robe de chambre, money can buy, made from silk in "Gentleman's Green". I trust you will cherish it, and I wish you both a long and happy future together. I love you.

'Next, is for you, Husband. Please come forward. I give you this most beautiful and treasured item. It is my own dad's watch which he wore on his wrist for his whole adult life. Mum has asked me to find it a safe home and, hon, there is nowhere safer than you. A fact which gives this whole family our unquestionable sense of security. I love love love you.

'And finally, for your gift, Miss Dora Pamela Battle . . . I'm afraid you have to get dressed and be in the car in five minutes to receive it . . . spit spot!'

For the first time in her life, Dora was ready on time and we sped off into Reading. She was very excited to know what it was. I was extremely nervous. Eventually, I stopped the car. 'Dora. I couldn't bring myself to trust anyone at "Pangbourne Ink", but I believe the guys in here are excellent . . .'

It was a tattoo parlour Lisa had recommended. Dora screamed.

'Oh my actual God, Mum! Are you going to let me?'

'Yep. And what's more, I'm getting one too. Come on.'

After a full hour of deliberating over snakes and roses and stars and dragons and spiky Celtic bands, a decision was made. A tiny heart for me, on my back, right in the middle, between the shoulder blades, and exactly the same for her. It bloody hurt, it really did, but now we are connected to each other. For ever. Mum and daughter. For always.

So, on my fiftieth birthday, I was branded as a mum, and happy to be so.

In the evening, we all went out for dinner at the local Italian. Husband wore his new watch <u>plus</u> his excellent new home-made regalia. Oscar wore his smoking jacket ... and alarmingly, an added turban. Pamela wore her best rabbit fur. Dora wore a low-backed slutty top to show off her tattoo, obviously still covered by a plaster, and I wore my new coat throughout the entire evening. We all got roaring drunk on too many limoncellos and rowed about <u>everything</u> noisily on the walk home. Once there, I took Poo and Elvis out for a last walk and was just returning at two minutes to midnight, when I stood on the opposite side of the road looking back at my house. I felt hugely grateful it was there. That house, containing all those beloved flawed people. I shuddered at the thought of how close I had come to losing them all. I would surely have lost myself had that been the case. Midnight. It wasn't my birthday any more and now, I knew, I had permission to get on with the rest of my life. No regrets.

EPILOGUE

On Sunday morning, I was up very early, about 5am, before anyone else was up. I got dressed. I had a cup of tea and headed out to the car. I turned on the ignition, put the car in gear, and headed out into the road. No one was about. It had been raining in the night, so it was very fresh and the sun was just starting to light up the world. I pulled over at the end of our road. I took the blindfold out of my pocket. It was one of those masks you are given on the plane so you can sleep. If I needed thrill and challenge, then I should have it now, in my fifties. I always wondered – would I do this if I wasn't scared? Well, I'm not scared any more. So go on, Mo, drive the route to work blindfold. Do it.

I take one last preparatory peek at the road ahead, put the blindfold on and pull out, slowly. Stay calm, change gear. Pull to a stop. Indicate left, pull away slowly, listening intently for other cars, heart beating so fast I can feel it in my throat. Pick up speed, steer, steer, steer. Past unseen shops, past unseen school. Indicate right for war memorial. Judge when to turn. Now? No ... keep driving. <u>NOW</u>. Turn. Seems fine, straighten up. Huge clunk, car lurches as it mounts the pavement. Slam on brakes. Stop. Take off blindfold. Yes, I had misjudged the turn and very nearly driven into a bloody great tree opposite the cricket pitch, but hey, I did complete nearly half the journey. Bloody hell! That's amazing! I look around, not a soul about. Thank God.

Until ... I look in the rear-view mirror and there, coming round the corner, on his racing bike with matching ergonomic helmet ... is Husband. Just behind. Following all the way, to check I don't hurt myself. Always there. At a safe distance. Keeping an eye out. Yep. This is my chap.

Thankfully, I seem to be in love with someone I happen to be married to. A mountain I haven't yet fully climbed. My husband.

Den.

From Nana P's recipe book

OSCAR'S BANOFFEE PIE

For the base
200g digestive biscuits
100g pecan nuts
100g butter, melted

For the caramel
100g butter
150g dark brown muscovado sugar
250mls double cream

For the topping
3 large bananas
300ml double cream
1 tablespoon icing sugar
1 teaspoon vanilla extract

Dark chocolate, grated

1. Put the biscuits and nuts in a plastic bag, and bash them up using a rolling pin. Mix in the melted butter.

2. Push the mixture into the base of the tin and flatten until the surface is even. Place into the fridge for 30 minutes. While it's in the fridge, start making the caramel. Melt the butter and brown sugar together. Once the butter is melted, add the cream and let it bubble away for 5 minutes until thickened a little, then leave to cool.

3. Spread the caramel over the biscuit base. Peel and finely slice the bananas and lay them over the caramel.

4. Whip the cream with the icing sugar and vanilla extract until it forms soft peaks, and then spread over the bananas.

5. Decorate with chocolate shavings and place in the fridge until ready to serve. Run a palette knife around the edge and gently remove the tin.

6. Take swig of home-made sloe gin. For cook.

MO'S BEETROOT CAKE

180g caster sugar

3 medium eggs

180g plain flour

180g ground almonds

50g cocoa powder

1 teaspoon baking powder

pinch of salt

200ml sour cream

1 teaspoon vanilla extract

200g raw, peeled and finely grated beetroot

Icing

170g icing sugar, sifted

2 tablespoons water

¼ teaspoon cream of tartar

1 medium egg white

½ teaspoon vanilla extract

drop of pink food colouring (optional)

Handful of hazelnuts to decorate, chopped

1. Preheat the oven to 180°C. Grease a 20cm tin with vegetable oil and line the base with baking parchment.

2. Whisk together the eggs and sugar for 5 minutes with electric beaters, until light and fluffy. Add the flour, almonds, cocoa powder, baking powder and salt. Beat to combine.

3. Beat in the sour cream and vanilla essence. Squeeze out any excess liquid from the grated beetroot and fold into the mixture.

4. Pour the mixture into the tin and bake for 50 minutes. Remove and cool on a wire rack.

5. Meanwhile, make the icing. Place all the ingredients into a bowl and place the bowl on top of a pan of simmering water until the sugar dissolves, stirring occasionally. Remove the pan from the heat and place on a heatproof surface and with the bowl still standing over the pan, whisk on a high speed until the mixture forms stiff peaks

6. Cover the top of the cake with the icing and scatter over the chopped hazelnuts.

7. Take swig of home-made sloe gin. For cook.

DORA'S PINEAPPLE UPSIDE-DOWN CAKE

For the topping
½ pineapple
55g soft brown sugar
6 glacé cherries

For the cake
170g self-raising flour
100g caster sugar
1 teaspoon of ground cinnamon
2 eggs, beaten
200ml milk
½ tsp bicarbonate of soda

1. Preheat the oven to 220°C. Grease a 23cm cake tin and line with baking parchment.
2. Peel the pineapple and slice into 6 rounds, each approximately ½ cm thick. Cut out the core from each and then place the pineapple into a large non-stick frying pan along with the sugar. Cook over a low heat until the sugar has dissolved and then turn

the heat up and let them bubble away for 10 minutes, turning occasionally.

3. Arrange the pineapple slices in the cake tin, in a neat pattern around the edge with one slice in the centre. Fill in the core of each slice with glacé cherries.

4. Combine the flour, sugar and cinnamon in a large bowl and create a well in the centre. Add the eggs and milk into the well and stir, pulling the flour into the centre little by little until combined.

5. Whisk in the bicarbonate of soda and then pour the mixture over the pineapple slices. Bake for 15 minutes, until set and golden.

6. Leave to cool in the tin for 5 minutes and then turn out on to a wire rack to cool completely.

7. Take swig of home-made sloe gin. For cook.

DENYS'S WHISKY CAKE

150g currants

150g sultanas

200g mixed peel

2 tablespoons whisky

1 tablespoon orange juice, plus zest of half an orange

100ml water

180g caster sugar

180g butter

3 medium eggs

180g self-raising flour

1 teaspoon bicarbonate of soda

1 teaspoon mixed spice

pinch of salt

100g chopped walnuts

Icing

60g butter, softened

210g icing sugar

1 tablespoon orange juice

1 tablespoon whisky

1. Soak the dried fruit in the whisky, orange juice, zest and water. Leave for at least 30 minutes.

2. Preheat the oven to 180°C. Grease two 20cm cake tins with butter and line with baking parchment.

3. Cream together the butter and sugar until light and fluffy, and then beat in the eggs, one at a time.

4. Beat in the flour, salt, mixed spice and bicarbonate of soda.

5. Finally fold in the walnuts, dried fruit and the liquid it has been soaking in. Divide the mixture between the two tins and place in the oven for 30 minutes, or until a skewer comes out clean.

6. Leave to cool for 5 minutes and then turn out on to wire racks to cool completely.

7. Meanwhile, make the icing. Place the butter in a large bowl and sift in a third of the icing sugar, beat until combined and then add the remaining sugar in the same way. Finally beat in the orange juice and the whisky. Spread a thin layer of icing on one cake, place the other on top and cover the top with the rest of the icing.

8. Take swig of home-made sloe gin. For cook.

ACKNOWLEDGEMENTS

Thanks to:

Louise Moore, for taking the plunge. And for cake. And for secrets.

Emma Kilcoyne, for constant encouragement and tuna tips.

Sue Perkins, for kicking me off.

Kathy Burke, for speed-reading and reassurance.

Sue Hunter, for not minding my handwriting, and for endless typing.

Ian Williamson, for consultation and advice.

Dr Cassie Cooper, for Kleinian guidance.

Diane and Nigel Bray, for being my top back-up team.

Millfield Val, for food-tech tips.

Debb Gabb, for keeping my chick safe in her coop.

Reevesy, Claire, Liz, John, Sarah, Colin, Sarah and all the team at Penguin for such care.

The Mighty B. F. for so much. So much.

Gareth Carrivick, who was always so full of life.

And finally, Len and Bill, for their patience and love.

'Beautiful' – Linda Perry
Copyright 2002 Sony/ATV Music Publishing LLC,
Stuck In The Throat Music.
All rights administered by Sony/ATV Music
Publishing LLC
All rights reserved. Used by permission.

'Sweet Dreams (Are Made Of This)'
Words & Music by Annie Lennox & Dave Stewart
© Copyright 1983 D'N'A Limited.
Universal Music Publishing MGB Limited.
All Rights Reserved. International Copyright Secured.
Used by permission of Music Sales Limited

'I Believe I Can Fly'
Words & Music by R Kelly
© Copyright 1997 Zomba Songs Incorporated, USA
Imagem Music.
All Rights Reserved. International Copyright Secured.
Used by Permission of Music Sales Limited.

'Between Yesterday and Tomorrow'
Written by Alan Bergman, Marilyn Bergman and
Michel Legrand
© 1991 F Sharp Productions Ltd

© Alamar Music Co.

All rights for Alamar Music Co. controlled and administered by Spirit Music Publishing, Ltd (PRS)

All rights reserved. International copyright secured. Used by Permission.

Questions with the author

With a bestselling novel firmly under her belt, Dawn French has battened down the hatches of her Cornwall home to start work on book number two. We sat down for a cup of tea with our author to ask her about the book, writing and what her readers can expect next . . .

DAWN FRENCH

Questions with the author

What was the turning point that made you realize it was time to start your novel?

I was writing *Dear Fatty*, which was my memoir, and basically realized that I enjoyed writing more than I ever thought I would. Because I've worked in partnerships and groups so much in my life, I didn't imagine that I'd enjoy a solitary job at all. But I completely loved it — I loved visiting my own imagination and so knew then that I would enjoy writing and I wanted to have a go at fiction.

How did you start your novel? Did you start with page one, or a particular character, or a list of ideas?

I started with page one, but I don't think I came to it completely blind. I think I'm the kind of person who percolates an idea — I don't write much down until I come to that page but I have been thinking about it a lot. I think about it when I go to bed, when I'm in my car, when I'm walking the dog — in any spare time I have. So, by the time I came to sit down and write that novel I knew the basic themes of it.

How different was the process of writing a novel in comparison with writing your memoir? Which was the most difficult?

The process is entirely different, because I knew the story of my memoir, because it was the story of my life. However, you realize that the very thing you think you know all about, which is your actual life, you really don't know — for example, dates (I'm particularly bad at dates), and you mix up people in your head, so you have to verify things. There are people you mustn't upset — perhaps you don't entirely tell every story about a particular Granny because you don't want to upset your uncles — so you have to be careful about what you write whilst at the same time being truthful.

Which was the most difficult? I'm not sure about that. I think probably the fiction because it was a brand new enterprise and I didn't know if I was capable of writing good fiction. I didn't even know if it was fiction that I was writing! I didn't want to copy anybody else's style; I wanted to create my own style and definitely have my own voice. You have to find the most natural, authentic and truthful voice that you can.

DAWN FRENCH

Questions with the author

Do you write in a particular place in your house?

I write in my office, where I'm sitting right now! When I saw this house, the minute I walked into this room I knew this would be my office. I knew I would look out at St Catherine's Castle and I would look up Fowey river and I would see boats coming by and it would be a cheerful place, even on a day like today when it's quite misty and grey. There's always something to look at; there's a lot of light that floods my desk and I have a really beautiful room I like being in. That's the room that I write in and I'm happiest writing here. I have written in my flat in London but it's a more grim experience — it feels like homework, whereas writing in Cornwall feels like my proper career.

Where have you found most inspiration for your ideas?

The answer to that is in my brain! Weirdly when I'm writing I feel connected to something that I'm not connected to in any other part of my life. In other words, weird things started to happen to me when I began to write fiction in that sometimes I would come up with words that I didn't actually know! Obviously I must know them, I must have read them, but they're not words that I would particularly use and I wasn't totally sure that I knew exactly what they meant. I know that sounds completely bloody weird but it is true, and it was moments like that I thought 'Oh, OK, I'm connected here in a way that I'm not connected normally.' It's like being very sharp in a way that you're not sharp usually. When it does happen, it's remarkable and it's a real buzz, so that's a reason to return to writing.

What is your writing routine? Do you need to set aside some time each day to write, or is it more fluid than that?

I'm a person of routine. I find that with writing I like to do office hours, and I like to start at my desk at nine and I stop for a bit of lunch and bad telly for an hour at lunchtime, and then I try to finish at five. I won't get up from that desk; I won't answer any long phone calls or anything like that during the day because it takes me completely away from the writing, so I prefer to do it like that. As I get older I would like to maybe start at seven in the morning and finish at noon – that would be great, and then

DAWN FRENCH

your afternoon is about your dog and your life and letting your ideas flood in rather than being chained to your desk, but at the moment I do office hours.

What have you enjoyed most about writing your first novel?

I think I have mostly enjoyed watching it take shape. Structuring it, realizing I was a third of the way through and hadn't started the main part of the story yet but was being delightfully distracted by everything else, and realizing I had to go back and start threading in a bit of tension, and so on. I enjoyed that very much — working it out and discovering that I could solve problems.

Did you suffer from writer's block at any point? How did you overcome it?

Yep — you suffer from writer's block every day — usually that first five minutes of the day and five minutes after lunch. There's not a block exactly, but I describe it as like going into a tunnel, and it takes a long time to get into that tunnel where everything else disappears and it's only about your book. Thus far (but I'm very new to this) I haven't suffered an utter block where I can't get going. Sometimes I can't get that first sentence right, and in the end I just remember that it's better to write anything than to write nothing at all and I can always return to it. Sometimes you just make yourself write the very least you're thinking and by the time you're on sentence four or five, and you're halfway down the page, you've got a bit of a head of steam up and you can go back and refine it. It is a bit frightening but very exciting at the same time.

Which is your favourite scene in the novel?

There are several. I very much like the scene where Mo sees herself in the reflection of a shop window and thinks that she is a bag of laundry, or somebody is, and then she realizes it's her. She thought she was wearing a very good, expensive grey coat but discovers that she actually looks like a ghost. It's just where Mo gets a bit of a wake-up call about how invisible and unimportant she's feeling, which is why she's so vulnerable, and why she can go ahead with her reckless behaviour.

I also like the scene where Mo has her pap smear because that is written from complete

DAWN FRENCH

experience of fear and terror about bosoms
being squished and fanny being probed!

I like Oscar's first session with Noel when Oscar
is absolutely convinced that he can make Noel
love him and goes in with a cocky assurance.
I also like Oscar with Luke, realizing he's made
a massive mistake: that Noel is a pointless object
of his affections but Luke is a worthy object.

I'm very fond of Dad's entry because it's the
only one and it's a very different one — a
muscular, heroic voice that comes slamming
into the foreground when Dad has been
unimportant and in the background.

And I also like the party scene where Dora
has a party where nobody really turns up except
a couple of goths and Oscar and his boyfriend
and she gets very drunk — I like that scene.

**How did the book change as you were
writing it?**

Because I was unsure that I could write a
novel, I checked a lot with my editor: I sent
her chapters and pages as I went along to
reassure me and to gauge how it was going.

I was inviting her input, but sometimes I
didn't want to hear some of the things she said,
like that I needed to include more dialogue.
But she was absolutely right and because I'd
chosen to write the novel in the form of diary
entries it would have been too easy for it to be
too internal. She made me open it up more
and make it more human and interactive,
and I enjoyed watching that change.

**What do you hope your readers will gain
from reading *A Tiny Bit Marvellous*?**

I hope that the readers will have a connection
with me — I hope that I'll get closer to the readers
and they'll get a bit closer to me by reading it. It's
very personal, this book. I don't mean personal in
the simplest sense that it's about me or anything
(it isn't), but it does have my imagination and my
style all over it and I'm inviting someone into a
one-way conversation with me. I don't know if
that's what other writers want, but I think that's
what I want. And I hope they have a laugh, really,
and that they're touched by something in it; that
would be fantastic if that were the case.

DAWN FRENCH

Questions with the author

How did you feel when you saw your finished book? Where do you keep your copy at home?

I was delighted when I saw the book finished, absolutely delighted: what was especially great about this book was that I loved working with the team on the cover and felt like we were all collaborating a lot, and there wasn't a moment where it felt like it was being hijacked into a direction I didn't like. It looked like the book I'd written; it didn't misrepresent it. It was lovely and stark and graphic — clear — I really liked that. Where do I keep my copy at home? I've got a little stack of them on a table and I've got one on my bookshelf I dig into every now and again.

What has been the most enjoyable part of publishing your first novel and the most nerve-racking?

I've enjoyed getting feedback: people writing to me or talking to me about the book, and I was always quite surprised that people had read it, even when I was going on their show to talk about it! It feels like a very personal thing has suddenly been made quite public. The most nerve-racking is the publicity, which is never my favourite thing to do.

Did you give out copies of your book to family and friends? Did they recognize themselves in any of the characters?

Yes, I gave out copies: first of course to my Mum, who the book is dedicated to; to my brother; to my best friend; and to a couple of people who I mentioned in the list of thanks/ acknowledgements. Nobody recognized themselves because nobody is there completely as themselves — they're there as amalgamations of people.

Did you read the reviews of *A Tiny Bit Marvellous*? What did you think of them?

I didn't read the reviews and I still haven't entirely, although a couple of them came to my attention by a route where I couldn't ignore them. Usually that happens if there's a good review — somebody will make sure you see it — but I'm just as wary of good reviews. I've come out of another career where it's all about reviews

DAWN FRENCH

and people having a lot to say about you so I've got quite a — it's not that I've got a thick skin, I've got a method, which is to not look, and to follow your own instincts, and to follow the positive or negative vibes you're receiving in your life and, very quickly without being too clever, you can pick up whether the reviews are generally OK or not OK. I knew I would get it in the neck from some people and I would definitely think that the more academic faction of the publishing world would be down on me like a tonne of bricks, but I don't even know if they were or weren't: and it's great not to know.

How does it feel to be recognized as an author as well as a TV personality?

Well that's an odd thing; I don't think I've earned that moniker yet. You are an author if you've written something, but whether you're a good author . . . the test of time will tell us that and that's what I would aspire to.

What can we expect next from the Dawn French pencil?

You can expect another novel, the tricky second novel, which I think will be very different to this one. I think it will be funny but I think it will be quite stylized and a bit less 'chummy'. Let's leave it at that!

Will you approach the second novel any differently?

I have approached it a bit differently because I've collated a group of characters who are unlike those in *A Tiny Bit Marvellous*, where I think I knew who the people were quite quickly and didn't need to research them much. With this novel I'm writing quite a lot of different characters who do jobs that I know nothing about. Why I have chosen to do that I don't know, because I've given myself quite a hard job. But I've had to do quite a lot of research and that has been fascinating. I've spent time in Ealing Hospital in the intensive care unit and that was pretty sobering; I also spent a lot of time with a woodsman . . . so I've been doing lots of interesting stuff that

I know nothing about. It's been a steep learning curve and it's been very good, very rewarding.

How would you feel if your book was made into a TV programme? Would you want to write it or star in it, or none of the above?

Well already people are asking me to make it into a TV programme but I'm reluctant about that at the moment because I might write more about those characters and I'd want to write more before I let it go. I probably would want to write it, or be involved with the writing — maybe be script editor. TV is very difficult because I see the book as quite filmic rather than for TV. Could be . . . I'm not sure yet.

DAWN's Reading List

Books that have inspired Dawn throughout her life:

Short Stories

Annie Proulx – 'Brokeback Mountain'
J. D. Salinger – 'For Esmé – With Love and Squalor'

Children's Titles

Joyce Lankester Brisley – *Milly Molly Mandy*
Anne Holm – *I am David*
Dodie Smith – *I Capture the Castle*
Eve Garnett – *The Family from One End Street*
Gerald Durrell – *My Family and Other Animals*

Adult Titles

Jane Austen – *Northanger Abbey*
Spike Milligan – *Puckoon*
Emma Donoghue – *Room*
William Boyd – *Any Human Heart*
Evelyn Waugh – *Decline and Fall*
David Niven – *The Moon's a Balloon*

Guilty Pleasure

Robert James Waller –
The Bridges of Madison County

DAWN FRENCH

Points for Further Discussion for
Reading Groups

🐑 The Battles are a dysfunctional modern family but come together when it matters most. Where in the novel do they show their strengths as a family unit, and what are their weaknesses?

🐑 Discuss the importance of the role Pamela plays in her family. What do the cakes say about the individuals she makes them for?

🐑 Dora is a hormonal teenager who projects a tough exterior. When do you see her vulnerable side?

🐑 Discuss the impact of the decision not to name 'Dad' until the end of the novel. What effect does this have on your perception of his character?

🐑 Look at the relationship between parent and child in the novel, looking at both Mo's relationship with Dora, and Oscar's relationship with 'Dad'. When do we see the roles in flux? Do the parent/child roles ever invert?

 Compare the ways in which Mo and Dora adapt and grow throughout the novel. What do they each learn about themselves and each other?

 Dora's relationships in the novel are often fragile. How does her relationship with her Mother compare to that of her friends and with X-Man?

 Discuss the character of Oscar, and his development throughout the novel. When are we allowed a glimpse behind his eccentric façade?

 Re-read the final scene of the novel, when Mo takes her journey to work. How does this summarize the relationship between Mo and Denys, and what does it say about how Mo has changed?

 To what extent do you think *A Tiny Bit Marvellous* is an accurate reflection on a modern-day family? What similarities can you see with your own family?

DAWN FRENCH

Loved **A Tiny Bit Marvellous?**

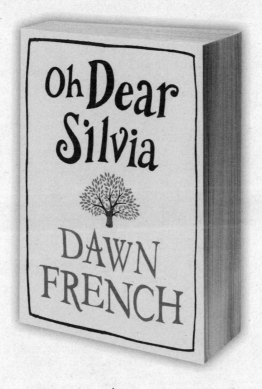

then read an extract of

Oh Dear Silvia – the new novel by DAWN FRENCH.

ONE

Ed

Wednesday 10am

He sits with a sense of being watched, although he himself is the watcher. Momentarily, the others have stepped outside so he is suddenly, shockingly, alone with her. It's odd for there to be no voices. No sound, save those of two human beings just being alive. He becomes acutely aware that for the first time in a very long time, he feels irrefutably more alive than her. She's always making sure you know she's chock-full o'life. She lives big and loud. Right to her fingertips. Her presently somewhat swollen fingertips. Look at them. Someone, perhaps a nurse, has tried to remove the coral-red varnish, but it is stubborn and has bled into her skin, revealing the nails beneath to be unbeautiful, nicotiney. Blotchy red fingers. Yellow nails.

She wouldn't like him to see such a personal thing, so he tries to stop looking . . . but of course he can't. He is transfixed by the unusual sighting. He feels her watching, and although she isn't and although he so wants to remain defiant, he looks away.

So. Here they both are again. Alone. They haven't been alone in a room for ... well, since they were married. What's that? About ... God ... What _is_ it now? Five years? Something like that.

There she is. Breathing.

Here he is. Breathing.

That's it.

Pretty much like it was at the end of the marriage, really. Two people occupying the same air. Nothing else in common. Just oxygen. He remembers when sharing breath with her was exciting, intimate. He would lie close to her in the night, happily breathing in what she breathed out. The breath of life, their joint breath from their joint life.

This breathing now, though, is very different.

He hears his own. It's quick and halting. It fits with his heartbeat, which is anxiously fast and occasionally missing altogether, when he finds himself holding his breath whilst urgent frightening thoughts distract him.

Her breathing is entirely unfamiliar. It's regimented and deep. Her lungs are rhythmically resonating loudly around the room, chiming in with the bellow-like wheezing of the machine. She's being breathed for, through a huge ugly tube in her throat.

Because Silvia Shute, despite all the supposed life in her, is in a coma.

TWO

Jo

Thursday 2pm

A dervish is whirling around Silvia's bed, gabbling and gesticulating wildly. Her explosion of curly grey hair bobs about busily as she moves. The too many strands of assorted, expensive but meant to look casual beads dance on her bosom, and the clack of her posh but meant to look like working boots resounds off the sparkly-clean-polished-all-the-way-under-the-bed-twice-a-day-check-it-on-the-time-sheet-no-bugs-here-mate floor. This is Jo, Silvia's elder sister. Her mouth has mistaken itself for a machine gun.

'It just bothers me darling, that when you do eventually wake up, I'm not even going to be able to tell you what happened because nobody seems to bloody know! You are probably the only one and will you even remember? God knows. Well obviously <u>God</u> knows, whichsoever God one chooses to align oneself with, of course. I can't remember now if you even believe in God, do you? Oh God, that's awful. No. I don't think you do. I <u>think</u> you're a hundred per cent not quite sure, aren't you? I remember you once saying you thought Jesus wore a blindfold to decide who would get the poorly babies, and how that was terribly unfair, but you were eleven, so you may well have updated your thinking since then.

'I know you like Christmas and weddings and church and stuff, but does that necessarily make you a Christian? It's probably got more to do with fabrics and lights and catering if I know you. Do I know you? That's the big question darling, because I can see all this . . . this hellish situation, there's going to be some major decisions I will probably have to make on your behalf.

'Oh God. Why did this happen?! What the hell were you doing out on your balcony? In the freezing cold? On your own? Have you started smoking again? Oh, darling, look at you . . .'

Jo leans over Silvia's bed, smooths her cheek and runs her fingers through her little sister's hair.

'Desperately need your roots doing, darling. Oh dear. What's happened? Where are you Sissy? Come on, come on. Wake up sweetheart. Wake up and see me. I'm here darling. I'm here for you. Always here for you. Big sister to look after you. Just as it should be. Big one looks after the little one. I promised Mummy I would, and I will.

'Come on now, try to wake up. The doctor says you're a long way away, but you're just asleep, aren't you? Very deeply asleep, that's all. Wake up one day, won't you? Yes. Yes, you will. Might be tonight. Or tomorrow. Or soon, anyway. Banged your head, didn't you, silly girl? Banged it when you fell. Does it hurt? They've cleaned it up pretty well. Shaved you a bit there darling, where it's sore, but not a problem, that'll grow back in no time. You've got lovely thick hair. And straight. Always wanted yours rather than mine. Mine's a mess. Yours is sleek, shiny. How hair is supposed to be. Not like this. Mattress has exploded on my head, you said. Everyone loves yours. Loves the colour.

'Come on now, you're just being a silly girl, pretending to be asleep like this. Snoozing. While we're all awake out here. You lazybones. Idle. Selfish. Selfish shellfish. Idle bridle. Lazy Maisie. That's you, isn't it?'

Jo acknowledges the catch in her voice and for the first time alone in the clean clean room with her still still sister, she submits to the tears that have been brimming since she heard the news two days ago. She doesn't want to cry. She knows that if Silvia is at <u>all</u> aware, she won't appreciate this pathetic show. She'd certainly tell her to 'butch up and get a grip', as she has done many times before.

Jo can't stop it though, it's the shock. This sort of thing doesn't happen to anyone she knows, ever. When she first heard the news, she felt as if she was suddenly a character in an American medical show. 'House' was calling her to say that her sister had fallen three floors and sustained a serious head injury. Thank you, Hugh Laurie . . . for giving me this terrible news in your inimitable forthright, some might say even cruel style. Thank God it's you, because now of course, I know it will all be alright for the simple reason that you will inevitably triumphantly and last-minutedly restore my stone of a sister to full health.

Sissy might even seduce him on waking, with her unique interestingness, and win him over to become Mrs Hugh House . . . hmmm.

That first shock of the phone call was awful. But this shock today, Jo thinks, the shock of actually seeing her lying there so motionless save for the hypnotic effort of the enforced breathing, is much much worse. No two ways about it, Silvia is nearly dead.

Look at her. Her skin never usually looks pallid like this.

She must not die. After all, Jo promised their mother to always have a care for her. Silvia shall not die before Jo. Otherwise Jo is even more of a bloody failure. If that's possible . . .

'Hold on, sweetheart. Come on! Keep living. We all love you . . . Well, I do. You know I do. We've had our moments Sis, but the loving you part has never ever been in question. You always love your little sister, don't you? Yes. You do. You have to. That's what you do. You just love them. Whatever they're like. Whatever they've done. However thoughtless or insensitive they might sometimes have been . . . however much they might have hurt you, sometimes carelessly, admittedly, but often purposely, you just keep right on loving them. Whatever you feel. You try to put their feelings first. They come first. Think of others before yourself. Always. Self comes last. Silvia must be protected.

'So that's what we're going to do. Keep you going sweetheart, at all costs. I'm not giving up on you. There'll be <u>something</u> that wakes you up. I've just got to find it darling, that's all. I'm going to try anything and everything, you wait and see, and one day I will find it and you'll open those beautiful big grey-blue eyes, and I'll be the first thing you see, and you'll know how much I cared and how much I tried, and you'll be grateful and maybe a tiny bit less unkind . . .

'I might well catch you looking at me often in the future, just knowingly, out of the corner of your eyes and I will know you are thinking, "Yep, there she is, my sister Jo, who saved my life, who didn't give up on me, who kept her promise. Who is, truth be told, a bit extraordinary and to whom I owe . . . well . . . everything, really."'

Jo picks up Silvia's heavy dead weight of a hand, noticing the red smudged fingers, and lifts it to her lips and kisses it very much.

THREE

Winnie

Thursday 4pm

Silvia is too hot. Tiny beads of sweat above her lip are the only sign, but it's enough for Winnie, her key nurse, to bring a cool muslin flannel to dab off the moisture and to then rest it on her forehead.

Winnie checks all the machines, could anything be wrong to cause Silvia to be hot?

The ECG monitor is beeping healthily. The read-out is correct.

The endotracheal tube is clear and the ventilator is functioning.

The venous line is in properly, she's getting all her fluids.

Drip drip. That's right.

The nasogastric tube is in place.

She clips a small grey claw on to Silvia's finger and, simultaneously, she deftly folds the large cuff around her arm so that she can check the blood pressure and the oxygen saturations together. She places the grey plastic gun-like infrared thermometer gently into Silvia's ear, and takes her temperature. It takes a moment . . . Winnie always feels like she is pointing a pistol right into the brain of her patients when she does this. She wouldn't say, because it shouldn't, but it amuses her.

Everything is normal. Good. Tick, tick on the clipboard.

Winnie relaxes and starts to sing. She is currently learning a new song for choir. It isn't really new, in fact it's an old traditional American song, but it's new to them, not in their repertoire, which is about three years old now. It's time Calvary Voices had something new. It's coming up to wedding season and they will be asked to sing all the time, sometimes at four weddings on any given Saturday, and Pentecostal services are long. Rarely are the choir invited to the wedding breakfast, so she can sometimes sing at four weddings with only a cold sandwich from the newsagents to sustain her small frame. And is it really right, she wonders, that choirmaster Claude receives £150 for every wedding, but that the choir only receive £10 each from it, and there's only ten of them?

She tries to banish all unchristian thoughts of what an evil selfish bastard Brother Claude might well be, by remembering that Brother Claude is also the official treasurer for Calvary Voices. So presumably there are overheads? On top of which, Brother Claude actually sings <u>with</u> them as well as being choirmaster. He is one of the ten, so he also gets a tenner each time. So . . . that's not good then.

As she toils away, around Silvia, she sings quietly, tenderly. She executes her work with great love.

'As I went down in the river to pray'

She washes Silvia's face

'Studying about that good ol' way'

She washes Silvia's arms

'And who shall wear the starry crown'

She washes Silvia's breasts and shoulders

'Good Lord show me the way'

She washes Silvia's fanny, careful not to dislodge the catheter

'Oh sinners, let's go down'

She changes the sanitary sheet under Silvia's bum, and washes her there

'Let's go down, c'mon down'

She washes Silvia's legs and feet

'C'mon sinners, let's go down'

She straightens up the sheets and tidies Silvia's nightie

'Down in the river to pray'

She brushes Silvia's hair.

When she's finished, she speaks out loud with a pronounced but gentle Jamaican burr.

'Dere you are, Silvia, nice 'n' fresh, yes? Now, we don't want you to be too hot, but I cyan't open the window due to possible cold or h'infection. BUT, mi cyan pull dis down here.'

She pulls down the blind.

'So dere, now you have no direct sunlight on you whatsoever PLUS, mi fetch you up de h'electric fan to cool you, yes? OK.'

She pats Silvia's foot.

She likes to stay in physical contact with her comatose patients at all times whilst she's in the room. It must be very lonely, she thinks, to be so locked away. She has seen this state time and time again, and although she is inured to the shock of it, she still empathizes anew with each fresh patient. No, _she_ isn't shocked, but _they_ are. They have just had all normal life snatched away in a heartbeat, and somewhere, deep inside the brain of this paralysed body, there is life. There are brainwaves.

Winnie saw them when the ITU intensivists and the consultant conducted the EEG scan the evening Silvia was first brought in. There were enough signs of life for them to hook her up, although she scored very badly when they measured the depth of her coma using the Glasgow Coma Scale which Winnie knows all about. It rates:

a. Whether she can open her eyes. She can't.

b. Her motor response. None.

c. Her verbal response. None.

But Winnie knows that just because Silvia doesn't show a response, it doesn't necessarily mean she is not aware. Sometimes Winnie notices the tiniest rise in heartbeat on the monitor when she comes into the room of one of her patients. Not Silvia. Silvia is pretty much spark out, and Winnie can't locate anything she could usefully feed back to the doctors or the family. That doesn't mean she won't though. You have to have two important attributes in this job: patience and vigilance. Oh, and add to those, hope.

Yes, hope, the most important thing of all.

The patients, the doctors, the families and the d'yam hospital itself will give up hope before Winnie does. Winnie's life is about hope. She brings bargain buckets of it with her to work every day. She knows that it's a certain truth, because she's seen it with her own two eyes, that often, it's only at the very edge of life and death that we truly live. Her privilege is to witness that phenomenon daily.

'Phew! You right Silvia, it too hot in here. Mi a burn up. I'll get dat fan, and some remover fi dem red fingers dere. Be right back darlin.'

The door slams shut. Silvia lies alone in intensive care suite number 5, like a marble sarcophagus.

A still, grey effigy.

Cold. But hot.